DEADLY DECEPTIONS

Also available from

LINDA LAEL MILLER

The Mojo Sheepshanks series
Deadly Gamble

The McKettricks series
McKettrick's Choice
McKettrick's Luck
McKettrick's Pride
McKettrick's Heart

The Stone Creek series
The Man from Stone Creek
A Wanted Man

**And in October 2008,
return to Stone Creek with**
The Rustler

LINDA LAEL MILLER

DEADLY DECEPTIONS

HQN™

ISBN-13: 978-0-7394-9341-0

DEADLY DECEPTIONS

My Dear Friends,

Welcome back to the crazy world of Mojo Sheepshanks, who sees way more dead people than she thinks is right. She's getting in deeper and deeper with hunky, semi-available cop Tucker Darroch, and in *Deadly Deceptions* she has a heartrending mystery to solve. If she's not careful, she could become a ghost herself!

I also wanted to write today to tell you about a special group of people with whom I've recently become involved. It is The Humane Society of the United States (HSUS), specifically their Pets for Life program.

The Pets for Life program is one of the best ways to help your local shelter: that is to help keep animals out of shelters in the first place. Something as basic as keeping a collar and tag on your pet all the time, so if he gets out and gets lost, he can be returned home. Being a responsible pet owner. Spaying or neutering your pet. And not giving up when things don't go perfectly. If your dog digs in the yard, or your cat scratches the furniture, know that these are problems that can be addressed. You can find all the information about these and many other common problems at www.petsforlife.org. This campaign is focused on keeping pets and their people together for a lifetime.

As many of you know, my own household includes two dogs, two cats and four horses, so this is a cause that is near and dear to my heart. I hope you'll get involved along with me.

With love,

Paula Eve Miller

To Josanne Lovick, with love and appreciation

DEADLY DECEPTIONS

CHAPTER ONE

I WAS SO INNOCENT THEN.

Don't get me wrong—I'd been through a lot, starting with the savage murders of both my parents, when I was only five years old. I'd been kidnapped and raised mostly on the road, by the late, great Lillian Travers, living under an alias that has since become more representative of who I really am than my given name—Mary Josephine Mayhugh—could ever be.

I'm Mojo Sheepshanks now, and as far as I can tell, I always will be.

Then again, you never know.

That's what I've learned since the day I sat in the back of an overcrowded church in Cave Creek, Arizona, on a hot day in early May, too shaken to cry. You just never know—about anything, or anybody.

The casket in front of the altar was painfully small, made of gleaming black wood, and it was open. The body of seven-year-old Gillian Pellway lay inside, nestled on cushions of white silk, clad in a blue ruffled dress, her small hands folded across her chest. I know it's what people always say, but she really *did* look peaceful, lying there. She might have been asleep.

She *wasn't* at peace. If she had been, her ghost wouldn't have been sitting in the folding chair next to mine, still clad in the single ballet slipper, pink leotard, tights and tutu she'd been wearing when she was murdered a week before, sometime after a rehearsal for an upcoming dance recital ended.

It wasn't as if I'd had a lot of experience dealing with dead people. Early trauma and the years on the road with Lillian notwithstanding, I'd led a pretty ordinary life. I wasn't psychic. I didn't have visions.

Then, one night in April, I'd awakened to find my ex-husband, Nick DeLuca, in bed with me. Not too weird—divorced people sleep together all the time. Except that Nick had been killed in a car crash two years before. I saw him often, over a period of a few weeks, and I probably owe him my life.

But that's another story.

Nick opened some kind of door, and I've been seeing ghosts ever since.

They're easy enough to spot, once you know what to look for. Their clothes are usually outdated, and they often seem lost, as though they want to ask directions but can't get anybody's attention. I encounter them all the time now—in supermarkets, busy restaurants, even in dog parks.

I wish I didn't, but I do.

I try hard not to make eye contact, but it doesn't

always work. Once they realize I can see them, they tend to get in my face.

That day, sitting through Gillian's funeral, I had mixed feelings. Of course it was a tragedy—the apparently random slaughter of a little girl. That goes without saying. But most of the people weeping in that church were crying more for themselves than for Gillian—because they'd miss her, because it might just as easily have been their own child lying in that coffin, because they thought death was an ending.

It might be simpler if it were.

As I said, I was innocent then. I'd figured out that death *wasn't* the final curtain, but the beginning of a whole new act in some complicated cosmic play. The proof was sitting right beside me, leaning against my arm. But the transition is rocky for some people, especially when it happens suddenly, or violently. Back then, I had no idea how many ghosts get caught in the thin, shifting, invisible web that separates this life from the next. A surprising number of them think they're dreaming, and wander around waiting to wake up.

Helen Erland, Gillian's mother, sat stiff-spined in a front pew, occasionally shuddering with the effort to hold in a sob. Her husband, Vince, wasn't there to share in her grief and lend support—he was in jail pending a murder charge. Though Mrs. Erland apparently had no family to lean on, the place was packed—many of the mourners, I suspected, were the parents of Gillian's classmates at school.

I wished I could tell Helen that Gillian wasn't really gone, but how exactly does one go about that? By tugging at the sleeve of the bereaved mother's cheap but tasteful black suit and saying, *Excuse me, but your daughter is more alive than you are?*

I don't think so.

So I sat there, and I watched and listened, and I wondered if the real murderer was present, gloating or guilt ridden. Although Gillian had yet to speak a word to me since she'd appeared in the backseat of my sister's Pathfinder soon after her death, she *had* indicated that Vince Erland hadn't killed her. It seemed more a matter of instinct than certainty.

Conundrum number two. How to explain to the police that they were probably holding the wrong man, and you knew this because the victim had shaken her head when you asked if he'd been the one, but either couldn't or wouldn't tell you who *had* ended her life. All without winding up in some psych ward yourself.

My gaze wandered to Tucker Darroch. He was sitting up near the front, with one strong arm around his ex-wife, Allison, her head resting on his shoulder. Their seven-year-old twins, Daniel and Daisy, friends of Gillian's, weren't present.

I knew what was going to happen, of course.

Allison would *need* Tucker.

And he would move back in with her, if he hadn't already.

Whatever had been starting between Tucker and me would be over.

I tried not to care. I wasn't in love with the man, after all. But we were definitely...involved.

The service was ending.

I squeezed Gillian's small hand, cold but substantial, and then Helen Erland rose shakily from her seat and walked to the coffin. With a soft wail of sorrow that pierced the lining of my soul, she laid a single white rose inside.

I felt Gillian pull away, and I tried to hold on, but it was no use. One moment the child was sitting beside me, the next she was standing at her shattered mother's side, her little face upturned, her whole being crying out in a silent plea. *I'm here, see me!*

What could I do?

Rush up there and gather a child no one else could see into my arms? Drag her back to the rows of folding chairs that had been set up in the rear of the church to accommodate the overflow?

There was *nothing* I could do. So I sat still, clenching my hands together, my face wet with tears.

Helen Erland, understandably focused on the body in the coffin, was oblivious to her real daughter, standing right beside her.

Gillian, I called, without speaking. *Come back.*

She turned a defiant glance on me, shook her head and grabbed ineffectually at her mother's hand. I was vaguely aware of a young woman at the periphery of my vision, a video camera raised to her face, and a slight shudder went through me.

Enduring the actual funeral was hard enough. Who would want to replay it?

Let this be over, I prayed distractedly. *Please let this be over.*

Gillian vanished, and did not return to her chair beside mine.

Tucker left Allison long enough to go to Helen, help her back to her place.

I couldn't stand any more.

I got up and slipped out through the open doors of the church, doing my best not to hyperventilate. I would have given just about anything to have one or both of my sisters there, but Jolie, recently hired as a crime-scene tech by Phoenix PD, was going through an orientation program, and Greer was caught in the throes of a rapidly disintegrating marriage.

So I was on my own. Nothing new there.

I took refuge under a leafy ficus tree, grateful for the shade, one hand pressed against the trunk so I wouldn't drop into a sobbing heap on the ground. I was dazed by the intensity of my mourning, and I didn't trust myself to drive. Not right away, anyhow.

The service ended.

People flowed past, murmuring, the men looking stalwart and grim, the women dabbing at puffy eyes with crumpled handkerchiefs.

The pallbearers, Tucker among them, carried

Gillian's casket to the hearse, waiting in the dusty street with its rear doors open like the black wings of some bird of doom, ready to enfold the child and carry her away into the unknown. The minister helped Mrs. Erland into the back of a limousine; I looked for Gillian, but she was nowhere around.

When a hand gripped my upper arm, I was beyond startled. I could no longer assume I'd been approached by another human being—not the flesh-and-blood variety, that is.

I turned and saw Allison Darroch standing just behind me, her eyes red rimmed from crying, her flawless skin alabaster pale. She had lush brown hair, pulled into a severe French twist for the occasion, and she wore a black sheath that accented her slender curves.

"What," she demanded in a furious undertone, "are *you* doing here?"

I swallowed, stuck for an immediate answer. I couldn't say I'd come to Gillian Pellway's funeral because the dead child had practically herded me there. Especially not to Allison, who clearly saw me as the Other Woman, even though she and Tucker had been legally divorced for over a year before I even met him.

Allison leaned in. "It's *sick*—this is a *little girl's funeral*—but you'll do *anything* to get close to Tucker, won't you?"

I'd never labored under the delusion that Allison and I would ever be friends, but I did respect her. She was a good, if overprotective, mother to the twins, and in her capacity as a veterinarian she'd recently saved Russell, a canine friend of mine, from certain death.

"I know Helen Erland slightly," I said, with what dignity I could muster, considering I still felt as though I might faint, throw up, or both. It was true, too, which admittedly isn't the case with everything I say. Helen clerked in a convenience store in Cave Creek, and I occasionally stopped in to buy lottery tickets or gas up my Volvo. "My coming here has nothing to do with Tucker."

"I don't believe you," Allison said.

"Back off," I replied, after reassembling my backbone vertebra by vertebra. "I have as much right to be here as you do."

Tucker appeared in the corner of my eye, handsome and anxious in his dark suit. His hair was butternut-blond and a little too long, like before, but he didn't look like the undercover DEA agent I knew him to be. His normal uniform was jeans, a muscle shirt and biker boots.

"Get in the car, Allison," he said.

She stiffened, gave me one more poisonous glare and walked away. Got into the big SUV parked at the curb.

For a long moment Tucker and I just stared at each other.

I figured it was his place to speak first, because he'd been the one to stumble into the hornet's nest.

On the other hand, there was a lot I wanted to tell him, because he was, after all, the only person in the world who knew I could see Gillian Pellway.

I bit my lower lip and stood my ground.

Tucker shoved a hand through his hair. Sighed. His green eyes were haunted, and I wondered how long it had been since he'd slept through a night. Certainly not since Gillian's body had been found, if appearances were anything to go by.

"Allison's pretty torn up," he said. "So are the kids."

I merely nodded.

"She asked me to move back in. Just for a while."

Tucker had a condo in Scottsdale, but he wasn't there much; when he was working, he tended to disappear into some mysterious underworld, one I knew little about.

My stomach pitched, and bile scalded the back of my throat. I swallowed and nodded again.

He moved as though he might take a gentle hold on my shoulders, or even pull me into his arms. Then, after glancing toward the SUV with its tinted windows, he looked at me again, his eyes begging me to understand. I figured his Harley, his usual favorite mode of transportation, was probably gathering dust in some garage.

"You're going to do it," I said.

Tucker thrust out a breath. "Moje, this isn't a reconciliation. Nothing like that. It's temporary—just until Allison gets over this. Daisy's having bad dreams, and Danny freaks if every light in the house isn't on all night long."

I thought of Gillian's silent insistence that Vince Erland wasn't her killer, and gulped back another throatful of bile. I believed her, and that meant the real murderer was still out there, perhaps already stalking another child. I shivered.

"Do you think the twins are in danger?" I asked when I could summon up enough breath. I cared about Tucker Darroch big-time, and I wasn't planning on sharing a bed with him as long as he was bunking in with the wife and kids, but Daisy attended the same dance school Gillian had, wore the same tiny-ballerina getup. Just thinking of that made me cold to the core.

"I don't know," Tucker said.

I took a step toward him, touched his hand. "See you," I told him.

He caught hold of my arm when I would have gone past him, climbed into my car and motored for Greer's place, on the chic fringes of Scottsdale. Until a week before, I'd lived in an apartment over Bad-Ass Bert's Biker Saloon, but following an unfortunate incident with a psychotic killer, I'd moved into my sister's guesthouse.

"What do you mean, 'see you'?" Tucker demanded.

I pulled my arm free, though I didn't make a show of it. I knew Allison was watching from the SUV, and I didn't want to spike her drama meter, which was already bobbing in the red zone. "I mean," I said evenly, "that while I certainly understand that you have to be there for your family, I don't intend to sleep with you in the meantime."

A muscle bunched in Tucker's fine, square jaw, and he nodded once, sharply. I thought he'd turn and walk away, but he didn't. His eyes searched mine, probing and solemn. "Have you seen Gillian again—since the day we talked on the phone?"

She'd been haunting me pretty much nonstop, but that was neither the time nor place to go into details. The way things were going, there might never *be* a time or place. "Yes" was all I said.

He absorbed that. Nodded again. "We have to talk."

"Not today," I answered.

"You're still living at your sister's place?"

The SUV's horn sounded an impatient, wifely little toot.

"Until further notice," I said, and this time when I started for my car, Tucker didn't try to stop me.

I WOULD HAVE LIKED nothing better than to go back to Greer's, strip to the skin and swim off some of my angst in her backyard pool, but I knew with my light, redhead's skin, I'd freckle and fry if I did. So I settled myself in the front seat of my Volvo, switched on the ignition and turned the air-conditioning up as high as it would go.

I sat, watching other people drive off in their cars.

The young woman with the video camera passed by, accompanied by another teenage girl with a mascara-streaked face.

The crowd consisted mostly of couples, though, going home to commiserate together.

Tucker and Allison among them.

I closed my eyes for a moment. They had each other. *I* had two distracted sisters and a very small ghost. Not much comfort there.

I rallied.

Told myself to get a grip.

Okay, so Tucker and I were on hiatus. Maybe we were even *over,* as I'd thought earlier. It wasn't as if I didn't have a *life,* after all. I'd recently started my own one-woman, kitchen-table detective agency, which I'd dubbed Sheepshanks, Sheepshanks and Sheepshanks, to give it some substance, and I'd inherited a biker bar. I had friends—so what if they were in Witness Protection and I was never going to see them again?

I sighed. My palms felt damp where I gripped the steering wheel.

Was there a *Damn Fool's Guide to Making New Friends?* I made a mental note to scour the bookstores and the Internet for a copy.

I shifted into Drive and pulled away from the curb, made a wide U-turn and headed for Bad-Ass Bert's.

Cave Creek isn't exactly a metropolis, so I was braking in the gravel parking lot the next thing I knew. Staring at the weathered walls of my saloon, cluttered with rusted-out beer signs. My old apartment was upstairs, and the last time I'd been in residence, I'd nearly been murdered myself.

Still, I missed the place, and it bugged me that I was afraid to stay there. I wasn't comfortable at Greer's, luxurious as it was. For one thing, I was worried that her husband, Alex Pennington, M.D., not exactly my greatest fan, might turn up beside my bed in a ski mask some dark night, and for another, Greer was really getting on my nerves. She had plenty of problems, including a cast on her left arm—some guy had tried to wrestle her into the back of a van in broad daylight just a few days back, and if Jolie hadn't been there to scald the perp with hot coffee, Greer would have been toast.

It wasn't as if she was out of danger, either.

One thing at a time, I thought. As if there was some universal crisis monitor out there someplace with a clipboard, making sure I didn't get overloaded.

Yeah. Right.

On an impulse, I pulled the keys from the ignition and got out of the car. Locked up and headed for the outside stairway leading to my second-floor apartment. Okay, I definitely wasn't ready to move back in, but I was up for a little immersion therapy. I was a grown woman, twenty-eight years old and self-supporting, and I'd survived some pretty hairy situations in my time.

I could stand walking through my empty apartment.

Sooner or later, I'd have to come to terms with the things that had happened there—some of them bad, some of them very, very good.

All the very, very good stuff involved Tucker, unfortunately. And it wasn't just the sex, either. We'd shared a lot of grilled cheese sandwiches in that apartment, swapped a few confidences, laughed and argued, too.

I climbed the stairs, and my hand shook only a little as I jammed the key into the lock and turned it. The door creaked on its hinges as I pushed it open, and I forced myself to step over the threshold.

Dark memories rushed me, left me breathless.

I switched on the light in the short hallway, even though it was three o'clock in the afternoon and the sun was blazing through every window.

My heart began to hammer as I moved into the living room. The atmosphere felt thick, smothering.

I half expected my dead ex-husband to appear, but he didn't.

Even *he* would have been some consolation that day.

I stayed close to the walls as I did reconnaissance, as cautious as if I were a member of some crack SWAT team staking out dangerous territory.

I sidestepped around the edges of the living room, the kitchen and finally the place I was most afraid to go—the bedroom. There was a peculiar humming thud in my ears, and my stomach kept bouncing up into the back of my throat.

I got down on my hands and knees, snagging my panty hose in the process, and peered under the bed. No monsters lurking there.

A tap on my shoulder nearly launched me through the ceiling.

I smacked my head on the bed frame and whirled on my knees, stoked on adrenaline, prepared to fight for my life.

It was only Gillian.

Her blue eyes glistened with tears. I wondered if she'd gone to the cemetery, seen her coffin lowered into the ground.

But no, there hadn't been time for that. And I knew there was no graveside service planned. Her mother and a few friends would be there, no one else.

I straightened and pulled her into my arms. I didn't even try not to cry.

She clung to me, shivering. She felt so small, so fragile. Ethereal, but solid, too.

"Talk to me, sweetheart," I whispered when I'd recovered enough to speak. "Tell me who—who did this to you."

She shook her head. Was she refusing to tell me, or was it that she didn't *know* who her murderer was? Yes, she'd denied her stepfather's guilt with a shake of her head, but that didn't mean she'd recognized her killer. He or she might have been a stranger. Or perhaps she hadn't actually seen the person at all; I wasn't even sure how or where she'd been killed. The police weren't releasing that information and there was no visible indication of trauma in her appearance, either.

Still, I had a strong intuitive sense that she was keeping a secret.

I got up off my knees, sat on the edge of the bed I was still too afraid to sleep in. Gillian perched beside me, looking up into my face with enormous, imploring eyes.

"Honey," I said carefully, "did you see the person who hurt you?"

Again, she shook her head, another clear no. There *had* been a slight hesitation, though.

I let out a breath. "But you're sure it wasn't your stepfather?"

She nodded vigorously.

I was about to ask how she could be so certain when the phone on my bedside table rang, a shrill jangling that made my nerves jump.

Gillian instantly evaporated.

I picked up the receiver more out of reflex than any desire to talk to anyone. "Hello?"

"It's Tucker."

I closed my eyes. Opened them again right away, in case some psycho was about to spring out of the woodwork and pounce. "What?" I asked, none too graciously.

He let out a sigh. "Look, I don't blame you for being upset," he said after an interval of brief, throbbing silence. "But we still need to talk."

"How did you know I was here?"

"I guessed."

"Liar."

"All right, I drove by after I dropped Allison off at home, and I saw your car in the parking lot at Bert's."

"Where are you?"

"Standing at the bottom of the stairway, trying to work up the nerve to come up and knock on your door."

"Don't," I said.

"Moje, we *need to talk*—about us, about lots of stuff. But today it's all about Gillian. I'm not planning to jump your bones, I promise."

"Okay," I heard myself say, taking him at his word. In fact, Tucker was about as easy to resist as a tsunami. "Come up, then. The door's open."

Tucker rang off, and I heard him double-timing it up the outside stairs.

I replaced the cordless phone on its base, stood, straightened the black dress I'd borrowed from Greer—it was the same one I'd worn to Lillian's funeral, not that long ago—and smoothed my wild red hair, which was trying to escape from the clip holding it captive at the back of my head.

"You should have locked the door," Tucker said, standing just inside my door in the tiny entry hall. He'd shed his suit coat, but he was still wearing the dark slacks, a crisp white shirt and a tie, the knot loosened. He looked like some next-dimension version of himself, just slightly off.

"As far as I know," I replied circumspectly, keeping my distance, "nobody is trying to kill me."

"Hey," he said with a bleak attempt at a grin, "given your history, that could change at any moment."

"Let's have coffee," I said, turning toward the kitchen. I needed a table between us if we were going to talk about Gillian, and something to do with my hands. "With luck, it hasn't been poisoned since I was here last."

Tucker followed me through the living room.

I felt a pang, missing Russell, a very alive basset hound, and my equally dead cat, Chester. Russell was in Witness Protection with his people, and Chester, after haunting me for a while, had gone on to the great beyond. Now he only haunted my memory.

My throat tightened as I grabbed the carafe off the coffeemaker, rinsed it at the sink and began the brewing process. I heard Tucker drag back a chair at the table behind me and sink into it.

"You've seen her again," he said. "Gillian, I mean."

I nodded without looking back at him. I couldn't, just then, because my eyes were burning with tears. "She was at the funeral."

Tucker didn't throw a net over me, for my own safety and that of others, or anything like that. He was the most rational man I'd ever known, and his brain was heavily weighted to the left, but as a child, he'd had an experience with a ghost himself. He'd believed me when I told him about seeing Nick, and Gillian, too.

I don't know what I would have done if he hadn't.

"She doesn't talk, Tuck," I said, groping to assemble the coffee. Open the can, spoon in ground java beans.

"She wouldn't," Tucker answered. "She was a deaf-mute."

I turned, staring at him, forgetting all about my wet eyes. He got up, took the carafe from my hands, poured the water into the top of the coffeemaker and pushed the button.

"I guess that shoots the theory that people leave their disabilities behind when they die," he said when I couldn't get a word out of my mouth.

"There's apparently some kind of transition phase for some people," I replied when I was sure my voice box hadn't seized and rusted. "In between death and whatever comes next, that is." I paused, moved away from him to get two mugs down off a cupboard shelf and rinse them out with hot water. "Why didn't you tell me Gillian couldn't hear or speak?"

Tucker leaned against the counter, his arms folded, the ancient coffeemaker chortling and surging behind him, like a rocket trying to take off but not quite having the momentum. Tilting his head slightly to one side, he answered, "It didn't come up, Moje. We haven't talked that much lately."

"She didn't see who killed her," I told him. "God, I hope it was quick—that she didn't suffer, or have time to be scared." I finally faced him. "Tucker, was she—was she—she wasn't—"

"She wasn't molested," Tucker said.

Relief swept through me with such force that my knees threatened to give out, and Tucker crossed the room in a couple of strides, took me by the shoulders and lowered me gently into a chair.

"How did she die?" I asked very softly. I didn't want to know, but at the same time I had to, or I was going to go crazy speculating.

Tucker crouched in front of my chair, holding both my hands in his. The pads of his thumbs felt only too good, chafing the centers of my palms. "You can't tell anybody, Moje," he said. "That's really important."

I knew that. I'd read *The Damn Fool's Guide to Criminal Investigation.* The police always keep certain pertinent details of any crime under wraps, for a lot of reasons, not the least of which is the danger of compromising the case if word gets out before the trial.

"Tell me," I said.

"Gillian was strangled," he told me. "With a piece of thin wire."

I swayed in my chair. "Oh, my God—"

"According to the ME, it happened quickly," Tucker said, but he looked as though he was thinking the same thing I was.

Not quickly enough.

"You're sure she ruled out the stepfather?" he asked when I didn't say anything.

I nodded. "I asked her twice."

"Moje," Tucker told me after rising from his haunches and taking a chair near mine, "he has an arrest record. Vince Erland, I mean. Solicitation of a minor—sexual context."

My stomach roiled. I slapped a hand over my mouth.

Tucker waited.

The coffee perked.

"He's a pedophile?" I asked, my voice coming out as a croak.

"We're not sure. The alleged victim was seventeen, and there was some evidence that she encouraged his advances. The charges were dismissed."

"But still…"

Tucker nodded grimly. "Still," he agreed.

"Gillian might have been mistaken," I murmured, "or maybe she simply didn't want to believe her stepfather, someone she trusted, would hurt her."

"Nine times out of ten," Tucker said, "the perp *is* somebody the victim trusts. Lousy, but true."

"But it could have been a random attack, right?"

"It could have been, but it probably wasn't."

"How can you be so sure?"

Tucker closed his eyes, opened them again. "Vince Erland picked Gillian up after the dance rehearsal. According to him, they stopped off at a supermarket on the way home and Gillian vanished. The report's on file—but he didn't call it in until he got back to the trailer. Most people would have been on the horn to 911 the *second* they realized their child was missing. Why did he wait?"

"I don't know," I said, pondering. "I didn't see this on the news, Tuck. That Mr. Erland was the last person to see Gillian—"

"It'll be out there soon enough," Tucker said. "His story is that he'd promised her a dog, and then had to go back on his word because he didn't have the money. He broke the news at the supermarket. She got mad and took off, and he thought she went home— it's a hike, but she probably could have done it."

"But the police don't believe it. That's why they're holding Erland."

Tucker looked conflicted. He probably knew a lot more about the case than he would admit, and he was deciding how much to tell me. "Partly," he said. "They're concerned for his safety, too. When it comes out that he was with Gillian just before she died, especially with his background, a lot of people aren't going to presume he's innocent until he's proven guilty. I don't need to tell you that emotions run high in situations like this. Some of the vigilante types might not be able to resist the temptation to take the law into their own hands."

I was still thinking about Gillian. She was a deaf-mute; she couldn't have cried out for help when she realized she was in trouble. Still, small as she was, she was determined, too. I believed she would have put up a struggle, however futile.

My heart ached, imagining that.

"Where was *Mrs.* Erland during all this?"

"Working," Tucker said with a shake of his head.

"No one saw anything? There must have been other shoppers in the store—clerks, passersby on the road..."

Tucker didn't answer.

"You're a DEA agent," I prodded. "How come you know so much about this investigation? Surely it isn't under federal jurisdiction."

"I resigned," he answered. "I'm with the sheriff's department now—homicide division."

"And right off the bat you were assigned to this particular case? Isn't that a conflict of interest, considering that Gillian and Daisy were friends?"

"Cave Creek is a small town," he reasoned quietly. "Helen Erland grew up here. Anybody who caught the case would have at least a passing acquaintance with the family."

I got up, because the coffee had finally stopped brewing, and poured a cup for Tucker and one for myself.

"I could help, Tucker," I said. "With the investigation."

Tucker's jawline immediately tightened. "No way," he replied tersely. "This is serious police work, Mojo. There's no place in a murder investigation for an amateur with a mail-order P.I. license and a stack of *Damn Fool's Guides* on procedure."

"Gillian came to *me*," I pointed out, generously

letting the gibe about my credentials pass. "There must be a reason."

Tucker, about to take a sip of his coffee, set the cup down with a thunk. A muscle bunched in his cheek. "I mean it, Mojo," he warned. "Stay out of this case."

"Too late," I answered. "I'm already in."

"How do you figure that?"

"You're the one with the badge," I admitted, "but *I'm* the one being haunted by a seven-year-old in a ballerina costume. I think Gillian's trying to help me figure out who killed her, and I wouldn't turn my back on her even if I could."

"Can't you just tell her to go into the Light, or something? Like that woman on TV?"

I sighed. "I wish it were that easy. Do you think I *like* having a little girl's ghost pop up every time I turn around? Gillian's not going anywhere, including into the Light, until she's ready."

Tucker paled under his biker's tan. Rubbed his palms together and stared as though he could see through my kitchen floor and into the closed bar beneath it.

"It's okay," I said.

I wanted to reach out, touch his cheek or his shoulder, but I didn't dare, because I knew where it would lead. We both needed comfort, and I was pretty sure any physical contact between us would be supercharged by grief and frustration. As much as I would have liked to lose myself in Tucker's lovemaking for a little while, if I did, I wouldn't be able to stand it when he went back to Allison.

"*What's* okay?" he rasped, understandably convinced that nothing ever could be "okay," in a world where children are murdered.

"Being relieved that this didn't happen to Daisy or Danny. It's a normal human reaction—and it doesn't mean you don't care about Gillian."

He glared at me. "Where did that come from? *The Damn Fool's Guide to Bullshit Psychology?*"

I sighed. "Go home, Tucker."

He did. He got up out of his chair and walked out, without another word or even a backward glance.

I should have been relieved, but I wasn't.

CHAPTER TWO

EVEN BEFORE Tucker's arrival I hadn't wanted to be alone in the apartment. After he was gone, the place seemed to yawn like some dark, uncharted cavern.

I emptied our cups, poured out the fresh coffee and shut off the machine. Then I snatched up my key ring, grabbed a couple of *Damn Fool's Guide*s off the bookshelves in my living room and boogied for the car.

When I arrived at Greer's fifteen minutes later, I parked in her brick driveway and, once I'd punched in the combination on the keypad by the back gate, skirted the main house. I simply wasn't up to seeing my sister just then.

The pool looked inviting as I passed, but the sun was still blazing, even though it was definitely headed west. *Later,* I promised myself.

The guesthouse, euphemistically called a "casita," was a three-bedroom, one-story territorial with all the conveniences—including a plasma TV that could be lowered out of the ceiling, a sunken bathtub with jets and a wet bar.

It was also blessedly cool.

I tossed my keys, purse and the stack of *Damn Fool's Guide*s onto the granite-topped counter separating the kitchen and combination living and dining room, and kicked off my high heels. Like the dress, they were Greer's, and they pinched my toes.

"Gillian?" I called.

Nothing.

I think I can be forgiven for being a little relieved that she wasn't around. And of course I knew she'd be back.

I proceeded to the master bath, stripped off the dress, chucked the ruined panty hose, started a lukewarm shower going and stepped naked under the spray. After I'd scrubbed and shampooed, I felt a little better. Wrapped in a towel, I padded back into the bedroom, lay down in the middle of the bed and allowed myself to air-dry.

I must have fallen asleep right away.

When I stirred to semiconsciousness, the room was nearly dark and my right big toe was clamped between two strong, cold fingers.

I choked out a strangled little shriek, wrenched free and shinnied to a sitting position with my back against the intricately carved headboard of the bed. Peering at the shadowy, adult-sized form—this was definitely not Gillian—I scrambled to cover myself with the towel.

"Alex?" I gasped, groping for the lamp on the bedside table. *Nick?*

I'd been meaning to shop for a gun—Jolie had promised to teach me how to shoot it—but there hadn't been time. Now I wished I'd bought one.

I flipped the switch, and light spilled into the room.

Greer was standing at the foot of my bed, wearing an oversize terry-cloth bathrobe, her cast bulging beneath one side. "You were expecting my husband?" my sister asked archly, raising one eyebrow.

I swore colorfully, finishing with a more moderate "*Damn* it, Greer, you scared me half to death!"

"I knocked," Greer said. "You didn't answer the door, so I came in. I *do* own the place, you know."

"As if you'd ever let me forget it," I snapped, getting off the bed in my towel toga and stomping into the bathroom to snatch my robe off the hook on the back of the door and yank it on. "You shouldn't sneak up on people like that, Greer," I ranted when I came out again. "If I'd gotten around to buying my Glock, you'd be *perforated* by now. And how come your fingers are so damn cold?"

Greer hadn't moved. Her blond hair was pulled into a ponytail, askew because she'd done it with one hand—on Greer, even that looked elegant—and her expression was stone serious. "I was digging through the freezer, looking for the tamale pie Carmen made before she left on vacation. When it wasn't there, I decided you might have nabbed it, so I came out here to find out."

"You could have just looked in my refrigerator,"

I pointed out, feeling only mildly guilty for stealing the tamale pie and dining on it, breakfast, lunch and dinner, until it was nearly gone.

"Why did you think it might be Alex who'd grabbed your toe?" Greer demanded suspiciously. Once she latched on to a subject, she was as tenacious as a pit bull with lockjaw.

"I'm not fooling around with your husband, Greer," I said. "If you won't credit me with any more honor than that, at least give me a few points for *taste*." I stomped out of the bedroom and through to the kitchen, where I opened the refrigerator door, yanked out the casserole dish with about three bites of tamale pie left in it, congealing under a curling crust of cornmeal topping, and slammed it down on the table.

"You never liked Alex," Greer accused.

"You're just figuring that out?" I countered. I took a half-empty bottle of white wine from the fridge next, uncorked it and poured two glasses—one for me and one for Greer. Mine was slightly fuller than hers. Okay, I was guilty of pie-napping, but I'd had a harder day than she had, so I figured it was fair.

Greer poked at the remains of the purloined pie with a beautifully manicured fingertip and made a face. "Yuck," she said, accepting the wineglass I offered.

I softened a little. "I could send out for a pizza," I suggested.

Greer took a sip of wine and made another face.

"At least you didn't steal *this* from me," she said. "My God, Mojo, how can you drink this stuff? It could double as nail polish remover."

I was used to my sister's wine snobbery. Her fruit-of-the-vine arrived in fancy crates, the elegant bottles artfully labeled and cosseted in wood shavings. Mine came from convenience stores and, if I was really feeling swank, supermarket closeout shelves. I usually got the boxed kind, in fact, with the handy-dandy little spigot built right in.

I didn't stoop to answer Greer's gibe. I simply opened the freezer compartment on my refrigerator, took out a frozen lasagna, single serving, low cal, low carb and low flavor, and handed it to Greer.

"Am I supposed to *eat* this?" she asked, raising both her perfectly plucked eyebrows this time.

"Since I only have one other option to suggest," I replied, "I'd go with eating, yes."

She blinked. "Do you have to be so nasty?" she asked.

I sighed. Shoved a hand through my hair, which was standing out around my head like the mane of some deranged lion because I'd fallen asleep while it was still wet from my shower. I'd probably need a whip and a chair to tame it. Maybe even a Weed Eater.

"Sorry," I said. "Bad day."

Greer slapped the frozen dinner down beside the casserole dish. "I suppose you think *mine* was wonderful? My life is a mess. Just last week I was accosted by an unknown assailant. My *arm* was broken. I haven't heard from my husband—for all I know, he's lying dead in the desert somewhere—"

"I went to a seven-year-old girl's funeral today, Greer," I said. Definitely trump card, but of course I didn't take any satisfaction in the victory.

"I forgot," Greer said, deflating. She pulled back a chair and sank into it.

"I wish I could," I answered.

Greer downed another slug of wine. Squeezed her eyes shut, and shuddered.

A little background on Greer. For one thing, she wasn't Greer Pennington any more than I was Mary Josephine Mayhugh. My abductor/mother, Lillian, had rescued her from a bus station in Boise when she was thirteen—more like sixteen, though she never admitted it—and unofficially adopted the runaway into our unconventional little family. I'd never known what or whom she'd run away from, but Lillian probably had. She'd have sent Greer back to her folks right away if home had been a good place to be.

Recently Greer had admitted she was being blackmailed, at least to Jolie and me, and she'd hired me to find out if her doctor husband was cheating on her. I'd followed up on a few leads, but with all that had been going on, I definitely hadn't earned my retainer.

I suspected, of course, that the broken-arm attack was connected to the blackmail, but I couldn't prove it.

I opened the freezer box, popped the contents

into the microwave and pushed the appropriate buttons. While Greer's supper nuked, I drew back another chair and sat down across from her.

Her eyes swam with tears as she gazed into her wineglass.

"Sooner or later," I said as gently as I could, given that my nerves were still quivering from the jolt she'd given me by gripping my big toe while I was sound asleep, "you're going to have to tell me the truth about who you are, Greer."

She gave an odd little giggle, followed by a hiccup. "Greer," she repeated. "Do you know where I got that name? Off a late-night movie on TV, starring Greer Garson. It was called *Julia Misbehaves,* and I almost went with 'Julia,' but 'Greer' had more pizzazz. I wanted to use Garson, too, but Lillian said that probably wouldn't fly. So I settled for Greer Stewart."

Considering how little Greer had told me about herself in all the years I'd known her, this was a revelation. I shouldn't have felt hurt because she'd obviously confided in Lillian, though probably not to any great extent and with a generous peppering of lies, but I did. Once, Greer and I had been close. Then I'd married Nick and she'd married Alex, and things had changed between us.

I had no clue why.

We'd both been playing parts, of course. And somewhere along the way we'd forgotten our lines.

"Who were you before you were Greer?" I persisted very quietly.

For a moment I actually thought she was going to tell me. Then she shook her head. "I know it sounds corny—like something from the late show—but that person doesn't exist anymore."

"Anything more from the blackmailer?" Talk about something from the late show. How often does a question like *that* come up in normal conversation?

Not that I'd know a normal conversation if I fell over it.

Greer bit her lower lip.

The timer on the microwave dinged.

I got up, pulled out the rubber lasagna and set it down in front of the woman I still thought of as my sister, for all the strange distance that stretched between us. I gave her some silverware and refilled her wineglass.

Tentatively she picked up a fork and jabbed it at the lasagna. I knew she was avoiding my eyes, and I was prepared to wait her out. I've got staying power—I once camped in front of a furniture store for three days to get the free couch they were offering as a prize at their grand opening. I was on the news twice, and Lillian, alarmed by the publicity, came and dragged me away fifteen minutes before I would have become the proud owner of an orange velour sectional, complete with built-in plastic cup holders.

Just one of the many reasons I have to be grateful to her.

"Greer?" I prompted.

"Yes," she said.

"Yes, what?"

"Yes, I've heard from the blackmailers—plural."

"When? What did he—they—say? Was it a letter, a phone call, an e-mail? Black-and-white eight-by-tens of you in some compromising position?"

Greer skewered me with a look. "This lasagna," she said, "is worse than the wine." But she kept eating. And she kept drinking, too, though I'd already lost interest in the vino. It *did* taste like vinegar.

"How am I supposed to help you if you won't tell me what's going on?"

"I didn't hire you because I'm being blackmailed. I hired you to find out if Alex is cheating on me."

"He is," I said, silently saying goodbye to the five-thousand-dollar retainer she'd given me, not to mention the other five I would have gotten when I turned in a definitive report. Actually, I was in pretty good financial shape for the first time in my life, because my demon ex-mother-in-law, Margery DeLuca, had forked over the proceeds of a life insurance policy Nick had taken out, in a fit of fiscal responsibility, with me as beneficiary. Still, Greer's payment represented my first earnings as a private investigator and for me that was meaningful.

Greer stiffened, peering at me over the lasagna and the cheap wine. "Do you have proof?"

"No," I said.

"Then the case isn't solved, is it? Maybe now that people aren't trying to kill you, you can get back to work." This was a reference to recent misadventures—so recent, in fact, that I still had little gummy bits of duct-tape residue on my wrists and ankles. I'd soaked and scoured, but they just kept appearing, as though they'd been hiding under my skin.

"Greer," I said.

"What?" She sounded testy. Could have been the leather noodles and the rotgut, but I didn't think so. Greer had been defensive, to say the least, since she'd stolen Alex Pennington from his first missus, closed down her hard-won interior design business and become the classic trophy wife.

"Talk to me. Who's blackmailing you, and why? More important, have you changed your mind about telling the police?"

The last time we'd discussed the issue, Greer and Jolie and I, she'd refused to involve Scottsdale's finest. Apparently whatever she'd done to get herself into this mess was bad enough that she was willing to risk her peace of mind, and maybe even her life, to keep it under wraps.

Suddenly Greer shivered, hugged herself. There *was* a distinct chill in the air, and I expected Gillian to appear, but she didn't.

Inwardly, I sighed. If the child didn't turn up soon, I was going to have to go out looking for her. Yes, she was a ghost—technically. But she was also a little kid, caught between two worlds, scared and alone. She'd witnessed her own funeral, too, and that must have been almost as traumatic as her murder.

"I did something terrible when I was young," Greer said. "Someone knows."

"What did you do, Greer?"

"I'm not going to tell you," she said, pushing back her chair to stand. Turning to flee, she stumbled a little. "I can handle this on my own."

I went after her. Caught hold of her good arm. "Greer," I pleaded, "listen to me. Somebody tried to nab you—you're obviously in real danger. What's going to happen if Alex pulls the financial plug, and you can't pay these people off any longer?"

She didn't answer. Trembling, she shook her head, pulled free and fled.

Some P.I. *I* was. I had a real way with people.

Disconsolately, I finished Greer's lasagna and what was left of the tamale pie. I'd barely touched my wine, so I poured it down the drain and went back to the bedroom to get dressed.

Five minutes later, sporting jeans, a tank top and a lightweight denim jacket, I fired up the Volvo and headed out to look for Gillian. It was after nine o'clock by then, and nearly dark.

I headed for the cemetery in north Scottsdale, where I knew Gillian had been buried. The place was fenced, but the gates stood open, so I drove in, considered the layout and parked. There were a few other people around—a couple of groundskeepers, a young man sitting cross-legged beside a tombstone and an old woman in a green polyester pantsuit and sensible shoes, arranging and rearranging flowers in an urn.

I didn't have to ask directions. I spotted Gillian right away, standing next to a new grave mounded with raw dirt.

I got out of the car, shoved my hands into the hip pockets of my jeans and approached.

Gillian couldn't have heard me, but she must have sensed that I was there, because she looked up and watched solemnly as I drew near.

I added another title to the growing list of *Damn Fool's Guides* I needed to acquire—one on sign language. I thought of how I'd asked Gillian about her killer, and she'd answered. Maybe she could read my mind—she'd responded at the funeral, when I'd mentally asked her to come back to where I was sitting—but it was more likely that she'd simply read my lips.

Duh. Mojo Sheepshanks, supersleuth. Not much gets by me.

Aware that she didn't want to be touched, and not too keen on being seen reaching out to empty air, should anyone happen to glance in our direction, I kept my hands in my pockets instead of cupping her face in them, as I wanted so much to do.

A single tear slid down her smudged cheek.

Because she'd lowered her head, maybe hoping to hide the fact that she was crying, I crouched on the other side of the mound so I could look up into her eyes. I steeled myself to see marks on her neck, left by the wire someone had used to strangle her, according to Tucker, but her flesh was unmarked.

"Hey," I said gently.

"Hey," Gillian mouthed silently.

It was a forlorn greeting, but at least she'd acknowledged my presence.

"Time to go home," I told her, forming the words very slowly and carefully. "You can stay at my place."

She stared at me, looking almost defiant. Her little hands were clenched into fists, and her stance told me she wasn't going anywhere, and I couldn't make her. True enough. She'd simply vanish if I made any sudden moves.

How do you bribe a ghost-child? Do you offer to buzz through the drive-in at McDonald's for a happy meal?

"You could watch TV," I said, after searching my brain for any scrap of kid lore. "I have a big one that comes down out of the ceiling when you push a button."

She signed something, but I didn't know what it was.

"She wants you to buy her a dog," a voice said.

I almost fell over, I was so jolted. I got to my feet and turned to see the young guy I'd glimpsed earlier, meditating beside a grave.

Duh, again. He was dead. The old lady with the flowers probably was, too. I made a mental note to pay more attention to my surroundings and not assume everybody I saw was alive.

He smiled.

I hoped he wasn't planning to follow me home. I had my hands full with one ghost—I didn't need two.

I swallowed. Stood up straight. "You're—"

"Dead," he said cheerfully.

"And you understand sign language."

He nodded. "I took a couple of special classes at the community college," he said. "I needed a service project to make Eagle Scout." He signed something to Gillian, and she eagerly signed back.

"Ask if she knows who killed her," I said.

"Whoa," he said, round eyed.

"Just do it, okay? It's important."

"I don't think we covered that in class," the boy replied. "But I'll try."

His hands moved.

Gillian's hands moved.

"She doesn't know," he said. "It happened really fast."

"Damn," I muttered. Then I took a closer look at him. He was wearing jeans and a red T-shirt, and he was even younger than I'd first thought. He probably hadn't even made it through high school before he passed away. "What's your name and when did you die?" I asked.

"I'm not sure when I croaked," he said. "I only

figured it out the other day. Up till then, I just thought I was having a bad dream."

I threw back my head, looked up at heaven. Why did God just allow these people to wander around, not knowing they were dead? Wasn't there some kind of intake system? Where were the angels? Where were the loving relatives, come to lead the newly deceased into the Light?

"But my name is Justin Braydaven," Justin went on. "I probably wouldn't be able to tell you that much if I hadn't read it off my headstone." He shook his head. "I've really been spaced lately."

"You didn't remember your name—but you can still communicate in sign language?"

Justin shrugged. "Maybe it's like riding a bike," he said. "You never forget how to do it, even when you're—" he stopped, swallowed "—dead."

I felt sorry for him, for obvious reasons. There was so much he was never going to experience. "I guess your date of death is probably on that headstone, too. Under your name."

"I was so glad to know who I was, I forgot to look for that."

"Justin, do you see a big light? If you do, you should go into it."

"No big lights," Justin said, sounding good-naturedly resigned.

Gillian began to sign again.

"She's back to the dog," Justin told me. "It's a big thing to her. Maybe there's one at the pound."

I thought about Vince Erland, promising his step-daughter a pet and then reneging. It would be easy to judge him for that, but the fact is, dogs and cats need a lot of things—shots, food, spaying or neutering, sometimes ongoing veterinary care. Those things aren't cheap.

The three of us started walking down a paved, sloping drive, in the general direction of my car. I was musing, Justin and Gillian were signing.

"Hey, lady!" one of the groundskeepers called to me, loading tools into the back of a battered pickup truck. "We're closing up for the night!"

I nodded. "On my way," I called back.

We passed the old lady, fussing happily with her bouquet. She didn't seem to notice us.

"She's been in a good mood since the flowers came," Justin informed me.

I drew up at the headstone where I'd first seen him, peered at the lettering.

He'd been dead for six years.

Where had he been all that time?

"Can I drop you off somewhere?" I asked, because I couldn't just leave him there.

After giving the matter some serious thought, Justin came up with an address, and we all piled into the Volvo—Justin, Gillian and me. I recall a few curious glances from the groundskeepers when I opened the passenger door, flipped the seat forward so Gillian could climb in back and waited until Justin was settled up front.

I smiled and waved to the spectators.

The smile faded as I drove out of the cemetery, though.

I was busy trying to solve the great cosmic mysteries—life, death, the time-space continuum.

No *Damn Fool's Guide* on that.

As it turned out, Justin lived—or *had* lived—in a modest, one-story rancher in one of the city's many housing developments. I swear, every time I leave town, another one springs up. There were lights in the windows of the stucco house with the requisite red tile roof, though the shades were drawn, and an old collie lay curled up on the small concrete porch.

When we came to a stop at the curb, the dog got up and gave a halfhearted woof.

"Justin?" I said.

"Yeah?"

"This is your folks' place, right?"

"It's home," he answered affably. Instead of opening the car door and getting out, he'd simply teleported himself to the sidewalk, leaning to speak to me through the open window on my side. The collie tottered slowly down the front steps. Its coat was thinning, and I saw lots of gray in it. "My mom lives here. My dad left a long time ago."

Hope stirred. If his dad was dead, he might come looking for Justin, show him the way to the other side. He was sure taking his sweet time doing it, though.

"Your dad passed away?"

Justin shook his head. "No. He just decided he didn't want to support a family."

My spirits, already low, plummeted. I blinked a couple of times.

"Your mom…" I paused, swallowed, wanting to cry. Was the kid expecting a welcome-home party? "She probably won't be able to see you, Justin."

Justin nodded. "I know," he said. "I just want to be where she is. See my old room and stuff. I couldn't figure out how to get back here, that's all."

The dog was near now, and it made a little whimpering sound that must have been recognition, then toddled over to nuzzle the back of Justin's hand.

"Hey," he said. "Pepper can see me."

"Not uncommon," I told him, drawing on my enormous store of knowledge about the ins and outs of the afterlife. "Animals have special sensitivities." I paused, gulped. "You'll be okay, then?"

Justin grinned, and I had a sudden, piercing awareness of just how much his mother probably missed him. If I'd had the guts, I'd have knocked on her front door and told her straight out that her son was still around. That he still cared, still wanted to be close to her.

But I didn't.

"What's your name?" Justin asked after leaning down to pet the dog. "In case I need to contact you, or something?"

"Mojo Sheepshanks," I said after briefly considering, I'm ashamed to admit, making up an alias.

"No shit?" he marveled. He stooped again, signed what was most likely a goodbye to Gillian and turned to walk away.

I sat at the curb watching as he and the dog, Pepper, headed for the house.

The front door opened, and a woman appeared on the threshold. I couldn't make out her features, but her voice was nice.

"There you are, Pepper," she called. "Come on inside now. Time for supper."

She obviously didn't see Justin, but he slipped past her, with Pepper, before she shut the door.

A lump formed in my throat.

The living-room drapes parted, and Justin's mother looked out at me.

Strange car in the neighborhood.

Not a good thing.

I shoved the car into gear and drove away.

Gillian, meanwhile, had moved to the front seat.

"I'm sorry, but I'm not getting a dog," I told her in a rush of words, careful to turn my face in her direction. "I live in my sister's guesthouse. She'd have a fit."

In that moment I was filled with a sudden and fierce yearning for my apartment. All right, I'd almost been murdered there. But it was *my* place, just the same. I could have a dog if I wanted. I could eat tamale pie for three days without feeling guilty—though stealing it would be trickier.

Did I mention that I never deliberately cook?

We made a detour, Gillian and I, and I zipped into a megabookstore to look for a *Damn Fool's Guide to Sign Language*. Sure enough, there was one, complete with the hand alphabet and lots of illustrations. Inspired, I grabbed a second volume from the series, this one on popularity.

I was only a *little* embarrassed to buy a book that had probably been written for grossly overweight computer nerds and aspiring middle-school cheerleaders, but, hell, there wasn't anything else for the socially challenged.

Back at Greer's place, I led Gillian to the guesthouse, and she immediately plunked down on the couch. No orange velour here—Greer's furniture was all decorator approved. True to my word, I brought the TV down out of the ceiling and cruised the channels until I found a cartoon.

Gillian was instantly engrossed.

I studied her ballerina outfit. If I bought her some clothes at Wal-Mart in the morning, I wondered, would she be able to wear them?

Nick, my ex-husband, had always shown up in the suit he was buried in. I had a feeling ghosts didn't have extensive wardrobes. Still, it was worth a try.

Gillian's leotard, tights and tutu were bedraggled, and she was still wearing just the one slipper. It haunted me, that missing slipper.

I wanted to cry every time I looked at her.

Which wasn't about the outfit, I know, but I needed to *do* something.

While Gillian watched TV, I brewed a pot of tea and sat down at my kitchen table to study *The Damn Fool's Guide to Sign Language.*

After two hours I knew how to say, "The cow is brown" and ask for directions to the nearest restroom.

Not very impressive, I know. But it was a start.

When I finally went to bed Gillian was still sitting on the couch, staring blindly at the TV screen.

CHAPTER THREE

GILLIAN WAS GONE when I got up the next morning, and the TV was still on. Closed-captioned dialogue streamed across the screen.

I sighed. Picked up the remote and switched to a news channel, clicking off the subtitle feature.

This was an act of courage. Because of my last excellent adventure, I'd been all over the media for days. That's what happens, I guess, when you suddenly remember who killed your parents when you were five years old, and the guilty parties try to shut you up before you can spill the proverbial beans.

That was last *week,* I told myself, but it wasn't much consolation.

The talking heads were prattling about obesity in children, and I regarded that as a positive sign. Nothing bombed, nothing hijacked. A slow news day is a *good* news day.

Trying to decide whether I ought to go to Wal-Mart for ghost clothes or run down another lead on Greer's cheating husband, I padded into the kitchen to start a pot of java. Greer's coffeemaker was state

of the art, unlike mine, and I had my choice of everything from cappuccinos and lattes to cocoa and hot
cider.

All I wanted was coffee, damn it. Plain, ordinary,
simple *coffee.*

Again I missed my apartment and the chortle-
chug of my own humble brewing apparatus.
Heebie-jeebies or not, I was going to have to bite
the bullet and go back. All this luxury was getting
to me in a big way.

I wrestled a single cup of caffeine from the sleek
monster machine, with all its shining spouts and
levers, and headed back to the living room, blinking
blearily at the TV screen as the theme shifted from
fat kids to Gillian Pellway's murder investigation.

Tucker Darroch's harried face appeared, close
up, then the camera panned back. He was wearing
a blue cotton work shirt, sleeves rolled to the
elbows, along with jeans and Western boots, and he
looked as though he'd like to be anywhere else but
in front of the sheriff's office with a microphone
practically bumping his lower lip.

"An arrest has been made, and yet the investigation continues?" the reporter asked. "Does that mean
you aren't sure you have the right man in custody?"

"Mr. Erland hasn't been formally charged,"
Tucker answered, tersely patient. "He's being held
for questioning."

"He's been in the county jail for almost a week,"
the reporter pointed out helpfully. She was ultra-

skinny—obesity clearly *wasn't* rampant among media types—and wore a pink suit with a pencil skirt and fashionably short jacket. Her hair was blond and big. "Doesn't that indicate that Mr. Erland is a prime suspect?"

Personally, I thought she was standing a tad closer to Tucker than absolutely necessary. I get sidetracked by things like that.

I took another slurp of coffee and reminded myself that I had no claim on Tucker Darroch. Oh, no. He still belonged to Allison, the divorce notwithstanding. While I'd tossed and turned in my lonely bed the night before, dreaming about dead people, he'd probably been snuggled in his ex-wife's arms.

I almost choked on the coffee.

"Mr. Erland," Tucker said evenly, "is a person of interest, not a suspect."

Copspeak, I thought. Tucker *couldn't* make a definitive statement regarding Erland's innocence or guilt—I knew it, Tucker knew it and so did the reporter, along with most of the viewing audience, a few flakes excepted. It was all rhetoric to fill airtime.

Translation: nobody knew jack-shit.

The interview ended.

The telephone rang.

A wild fantasy overwhelmed me. It was Tucker, I decided, calling to ask if I'd seen him on TV.

As if he'd ever do that.

"Hello?" I cried into the cordless receiver I'd snatched up from the coffee table.

"Who is this?" an unfamiliar female voice demanded.

I bristled, disappointed. "You first," I said. "After all, *you're* the one who placed the call."

There was a short standoff, and I was about to break the connection when the caller relented.

"My name," the woman said, "is Mrs. Alexander Pennington. And I'm looking for Mojo Sheepshanks."

I hadn't had all that much coffee. It took a moment for my brain to grope past Greer, the only "Mrs. Alexander Pennington" I knew, to the ex-wife with the drinking problem. I'd met her once at Fashion Square Mall, and her image assembled itself in my mind—overweight, expensively dressed, too-black hair worn Jackie O bouffant.

"This is Mojo," I said, against my better judgment. "What do you want?"

All right, maybe that question *was* a little abrupt, but it was direct and to the point. The first Mrs. Pennington knew I was Greer's sister, and that meant she'd probably called out of some codependent need to harangue the trophy wife in a flank attack. It's always better to be direct with that kind of person.

"I understand you're a private investigator now," Mrs. Pennington #1 said with drunken dignity. I wondered if she was still under the influence of last night's cocktail hour, or if she subscribed to the hair-of-the-dog-that-bit-you theory and had started the day with a Bloody Mary.

I closed my eyes. Damn all that TV coverage, anyway. Why had I touted myself as a P.I. every time I got in front of a camera? Now people actually expected me to solve things. "How did you get my number?" I asked.

"You're in the book."

Right. And I'd programmed my phone at the apartment to forward calls to Greer's guesthouse. I needed more coffee.

"Yes," I said, scrambling for a little dignity of my own.

"I'd like to hire you."

"That would be a conflict of interest, Mrs. Pennington," I said, intrigued in spite of myself. "As you know, your ex-husband is currently married to my sister."

"I'm aware of that," she replied moderately. "Believe me. This is a separate matter, and it's delicate, which is why I would prefer not to discuss it over the telephone."

It finally occurred to me that Mrs. Pennington-the-first might be one of Greer's blackmailers. As I said, I hadn't had enough coffee.

While it seemed like a stretch, hell hath no fury like a woman scorned and, besides, you can dig up dirt on just about anybody if you have the resources to hire enough muscle to do the shoveling.

Suffice it to say that an instinct kicked in. There

was something important going on under the surface here, and I had to find out what it was.

"When did you want to meet?" I asked.

"Noon today," Mrs. Pennington answered readily, reeling off a posh address not that far from Greer's. "I'll have Carlotta serve her special lobster salad, so don't eat before you get here."

I wasn't sure eating anything prepared under the *grande dame*'s roof would be smart, but I liked lobster, and my budget didn't allow for much of it. I had my stash in the bank, thanks to Margery DeLuca, but I didn't plan on blowing it on seafood.

"Noon," I repeated cautiously. I'd scrawled the address on the front of a *TV Guide*.

"I'd rather you didn't tell your sister about this meeting, if you don't mind," Mrs. Pennington went on. "At least, not immediately."

"I can't promise that, Mrs. Pennington," I said, frowning. Elsewhere on the *TV Guide* cover someone had written, in lopsided, childish letters, "DOG."

Gillian, of course.

She could write? Not much, probably, since she was only seven. Still, the word opened up a whole new realm of possibilities. Mentally I added an item to the shopping list in my head.

"Call me Beverly," Mrs. Pennington said.

I wasn't planning an ongoing relationship with Beverly Pennington, but calling her by her first name would certainly be less awkward, given that on the rare occasions the words *Mrs. Pennington* came to my mind, it was always in reference to Greer.

"Beverly it is," I agreed.

We said our goodbyes, and I hung up. After a glance at the clock I took a quick, cool shower, donned a blue-and-white-print sundress with spaghetti straps and a pair of sandals and subdued my hair with a pinch clip. Tufts stuck up on my crown, giving the do a decidedly *un*done look, but hey, it wasn't as if I was a TV reporter or anything. I was a *detective,* Tucker's snide remarks about my mail-order license aside.

I was sort of expecting Gillian to materialize in the front seat of the Volvo as I backed out of the driveway, but it didn't happen. I hoped she hadn't returned to the graveyard to hang out. I was no expert on ghost behavior—maybe she'd gone home, the way Justin had, or to her school, or any one of a number of familiar places—but I'd found her at the cemetery once before.

All those possibilities stuck in the bruised places in my heart like slowly turning screws.

I couldn't go to the school, or to the Erland home—at least, not without an excuse, and I hadn't thought of one yet. I'd take a spin through the cemetery, though, I decided, on my way to Wal-Mart.

My cell phone jingled inside my purse as I was pulling onto the 101, heading south. I upended the bag and fumbled for the phone, afraid to take my eyes off the road. Arizona drivers, I've gotta tell ya, are stone-crazy. Maybe it's the serotonin, from all that sunlight. Seasonal affective disorder in reverse. Maybe it's the flat, straight roads. Whatever it is, most of them drive like maniacs, and last time I checked Phoenix was the number one city in the country for red-light fatalities.

"Hello?" I said, swerving to avoid a white Expedition crossing in front of me to make a last-moment exit. "Tucker?"

I hadn't dared to glance at the caller ID panel before I answered; even a split second could have meant months in traction, and I don't have that kind of spare time.

"Sorry," Jolie said. "It's only your sister. You know, the black one?"

I was glad to hear her voice. "Yeah," I replied, grinning. "I remember. What's up?"

"I'm on the job," Jolie answered, and from the change in her tone I figured she must have cupped the phone with one hand, hoping her voice wouldn't carry. For Jolie, "on the job" probably meant she was standing over a body. "Moje, this is bad."

"What?" I asked, navigating the road leading to the cemetery. If I wasn't careful, I'd end up checking in for good, and the adrenaline rush brought on by Jolie's words wasn't helping.

"I can't talk long," Jolie said, hush-hush. "The short version is I'm standing in the desert about twenty yards from a corpse, and I'm ninety-nine percent sure it's Alex Pennington's."

The Volvo's tires squealed as I wrenched the car off the road, came to a stop in a restaurant parking lot. I was shaking. "No!"

"Yes," Jolie replied with a sigh. "The uniforms are here, and homicide is on its way. But it's Alex, all right. I'd know that asshole anywhere."

"Who found him? How was he killed?"

"Gotta go," Jolie chimed, and hung up.

Something Greer had said the night before stung my brain. *For all I know, he's lying dead in the desert somewhere.*

"Shit," I said to my empty car.

She couldn't have done it. She *couldn't* have killed Alex. The Greer I knew, while self-absorbed and famously high maintenance, simply wasn't capable of that.

I shook off the agitation and switched the dial to damage control.

How was I going to break news like this to Greer? Even though she'd hired me to get the goods on Pennington, I knew she loved the guy, even hoped to have a family with him, which was why I didn't seriously entertain the notion that she might have killed him. I also knew she was still hoping he'd come out pure on the other end of my investigation. Instead, he'd come out *dead.*

A new and even more alarming thought elbowed its way to the forefront of my mind. What if he haunted me?

Goose bumps sprouted on my forearms, and

even though it was a hundred degrees outside, I felt as though I'd just stepped into a meat locker.

I did some deep breathing—*Damn Fool's Guide to Relieving Stress*—and waited until the shaking subsided.

What to do?

Motor back to Greer's and wait, pretending I didn't know Alex was a goner, until the police called or dropped by to tell her what had happened?

For one thing, I couldn't pretend that well. For another, Greer probably wasn't home. Even though she had a cast on her left arm, she attended her yoga class faithfully every morning, had lunch out and then went shopping.

When I was steady enough, I drove back out onto the street and went on to the cemetery. I could call Greer on her cell phone, but what would I say? *A body's been found in the desert and Jolie is ninety-nine percent sure it's Alex?*

What if it *wasn't* Alex? Okay, it was almost a sure thing, but there *was* that one-percent factor.

I bit my lip. Drove through the cemetery gates.

The old lady was there, still fiddling with her flowers.

But there was no sign of Gillian.

Half-relieved, I turned around and fixed my internal GPS on Wal-Mart.

Cell phones were a no-no in yoga class, which meant I wouldn't be able to get through to Greer anyway, and I still didn't know what I'd say if I did.

The parking lot at Wally World was crowded.

I wedged the Volvo in between a tangle of shopping carts and an old car with a Confederate-flag sunscreen, and sprinted for the entrance. I was in no particular hurry, though, since I had almost two hours before my lunch date with Beverly Pennington, and I was probably going to break that, anyway.

After all, she'd been married to Alex, and they had several grown children. However acrimonious the divorce had been, she was in for a shock. I didn't want to be there when she got the news.

I took a cart, wheeled into the store. Two old guys in blue vests welcomed me to Wal-Mart. One of them was dead, but he seemed happy enough.

I guess there are worse ways to spend eternity.

I headed for the children's section, picked out two pairs of jean shorts and two T-shirts that looked as though they'd fit Gillian, along with some tiny white sneakers. Then it was on to the toy department, where I chose a blackboard and a box of colored chalk.

The whole thing took under fifteen minutes, which left me with a serious gap in my schedule. I paid and left the store with my purchases.

Gillian was sitting in the front seat of my car when I got back.

"Look," I said, holding up a blue plastic bag. "I bought you a change of clothes."

She gave me a piteous glance, turned in the seat and wrote "MOM" in the dust on my dashboard with the tip of one finger.

I got the blackboard out of its cardboard box and handed it to Gillian, along with the chalk.

She blinked, looked at me curiously, then extracted a pink stick of chalk from the box and wrote "MOM" again.

I sighed, got into the car and fastened my seat belt. Started the engine. Alarming thought number seventy-two struck in the next instant. I took Gillian's chin in my hand, turned her to face me.

"Was your mom the one?" I asked slowly. "The one who hurt you, I mean?"

Gillian's eyes widened, and she shook her head.

"Do you know where she is now?"

She rubbed out "MOM" and replaced it with "WURK."

Work? Helen Erland was at *work,* the day after her child's funeral, selling cigarettes and auto air fresheners and propane tanks for people's barbecue grills? "Why didn't you just pop in on her, the way you do with me?"

Gillian's chest moved with a silent sigh.

"Okay," I said. "I'll take you there. But she still won't be able to see you, Gillian. Are you sure you want to do this?"

Gillian nodded. Erased "WURK" and wrote "DOG."

"No dog," I said without conviction.

Gillian underlined the word with a slashing motion of her hand and looked stubborn.

"We'll see," I told her.

We headed for Cave Creek, and sure enough, her mother was behind the counter at the convenience store, wearing a pink cotton smock with a company logo on the pocket. She looked wrecked—her eyes were puffy and swollen from crying, and she hadn't bothered with the usual heavy makeup. She seemed younger without it. Her hair, blond like Gillian's, was pulled back into a ponytail, and even though she was pale, there was a tragic prettiness about her.

I bought a forty-four-ounce diet cola, feeling nervous, while Gillian stared at her mother with a longing that made me ache at a cellular level.

"You were at Gillian's funeral," Helen said, blinking as though she was just coming out of a stupor. "I saw you."

I nodded. Put out my free hand. "Mojo Sheepshanks," I said. "I come into the store sometimes. I'm so sorry, Mrs. Erland—about Gillian."

She blinked. Retreated into herself a little. I'd seen the expression before; any moment now, the blinds would be pulled and the lights would go out. "You're the one who was on TV."

"Yes," I answered.

"You're a detective," she mused.

"A private investigator," I clarified.

She leaned partway across the counter and spoke in a low voice. "My husband did not kill our daughter," she said. "Vince would never have hurt Gillian."

I didn't know what to say to that, so I didn't say anything.

Fresh tears sprang to Helen Erland's eyes. "The police think Vince is guilty," she whispered desperately. "They're not even looking for the real murderer!"

I thought of Tucker. Whatever our differences, I knew he was a good cop. He'd be looking for the killer, all right. I let the remark pass, since I wasn't there to argue. "I know you must have been asked this question over and over again, until you wanted to scream," I said gently. "But do you have any idea who might have done such a thing? Besides your husband, I mean."

She sniffled, snatched a handful of tissues from a box behind the counter and swabbed her face. Her skin looked raw, as though she'd tried to scrub it away. "It must have been a drifter, someone like that," she said. "Nobody who knew Gillian would want to hurt her." There was a short pause. "She was such a brave little thing. She couldn't hear, you know, or speak, except in sign language. But she did everything the other kids did—even ballet. She told me she could *feel* the music, coming up through the floor."

I swallowed. I could have used a handful of tissues myself just about then.

"I'm so sorry," I said again.

"Everybody's 'sorry,'" Helen Erland replied, almost scoffing. "That won't bring her back."

I nodded, looked away, blinked rapidly until my

vision cleared. "I wish there was some way I could help," I said, thinking aloud.

"I work in a cash-and-dash," Mrs. Erland said, peering at me from beneath an overhead cigarette rack on my side of the counter. "I can't pay you much, but if you want to help—if you weren't just saying that—there *is* something you can do. You can find out who killed my baby girl."

I felt Gillian's hand creep into mine, and gave it a subtle squeeze.

I remembered Tucker's warning the day before, in my apartment. *I mean it, Mojo. Stay out of this case.*

"This is a matter for the police, Mrs. Erland," I said. "Not a private detective."

"The *police*," Helen mocked. "They think they've got the killer. They're just going to *pretend* to investigate until all the media hype dies down. Then Vince will spend the rest of his life in prison—if he isn't executed—and whoever did this will go free."

I wondered how much of the conversation Gillian was taking in. She couldn't hear, and being dead hadn't changed that, but she'd probably learned to read her mother's every expression, not just her lips.

Her fingers tightened around mine.

"I'll look into it," I heard myself say. It wasn't the fee that prompted this decision—there wouldn't be one. And it wasn't the chance to learn by experience, so I'd be a better detective. Gillian wasn't going to rest if the killer wasn't found. That had to be the reason she was hanging around. "But I can't promise anything, Mrs. Erland."

A semblance of hope sparked in Helen's sorrow-dimmed eyes. "Just do what they're *not* doing," she said.

I knew she was referring to the police again, and I nodded. "You'll have to help me. Answer lots of questions. And if you can get me in to see Mr. Erland, I'd like to talk to him." Read: size him up.

She nodded almost eagerly. "I get off at six," she said. "Maybe you could come by my place, and we could talk. I'll call Vince's public defender and ask if he can arrange a visit."

I nodded, but my mind had drifted to the body that was probably Alex's. Greer's world was about to collapse all around her, and I'd need to be there to help gather up the pieces. Not that she'd be grateful—comforting her would be like trying to bathe a porcupine.

"When's your next day off?" I asked.

"I don't have any days off," Helen answered. "I took every shift I could get. Staying home makes me—well, I can't stand it. There are too many reminders, and with Vince gone, it's even worse."

"I'll stop by tonight, then," I said. Jolie would be off work by then, if it didn't take too long to process the crime scene. She'd have to be the one to bathe the porcupine. "Your place, around six-fifteen?"

Helen nodded and gave me directions.

I turned to leave, glancing at my watch, and I

wasn't surprised when Gillian didn't follow. The poor kid wanted to be with her mother.

My throat knotted, and I wiped my eyes with the back of one hand.

I felt a little pang as I drove past Bad-Ass Bert's, too. I'd finally worked up my courage to move back into my apartment, but it wasn't going to happen any time soon. I'd have to stay at the guesthouse, in case Greer needed me.

Shit. I really wanted to go home.

It was still too early, but I headed for Beverly Pennington's place anyway. It was an upscale condo in a gated community, and there were police cars clogging the entrance. The sheriff's department, Phoenix and Scottsdale PD—the gang was all there.

I made an executive decision and canceled lunch.

No lobster for me. Maybe I'd spring for a box of fish sticks.

Jolie called again just as I was pulling into Greer's driveway.

No squad cars in evidence there, anyway. And no sign of Greer's pricey SUV.

Call me callous, but I was relieved.

"Was it Alex?" I asked, without a hello.

"Yes," Jolie said.

I swore. There'd been, as they say, no love lost between Alex Pennington and me, but I wouldn't have wished him dead. And Greer was going to come unglued when she found out. "What happened?"

"He must have pissed somebody off, big-time," Jolie said. "The term 'riddled with bullets' has new meaning."

"Where are you?" I whispered loudly, getting out of the Volvo.

"In my car, headed for Greer's," Jolie replied. "Where are you?"

"Waiting for you at Casa Pennington," I said, punching in the security numbers on the back gate with a stabbing motion of one finger. "Are there any leads?"

"The suits don't discuss things like that with lowly crime-scene techs," Jolie answered. "Right off the top of my head, though, I'd say they haven't got a clue."

"If that was supposed to be a play on words, it bites," I snapped.

"Moje?"

"What?"

"I'm on your side."

"Greer is going to *freak*."

"Maybe," Jolie said.

"What do you mean, 'maybe'?"

"She's the *wife*, Moje. She and Alex haven't been getting along lately. She's automatically a suspect."

I dealt with another jolt of adrenaline. Yanked open the front door of the guesthouse and went in. "You mean a person of interest."

"That's a bullshit, politically correct term for *suspect*," Jolie told me.

"You don't think she could actually have *done* this?" I challenged, furious because the possibility, so readily dismissed before, suddenly seemed more viable.

"What do we really know about Greer?" Jolie asked reasonably. "She's a *stranger,* remember? And she's being blackmailed—she told us that herself—so it's safe to assume we might find some nasty surprises if we went poking around in her background."

"She's our *sister,*" I argued.

"That doesn't mean she isn't a killer," Jolie pointed out.

"She wouldn't!"

"Wouldn't she?"

"Jolie, *stop.* You *know* better than to think Greer—*Greer*—is some kind of monster!"

"Chill, Moje. I'll be there in half an hour. We can talk more then."

She hung up.

I hung up.

I flung the phone onto the couch and nearly hit Justin Braydaven, who must have blipped in while I was pacing and ranting at Jolie.

"What are you doing here?" I asked.

"I don't know," he said. "I just thought about you, and here I was."

I stopped. I'd meant to look Justin up on Google,

find out how he'd died, but I'd been too busy. *No time like the present,* I thought. Greer wasn't home, the police hadn't arrived and Jolie was still thirty minutes out. I went to the computer, a laptop I'd borrowed from Jolie since my desktop was still at the apartment, and logged on. There was the daily threatening e-mail from my ex-husband's girlfriend, Tiffany, who had been riding with Nick the night he died. She'd been thrown through the windshield and permanently maimed, and for some mysterious Tiffany reason, she blamed me for her disfigurement.

I tucked the message into the Death Threat file and forgot about it.

"My mom isn't doing too well," Justin said.

I looked back at him over one shoulder. "Are there any other kids in the family?" I asked hopefully.

Justin shook his head. "Just me and old Pepper," he said sadly, "and he's about on his last legs. Poor old dog. If I died six years ago, that means he's almost fourteen. When he goes, I don't know what Mom will do."

I went to the Google page and typed Justin's full name into the search line. "Does she have a job? Hobbies?" *The Damn Fool's Guide to Insensitivity,* page forty-three. But I was trying.

Justin didn't seem offended. He simply sighed and said, "She works at home, doing billing for a credit card company in a back bedroom. And her hobby is ordering stuff off QVC."

There were something like seven *thousand* references to Justin on the Web, according to Google, but I wasn't going to have to wade through them. The first one told the story.

"You were killed in a drive-by shooting," I said. There it was again, that ole sensitivity o' mine.

Justin winced. "What was I doing at the time?"

"Waiting for a streetlight to change after a concert," I answered, turning in my chair. "If it's any comfort, they caught the perp. He's doing life in the state pen."

Justin absorbed the news with admirable ease. "Then I guess I'm not hanging around here waiting for my killer to be caught, like Gillian is."

My heart seized. "Did she tell you that's why she's here? In sign language or something?"

"No," Justin said. Then he reached for the TV remote, lowered the screen expertly and flipped to a rock-video channel. "You had me ask her if she knew who killed her. It was no great leap to guess why she's still around. The question is, why am *I* still around?"

I thought I knew the answer to that one, though I wasn't about to say so.

I do have *some* sensitivity, after all. There are moments when I positively exude it.

Justin hadn't gone into the Light, if there was such a thing, because his mother couldn't—or wouldn't—let go.

CHAPTER FOUR

MY CELL PHONE RANG AGAIN. Justin picked it up off the couch cushion and tossed it to me. I checked the caller ID panel.

Tucker.

"Hello," I said, trying not to sound breathless.

"There's some bad news coming down, Moje," he replied.

"I know," I responded. "Alex Pennington was found dead in the desert today. Full of bullet holes."

Too late, I realized I'd made a mistake. I wasn't supposed to know Alex had been pumped full of lead. And Jolie would get in a lot of trouble, maybe even lose her job, if I answered Tucker's inevitable question.

"How did you find out?" he asked.

I closed my eyes. Opened them again. Logged off the Internet. "I'm a detective," I said lamely. "I have my sources."

Tucker thrust out an exasperated sigh. "Yeah," he retorted. "Your sister, Jolie, the crime-scene tech. She's *so* lucky you're not talking to any other cop on the planet right now. Look it up in one of your *Damn Fool's Guides*, Moje—this is a *serious* breach of ethics."

"Got it," I said. "But isn't it a breach of ethics for *you* to call and tell me about Alex's death before the next of kin has been notified?"

He laughed, but it was a raw, broken sound. "You have a point," he said. "I hate it when you're right."

"Get used to it," I replied. "It happens at least sixty-five percent of the time."

"*Damn Fool's Guide to Stupid Statistics?*"

"Very funny. Hilarious, in fact."

"I'm going crazy, Moje. I need to see you."

"Are you still living with Allison?"

"Yes."

"Sorry," I chimed, with a brightness I certainly didn't feel. "All booked up."

"Moje, be reasonable, will you? I'm not sleeping with her."

"So you say."

"You don't believe me?"

My eyes started to burn. "I want to. I really do. But the map of *that* emotional territory is clearly marked 'Here be dragons.'"

Tucker didn't answer. What could he have said?

"How's the investigation going?" I asked, to get things started again. I wanted to hold Tucker in my arms, get naked with him and lose myself in the wonderful world of multiple orgasms. I couldn't, because even if he *wasn't* having sex with Allison, he was in too deep. So I settled for stretching the conversation as far as I could, just so I could hear the sound of his voice.

Pitiful.

"It's not," Tucker said glumly.

I decided it might be in my best interests to be forthcoming about my plans to visit Helen Erland that evening, though I wasn't about to let him know she was trying to arrange for me to see Vince in jail. He would have blocked that, on general principle. He'd hear about it after the fact, of course, but by then it would be too late.

I threw him a bone. *Part* of the truth. But, hey, that's better than nothing, isn't it?

"Mrs. Erland asked me to investigate Gillian's murder," I said, and braced myself for meteor impact. Oceans were going to overflow. Continents would shift. A new ice age would begin.

And here's me, the flash-frozen mammoth with fresh grass in its mouth.

"When," Tucker countered evenly, "did you speak with Helen?"

"Today at the convenience store where she works," I answered after swallowing. "Gillian appeared in my car at Wal-Mart, and she wanted to see her mother. So I took her there."

"Mojo, if you compromise this case—"

"I might *solve* it, you know."

"As far as the sheriff's office is concerned, it *is* solved."

"Not what you said on the news this morning, Detective Darroch."

"Look, Mojo, there's an *official* investigation going on here, and it's delicate."

I ignored that. I was in charge of the *un*official investigation. "Helen doesn't think he did it. Vince, I mean. And neither does Gillian."

"Helen is out of her head with grief, and she doesn't *want* to believe Erland's guilty. As for Gillian—well, I hate to tell you this, Sheepshanks, but ghost testimony doesn't hold up in court."

I glanced in Justin's direction, hoping he'd left.

He was still sitting on the couch, and he was listening. For all I knew, he could hear Tucker's side of the conversation as well as mine.

"It's not easy being a ghost," I said.

Tucker sighed again. He sighed a lot whenever we talked about my strange new talent for seeing dead people. I could only conclude that he wanted me for my body, not my mind.

It was a sure bet it wasn't my detective skills.

"Moje," Tucker said. "I'm not sleeping with Allison."

I would have replied, "And I'm not sleeping with you," if Justin hadn't been there, taking it all in.

"Whatever," I answered.

"Stay away from Helen Erland."

"No. But thanks for the input."

"Mojo—"

I hung up.

"I could find out if he's sleeping with her," Justin said.

"Justin," I answered, "don't help."

He grinned. "It's not like I don't have time on my hands," he reasoned. "I could help you solve the case, too."

"How?"

"By spying on people. I'm invisible to most of them, remember. That could come in very handy."

"I've got a better idea, Justin," I said. "Go home."

"I can't. My mom's too sad. It's a bummer."

"That isn't the home I was talking about."

"I have to wait for Pepper," he told me decisively. "He's old and he might get lost or something. It won't be long, and I might as well make myself useful in the meantime."

My throat closed and my sinuses clogged up instantly.

"Do you think they let dogs into heaven?" Justin asked. "Because I'm not going if they don't."

I started to cry.

Justin blipped out.

Alive or dead, men can't stand tears.

JOLIE ARRIVED while I was rooting through the cupboards looking for something that could reasonably be expected to morph into lunch.

"You look terrible," she said after letting herself in.

"Do you think dogs are allowed in heaven?" I asked.

"Sit down," Jolie ordered. "You're a train wreck."

I slumped into a chair at the kitchen table.

Jolie washed her hands at the sink—a good thing, since she'd probably been dropping pieces of Alex Pennington into evidence bags all morning—and opened a can of soup. "Greer's not back from shopping yet?" she asked, getting out a saucepan.

I shook my head.

"It will be interesting to see how she reacts to the news," Jolie said, plopping the contents of the soup can into the saucepan. "Do you ever buy groceries?"

I ignored the grocery gibe. Jolie *cooked.* It made sense that she had a fixation with supermarkets. To me, they were just places where I ran into crazy stalkers and dead people. "Greer," I said evenly, "did *not* riddle Alex with bullets and leave him to rot in the desert."

"Don't be so free with the gory details, okay? I could get fired if anybody finds out I called you from the crime scene."

Guilt washed over me. I bit my lower lip. Who needs collagen when you can get the plump look by gnawing on yourself? "I might have let something slip to Tucker," I confessed.

Jolie stared at me, her eyes going huge and round. She was beautiful, even clad in khaki shorts, a Phoenix PD T-shirt and hiking boots. Her long hair, done up in about a million skinny braids, was tied back with a twisted bandana. "Mojo Sheepshanks," she said, "you *didn't* tell him I told *you* about Alex?"

"He guessed," I said.

"Right," Jolie snapped, glaring.

"Not to worry," I said, holding up two fingers pressed close together. "He and I are like *that*."

Jolie swirled an index finger around one temple. "You and Tucker are like *this*. Both of you are crazy!"

"Tucker isn't," I said.

Jolie turned back to the soup, her spine rigid.

"You're going to have to sit with Greer tonight," I told her. "So I hope you don't have any plans."

Jolie didn't look at me. "And where will *you* be?"

"I have some investigating to do."

Jolie muttered something I didn't quite catch, but I thought I heard the words *real job* in there somewhere.

"I'll be back as soon as I can," I said. "And how hard can it be to hang out with Greer for a couple of hours?"

Jolie rounded her eyes at me.

Just then the front door crashed open, and Greer came in. She went immediately to the cupboards and started ripping through them, a one-armed marauder. She found a package of Oreos—Nick liked to smell them, and even though I seriously doubted he'd ever be back, I kept them around just in case—and started stuffing them into her mouth, two at a time.

I figured a size-twenty-two wardrobe might be

one of the dark secrets hidden in my foster sister's mysterious past.

"Alex is dead," she said, spewing crumbs. "He's *dead!*"

Jolie and I exchanged glances.

"Sit down, Greer," I said as Jolie pulled back a chair and pushed her into it. Greer looked up at us, her mouth rimmed with cookie dust.

"What?" I threw in when nobody spoke, hoping it sounded as if the news had come as a shock.

"The bastard isn't off boinking some floozy," Greer informed us, wild-eyed. "He's a cadaver!"

"Calm down," I said, "and tell us what happened."

Greer's eyes filled with tears. She opened her mouth, shoved in three more Oreos and tried to talk around them. "I just got a call from the police," she said, the words garbled. "Some hikers stumbled across Alex's body in the desert this morning. He'd been *shot.*"

I tossed Jolie a *See? She's surprised* kind of look.

Jolie took the soup off the burner and set the saucepan aside.

"What am I going to do?" Greer asked.

Jolie pulled up a third chair and sat down. "You can start by telling us whether or not you killed him," she said.

Greer gasped, and then went into a choking fit. Obviously she still hadn't swallowed all the Oreo residue.

I jumped up and pounded on her back, while Jolie got her some water.

"Killed him?" Greer gasped once she'd recovered the ability to breathe.

"The man was probably cheating on you," Jolie said evenly after flinging a shut-up glance in my direction. "He'd moved out and you hired Sherlock here to get the proof. The police are going to want to know if you offed him, Greer, or paid somebody else to do it."

Greer bolted for the bathroom.

Power vomiting ensued.

"Good work," I told Jolie in a harsh whisper. "Why didn't you just ask her how much she stood to inherit and when she plans to remarry?"

Jolie glowered me into silence.

We both got up and tracked Greer to the bathroom.

She was on her knees, with her head over the toilet bowl, dry heaving.

When she stopped, I soaked a washcloth in cool water and squatted to wipe off her face.

Jolie flushed the john and spritzed the air freshener.

"You can't possibly think I would murder my own husband!" Greer sobbed as Jolie and I helped her to her feet. I looked at her cast, due to come off in a few weeks, and wished it had been on her right arm instead of her left. If it had been, she couldn't have shot Alex.

"Look, Greer," Jolie said fiercely, though she was stroking Greer's back as she spoke, "the cops

will give you a day or two to catch your breath, then
they're going to be in your face, wanting a lot of
answers. *Talk to us.*"

"*I didn't kill Alex!*"

We ushered her back to the living room and sat
her down in a leather armchair, facing the empty
fireplace.

"You can tell us if you did," Jolie said. "We'll
help you."

Greer shook her head. "It was probably that bitch
Beverly," she said. "I need wine."

"No, you don't," Jolie argued quietly. "I know
you've had a shock, and I'm sorry. But you can't
afford to crawl into a bottle and pretend none of
this is happening, because it *is*. When did you see
Alex last?"

Greer considered. "The day after Lillian's funeral," she replied. "He came by to pick up some
of his things. He said he wasn't really leaving—that
we just needed some time apart to get perspective."

Greer might have been getting perspective, I
thought. Alex had probably been getting nooky
instead.

"Where was he going?" I asked after a sour
glance at Jolie, thinking *hey,* I'm *the detective
around here.*

"He said he'd be staying at the Biltmore."

That figured. The Biltmore is posh—nothing
but the best for Alex Pennington, M.D., and the
bimbo du jour.

"Did you check?" Jolie pressed. "Call the hotel to find out if he was really there alone and not staying with a girlfriend?"

Greer's right hand knotted into a white-knuckled fist. *"No,"* she said, gazing up at me. "I paid *Mojo* to do that kind of dirty work."

"I *was* a little busy," I pointed out.

"I want my retainer back," Greer said.

"Fine," I told her.

"Stop bickering," Jolie said. "Both of you!"

Greer and I both subsided.

"A man is dead," Jolie informed us. "Let's stay on the subject."

Greer let out a wail.

A man is dead, I thought with a mental snort. Gee, maybe I ought to offer Jolie a partnership in Sheepshanks, Sheepshanks and Sheepshanks. She had such a keen eye for detail.

But then, she'd expect a paycheck.

Back to sole proprietorship.

"I think Beverly killed him in a drunken rage," Greer said with frightening clarity. "Alex just spent a fortune to send her to some fancy rehab center, but I'll bet she was swilling gin on the plane back. Are there any more cookies?"

The whole conversation went like that. I wondered why anybody would want to be a cop—or a private investigator, for that matter. And I seriously considered applying for a blue greeter's vest at Wal-Mart. The dead guy and I would probably get along fine.

AT SIX-FIFTEEN that evening I pulled into Helen Erland's dirt driveway. She lived in a double-wide on one of those acre plots with "horse facilities," meaning pipe fences, a rusted feeder and a beat-up tin roof the animals could stand under to get out of the merciless Arizona sun. When the place had been new, it was probably pretty remote; now it was surrounded by the ever-encroaching stucco houses people like Helen couldn't afford.

There weren't any horses.

Before I could knock, the inside door opened and Helen peered out at me through the screen. She was wearing baggy shorts and a short-sleeved plaid shirt, and her feet were bare, with blue foam cushions wedged between the toes. Not too grief stricken for a pedicure, then, I reflected, and instantly hated myself for thinking that way.

Lillian used to tell Greer, Jolie and me that you couldn't help the thoughts that came into your head, but you didn't have to let them stick around.

"Thanks for coming," Helen said, stepping back so I could come inside.

Gillian was sitting in a little rocking chair over by the fake fireplace, the kind with light-up logs inside.

I didn't acknowledge her, of course, until Helen turned away to clear some laundry off one end of the couch so I could sit down.

Gillian returned my thumbs-up signal—I guess

it qualified as sign language—but she looked so sad and small sitting there.

I sized up the living room. Despite the laundry, it wasn't messy. The carpet looked clean, and there was no dust on top of the TV, which was muted but on, or beer cans on the coffee table. An electric picture of Jesus and the apostles in a boat filled most of one wall, but the plug was pulled.

"That belonged to my mother," Helen said fondly, having followed my gaze. "It's awful, isn't it?"

Before, I'd just felt sorry for Helen Erland. Now I began to like her. But I wasn't stupid enough to dis a picture of Jesus, even if it did light up.

"Mom treasured it," Helen went on when I didn't comment. "I keep it around because it reminds me of her."

I nodded. I barely remembered my own mother, since she'd died when I was small, but I'd just lost Lillian, and her ratty old chenille bathrobe was hanging in my closet at the apartment. I had her tarot cards, too.

I understood about keeping things.

"You want a beer or a soda or something?" Helen asked. She was a little nervous. Putting me on the trail of Gillian's killer had probably seemed like a good idea at the time. Now I figured she was having second thoughts.

"Diet cola, if you have it," I said.

Helen got up and pigeon-toed it into the kitchen. Her toenails glowed neon-pink.

Gillian and I exchanged looks again.

I signaled for her to leave the room.

She shook her head and sat tight in the little rocker.

"Tell me about your husband," I said when Helen came back and handed me a cold can of soda. "I understand he was arrested for solicitation of a minor."

"That was before I met him," Helen said. "And he said *she* came on to *him,* that girl."

I decided I'd never get the straight story on that from Helen, and made a mental note to look elsewhere. Like straight into Vince Erland's eyes, when and if I got to speak to him. I *did* say, "Men sometimes lie about things like that."

Helen flushed. "Vince didn't do it," she reiterated. "He didn't proposition a teenage girl, and he sure as hell didn't kill Gillian."

"Let's go back even further," I said moderately, popping the top on the diet cola. Gillian's last name was Pellway, not Erland, so there must have been an ex-husband or a boyfriend in the picture. "You were married before, right?"

Helen tested her toenails for dryness and pulled the blue foam cushions out. Set them carefully on the end table beside the old leather recliner and sat down. A dull flush rose under her ears. "Yes," she said. "To Benny Pellway. He's doing twenty to life in the state pen for armed robbery."

I didn't need to take notes. *The Damn Fool's Guide to a Photographic Memory.* "He's Gillian's biological father?" I asked.

Helen lifted her ponytail off her neck and fixed it to the top of her head with a pink squeeze-clip. "Yes," she said.

"Are there any other children in the family?"

Helen shook her head, and her eyes brimmed with tears. "No," she replied. "Vince and I were talking about having a baby, though."

"Where does Vince work?" I was miles behind the police, I knew, but I could still ask his fellow employees what kind of man he was. And it was always possible that Tucker and the others might have missed something.

"He was between jobs," Helen said. Her chin jutted out a little way, as though she expected me to denounce Vince Erland as a bum, and she was prepared to defend him.

"How far between?" I asked.

"He worked for a furniture company, delivering couches and stuff, until about six months ago," she said. "Then he got downsized."

"Do you have any family pictures or albums or anything?" Except for Jesus and the disciples, the paneled walls were bare.

Helen sniffled, got up out of the chair and opened the cabinet under the TV. Brought out several framed school photos of Gillian, along with a couple of thick albums.

"I had to put them away," she said, referring to the shots of a smiling Gillian, posing against a plain blue background.

"I understand," I told her.

Gillian began to rock slowly in her little chair.

"It's the oddest thing, the way that chair moves on its own sometimes," Helen said.

"Probably a draft," I answered, unable to look at her.

"Probably," Helen agreed with a sigh.

I turned to the albums. There weren't a lot of pictures, and most of them were old. In one, a couple in sixties garb stood beaming in front of what looked like the same double-wide we were sitting in.

"My mom and dad," Helen explained, her face softening. "This was their place. It was new back then."

I swallowed, thinking of my own dead parents. "They're both gone?"

"Both gone," Helen confirmed.

I flipped more pages. Helen, growing up. Helen, on horseback, then dressed for a dance, then graduating from high school. Helen, standing with a smarmy-looking guy in a wife-beater shirt and cutoff jeans, holding a baby in her arms.

Benny Pellway *looked* like the kind of guy who ought to be doing twenty to life in the state pen. I decided to make sure he hadn't escaped. Shortcut: ask Tucker. The police would have checked that first thing.

After that, the snapshots were mostly of Gillian, usually sitting alone on a blanket, clutching a ragged stuffed dog.

"She always wanted a pet," Helen said with painful regret. She'd been leaning in her recliner so she could see the pictures, too.

Gillian signed a word, and I was pretty sure it was *dog*.

My throat squeezed shut again. "She's here," I said. I hadn't planned on saying that—it just came out of my mouth.

"What?" Helen asked, blinking.

I figured she was about to throw me out, but it was too late to backtrack. "I can see Gillian," I said. "She's sitting in the little rocking chair by the fireplace."

Helen turned in that direction. Signed something.

Gillian duplicated the sign eagerly.

I love you.

I hadn't gotten very far in my studies, but I knew that one.

My heart sort of caved in on itself.

Helen got up, walked toward the chair.

Gillian instantly vanished.

What did *that* mean? I wondered.

I knew Gillian wasn't afraid of Helen Erland. She obviously liked to be with her, wanted very much to get her attention somehow. Maybe just to say goodbye.

"Is she still here?" Helen wondered softly.

"No," I said.

Helen, standing in the middle of the living room now, turned to study me narrowly. "Are you some kind of psychic or something?"

"No."

"But you saw my Gillian?"

I nodded. Looked up at the electric Jesus picture and had a sudden, strange urge to plug it in. "Yes."

"Can you talk to her?"

"She doesn't speak, but she reads my lips sometimes. And she wrote 'Mom' in the dust on the dashboard of my car yesterday. That's why I came into the store. Because she wanted to see you."

Helen's legs buckled, and she dropped heavily to the floor, landing on her knees.

I knew she hadn't fainted, so I stayed where I was. Waited.

It was an intensely private moment, to say the least, and I felt bad for being there to see it.

Tears poured down her face. "My baby," she whispered. "Oh, my baby."

I didn't say anything.

Helen looked up at the light-up picture. "Why?" she demanded. "Why is she just wandering around, lost? Why isn't she in heaven?"

I wasn't sure if she was asking me or Jesus. Both of us, probably.

I looked at the picture, too. *The ball's in Your court, Big Guy,* I thought.

"I don't know for sure," I answered when I could get the words past the lump in my throat, "but I think it has to do with finding her killer." Justin's mother, Mrs. Braydaven, crossed my mind. Helen Erland had just seen her only child buried. She wasn't ready to hear that she'd need to let go of Gillian at some point.

Helen turned again, studied me, still on her knees in the middle of the living room. She opened her mouth, but before she could say whatever she'd intended to, the front door opened and a slim teenage girl walked in without bothering to knock.

Seeing Helen kneeling, her face wet with tears, the girl turned on me. "What did you *say* to her?"

I remembered catching a glimpse of her at Gillian's funeral. She'd been with the camerawoman.

"It's all right, Chelsea," Helen said, getting up. "This is Mojo Sheepshanks. She's a private investigator. Mojo, this is Chelsea Grimes. She's—she *was* Gillian's babysitter."

Chelsea studied me suspiciously. She had short blond hair, blue eyes and wore a skimpy pink T-shirt— the kind that leaves most of the stomach showing— and low-cut jeans. A silver ring glinted from her belly button.

On most people, the bare-belly look is unflattering. On Chelsea Grimes it definitely worked. She was probably only sixteen or seventeen, and she was clearly protective of Helen.

"Helen's been through a lot," Chelsea said. "She doesn't need somebody over here giving her a nervous breakdown."

I stood, still holding the photo albums.

"Chelsea, it's okay," Helen said.

Chelsea followed me outside to my car. The way she picked her way over the gravel finally clued me in that she was barefoot. Since there wasn't another vehicle in sight, I guessed she must live nearby, but it was possible someone had dropped her off.

"Look," Chelsea said, "the cops have been all over Helen since they found Gillian. Her husband is *in jail.* Cut her a break and don't go asking her all kinds of questions, okay?"

I was too tired and too despondent to smile. "How long were you Gillian's babysitter, Chelsea?"

"Forever," Chelsea said, cocking a thumb toward a cluster of spindly eucalyptus trees. I could see the outline of a small house beyond. "I live just over there, with my mom."

I nodded. Opened the passenger door of the Volvo and set the photo albums carefully on the seat. "Do you think Vince Erland killed Gillian?"

Chelsea flushed. "The police already asked me that," she said. "About a million times. And the answer is *how should I know?* I told them that. I told Tucker. Vince never put the moves on me, but he's a sleazeball, so anything's possible."

I told Tucker.

"You know Tucker Darroch?"

"Yes. I *know* Tuck—Mr. Darroch. I babysit Daisy and Danny sometimes."

Cave Creek is a small town. It wasn't a surprise that Chelsea knew the Darrochs and looked after their children. It *did* bother me a little that she'd referred to Tucker by his first name.

But then, she'd called Helen Erland "Helen."

Manners have changed since I was a kid.

"Why is Vince a sleazeball?" I asked.

Chelsea shrugged. "He can't hold a job, but he sure doesn't mind spending whatever Helen brings in on beer and cigarettes. My dad was like that, but he had the good manners to shoot himself in the head three years ago—problem solved. Except that my mom's still in the market for another loser."

"You're pretty bitter," I said, "for somebody so young."

"You would be, too, if you were me," Chelsea said. "I can't wait to get out of this hole. One thing's for sure—I'm never going to hook up with some bum who can't even support his own family."

"I guess Vince promised Gillian a dog, and then went back on his word," I said, testing the ice.

"I could have told her not to believe a word he said, if I knew how to speak sign language." She huffed out a disgusted sigh. "Even *Tucker,* hot as he is, moved out on the wife and kids and took up with some slut who lives over a biker bar."

"Is that so?" I asked moderately.

"You can't trust them," Chelsea went on. I was surprised by all the chatter, given that she'd been so protective of Helen Erland a few minutes earlier. I let the whole slut issue slide. "Men, I mean. Not even the 'good' ones."

"Right," I said.

Evidently finished, she turned and stomped back inside.

I got behind the wheel and backed out of the Erlands' driveway, onto the road.

I'd call Helen Erland later, I decided, and see if she'd spoken to Vince's lawyer about that visit.

CHAPTER FIVE

TUCKER'S SUV WAS SITTING in the driveway when I got back to Greer's, and I felt a leap of anticipation, square in the center of my heart, before it occurred to me that he might be there on official business. As in, arresting Greer. If Alex's body had been found in the desert, outside the city limits of both Scottsdale and Phoenix, then the jurisdiction belonged to Maricopa County, and the sheriff's department would lead the investigation.

Full of dread, I approached Greer's front door instead of heading for the guesthouse out back. The doorbell bonged through a ponderous sequence, and it was Jolie who opened up.

"He's here," she whispered. "Tucker."

I nodded, cocked a thumb to indicate that I'd seen his rig.

"Be careful what you say," Jolie told me.

I rolled my eyes. People tell me that all the time. You'd think they'd figure out that I never listen.

Greer was enthroned in her massive living room, with its beamed ceilings and imported tile floor. Authentic Navaho rugs hung between museum-quality paintings on the white walls, and there was one in front of the fireplace, too.

Tucker sat in a high-backed leather chair, in jeans and the blue cotton shirt he'd been wearing on TV that morning, his left ankle propped on his right knee. He'd been studying a sheaf of papers, but when I entered the room he looked up. Smiled with his eyes, if not his mouth. Started to get up.

I shook my head, motioned for him to stay seated. Tore my gaze from him and shifted my attention to Greer. She looked so bereft, so insubstantial sitting there, a wad of tissue crumpled in her right hand, that the image of Gillian in her little rocking chair back at Helen Erland's double-wide did a fade-in on my mental screen. For one terrible moment I thought Greer was dead, and I was seeing her ghost.

She must have heard the doorbell, but when she looked up, she seemed surprised that she wasn't alone in the room. The expression in her eyes reminded me of some wild thing, hunted down and trapped. Cornered, with no hope of escape.

I went to her, sat on the arm of her chair and slipped an arm around her. "What's going on?" I asked mildly after giving both Jolie and Tucker a glance that said I'd protect my sister—even from them.

"Tucker's here to ask some routine questions," Jolie said before Tucker managed to reply.

He sighed and rubbed the back of his neck. Set

the papers aside. Reports, probably. Or were they copies of Alex's insurance policies—or perhaps his will?

A shudder strolled down my spine, then shivered right back up again to tingle on my nape. I waited.

Tucker stood. Shifted slightly on the soles of his beat-up cowboy boots. I remember wondering, completely out of context, if he'd sat on the edge of Allison's bed that morning to pull on those boots. If Allison had been the one to tell Chelsea he'd left his family for a "slut who lives over a biker bar."

"I'm sorry for bothering you at a time like this, Mrs. Pennington," he said, though he was looking at me as he spoke, not Greer. He took a card from his shirt pocket, laid it on the end table on top of the papers he'd been reading. "If you think of anything you figure I should know—anything at all—call me."

Greer nodded numbly. Even without seeing her face, I knew she'd disconnected. Tucker was no more real to her than the dead greeter at Wal-Mart would have been.

Tucker's eyes connected with mine, held.

"You see Detective Darroch out," Jolie told me, briskly efficient. "I'm going to help Greer upstairs. She needs to rest."

I nodded, watched as Jolie got Greer on her feet and steered her toward the curving stairway.

Tucker could have found his own way out, of course, but he waited for me.

"We need to talk," he said, repeating what had

become his stock phrase, when we were outside, with the door closed behind us. "Your place? Or we can get some dinner somewhere."

I knew Gillian or Justin, or both of them, might be in the guesthouse, waiting for me to come back. I could have dealt with that, but adding Tucker to the mix was just a shade more than I could handle.

"Dinner," I said. "If you're buying."

He grinned wanly, looking sort of like the old Tucker, but not quite. I wondered if it was the new job that had changed him, or sharing a house with Allison and the kids. I longed for the good old days, before I'd started seeing dead people, before—well, just before. "I'm buying," he assured me. "Things a little slow in the detective business, Sheepshanks?"

"I have to give back Greer's retainer," I admitted. He knew my sister had advanced me five thousand dollars to find out if Alex was being unfaithful, with another five grand to follow if I got the goods on him—I'd bragged about it. After all, it was my first case. Since I didn't want to tap in to Nick's insurance money, I'd probably have to hit the casino and work the slot machines for some ready cash. I have a talent for making them pay, but I'll get to that later.

We'd reached Tucker's SUV, and he opened the passenger door for me, waited while I climbed in and snapped the seat belt in place.

"I guess Pennington's getting killed sort of threw a wrench in the works," Tucker said. "But at least now you know he's not cheating on your sister."

I didn't answer until he'd rounded the SUV and gotten behind the wheel. Started the engine. "Isn't it a little soon for you to be questioning her?" I asked tightly. "After all, they only found the body this morning."

"Write this down and hide it in the secret compartment of your magic detector ring, Moje," Tucker answered, backing out onto the street. "It's important to question everybody who might have been involved in a homicide, or have any knowledge that might be helpful for the case, before they've had a chance to think about it too much."

I folded my arms. "You did notice, didn't you, that Greer has a cast on her arm? How do you figure she could have muscled Alex out into the desert and then shot him?"

"She didn't have to do all that," Tucker pointed out, watching the road. "She could have hired somebody."

"So could the *other* Mrs. Pennington," I said. I felt a pang. I'd have to call Beverly in a few days and offer my condolences. We weren't friends, or even acquaintances, really, but she'd wanted to hire me. While my reasons for not showing up for lobster salad were obvious, and thus required no explanations or apologies, I wanted to acknowledge her in some way.

"Scottsdale PD is on that one," Tucker replied, "and Phoenix is checking the Biltmore angle."

"It's a joint investigation, then?"

"More like a cooperative effort," he said. "Can we not talk about this?"

"What do *you* want to talk about?" I asked, and maybe I sounded a little terse. "My sister's estranged husband was found in the desert, strafed with bullets. A seven-year-old dead girl is following me around, and I don't really know what she wants. Excuse me if things like that tend to distract me from the really *important* issues, like how you want to live with your ex-wife and boink *me* in your spare time."

Tucker whipped the SUV to the side of the road so suddenly that the tires screeched, and dust billowed all around us. I was glad the windows were rolled up, because I didn't want to have to wash my hair again.

"I am not *living* with Allison!" he snapped. Then he thrust out a sigh and shoved a hand through his hair. "Not the way you mean, anyway."

"Okay," I said calmly. After all, *one* of us had to keep it together. "Let's assume you're telling the truth. You're sleeping on the couch, or in one of the guest rooms. Except for holding Allison when she cries, because she's so upset over what happened to Gillian—and who wouldn't be?—you haven't touched her. I can buy all that, Tucker. I really can. And I wouldn't ask you to do any of this differently. But while you've got one foot in your marriage to Allison, you're not putting your boots under my bed."

"Who's going to hold *you* when *you* cry, Moje?"

The question broadsided me, with an impact that literally knocked the breath from my lungs.

Tucker leaned across the console, caught my face in both his hands and turned my head so I had to look at him. "Who, Moje?"

Another shiver went through me, stronger than the one I'd felt a few minutes before, in Greer's living room. Strong enough to rattle my bones. "Nobody," I said bleakly.

Someone swerved out around us, honked impatiently.

We ignored them.

And Tucker kissed me, gently at first, then with tongue.

I know I should have pushed him away, but I didn't. Because I'd cried a lot in my life, and just once, I wanted someone—Tucker—to hold me. To say everything would be all right, even if it was a lie. I just wanted to believe it for a little while, until I could get my equilibrium back.

As Tucker deepened the kiss, fiery sensations shot through me, hardening my nipples, making me squirm on the car seat. We both had all our clothes on, but I was already expanding to take him in. I was moist and achy, and my nerve endings jumped and crackled under my skin. My skeleton began to melt from the heat.

It was Tucker who drew back, still holding my

face between his hands, and said, "My place is five minutes from here. Do you still want dinner?"

I hesitated.

He lowered one hand to cup my breast, rubbing the side of his thumb slowly back and forth across my nipple. "Moje?" he rasped.

I whimpered, arched my back.

Tucker dropped his hand from my breast to my thigh. Bunched the soft, skimpy fabric of my sundress and pushed it up. Caressed me through my panties before slipping his fingers inside to play with me.

"This—is—entrapment," I protested, dizzy.

"I want to put my mouth where my fingers are now, Moje," he told me. "And suck on you until you come. And then come again. And again—" He began a slow, swirling motion with his hand. My knees fell apart, and I thought about his lips and tongue on me, and I stiffened with a small, sharp orgasm, over too soon. Instead of satisfying me, it left me desperate for more.

I gave in. "Your place," I said.

We were at his condo in Scottsdale in three minutes, not five, but we didn't get any farther than the garage the first time. Tucker got out of the SUV, came around to my side, helped me down, since my knees were wobbly.

I thought we'd go inside, but Tucker opened the rear door of the SUV, got me around the waist and hoisted me onto the backseat.

"What—?" I began, need-fogged.

He laid me down sideways on the seat, and then I *knew* what.

He pushed my dress up around my waist, tore off my shoes and yanked down my panties. I was groaning by then, writhing on the seat like a first timer on prom night.

Tucker set my heels on the seat, held my knees apart and started kissing my bare belly. His hands moved farther up under the dress, under my bra. It was going to be the full treatment, and the need I felt went way beyond the physical, into something much deeper.

I began to buck beneath him, my body making pleas I was too proud, even then, to put into words.

I felt his breath on me and tried to raise myself to him, and he parted me then, and flicked me with the tip of his tongue. I gave a strangled shout of pleasure and spasmed.

He chuckled. "Entrapment, huh?" he murmured hoarsely. "Can't have that."

"*Tucker,*" I gasped.

He rolled my swollen clitoris between his lips. Tongued it a little. "Hmm?" he asked.

He made me tell him what I wanted. No, sirree, no entrapment here.

I plunged my hands into his hair and pulled him to me, held him there.

Tucker chuckled again, but then he got down to business in earnest. I moaned as he alternately teased and feasted, shouted when he brought me to the first raw orgasm.

I hoped the neighbors weren't home. I must have sounded like a she-wolf howling at the moon, but I couldn't help it.

While I lay shuddering in the sweet aftermath, I was vaguely aware of Tucker taking off my dress, and then my bra. I started to scoot backward on the seat, so he could climb into the SUV and take me, lover's lane-style, but he stopped me. Brought me back to the edge, draped my limp legs over his shoulders and started nibbling at me again.

I gasped his name. Grasped at his shoulders. Tried to tug him upward, on top of me.

I needed him inside me; as shattering as that first real release had been, it hadn't satisfied me. Nothing would, except the long, powerful strokes of what was probably pressing hard against the front of his jeans by then. The spill of warmth inside me when he finally let go.

But it didn't happen that way.

I came again.

And then again.

When he finally reached the point where he couldn't wait any longer, I was dazed, everything inside me warm and soft and loose.

I watched his face, his magnificent face, as he opened his jeans, freed himself, and I crooned in stupefied anticipation as he took me by the waist, sat me up and then lowered me onto him.

I'd made love with Tucker a hundred times, but it was always a shock how big he was, how hot and hard. Wide awake, all my senses suddenly back on hyperalert, I wrapped my legs around his middle, clasped my hands behind his neck and leaned back slightly, ready for the ride.

And what a ride it was.

We started out slowly, every stroke something to be savored, but as the friction increased, so did our pace. Tucker pressed me back against the seat and slammed into me until, in the same moment, like two universes on a crash course, finally colliding, the whole order of the cosmos was changed.

Tucker gave a low, hoarse cry.

I clawed at him with both hands, drowning in fire.

After the Big Bang, there were a few more implosions as I descended, convulsing against Tucker each time. When it was finally over, I fell back on the seat, utterly exhausted, and he lay half on top of me, gasping for breath.

While we recovered, I wound my fingers in his hair and cried.

Presently he lifted his head from my stomach. "What?" he asked gently.

"You know what," I told him.

He sighed, lifted me again, set me on my feet on the cold garage floor, and gathered me into his arms. "It'll be okay, Moje," he told me in a ragged whisper, his breath like a warm breeze against my temple.

It was a lie, of course.

But I wanted—needed—to believe it, so I did.

We shared a shower after that, soaping each other up and kissing and groaning a lot, but neither of us had the knee power to make love standing up, not after the episode in the garage.

Tucker's bed was neatly made when we got into it. Hours later, when something awakened me, the covers were on the floor and the pillows were in odd places.

I realized the unwanted thing prodding at me, nudging me out of a semicomatose state, was a ringing telephone.

With a muttered curse Tucker raised himself onto an elbow and groped for the cordless receiver on the nightstand. Stuck it to his ear.

"Darroch," he growled.

Lying beside him, facing his back, I knew, even before his spine stiffened, that it was Allison calling. I couldn't make out her words, just the hurried, slightly shrill tone of her voice.

Tucker listened. I wanted to touch him, but I knew he'd flinch if I did, and I couldn't have borne that.

What he said to Allison surprised me, though. Big-time.

"I'm with Mojo."

I blinked.

Silence on Tucker's end, a diatribe on Allison's. I can't describe the sound—it was more of a feeling, like a stripped live wire twisting and crackling on the ground in a pouring rain.

"We're not *married* anymore, Allison," Tucker said when she gave him a chance.

Something else from Allison.

"No," Tucker told her. "I will not put her on." More listening, followed by a sigh.

I got up, wishing my dress and underwear weren't scattered all over Tucker's garage. It's hard to make a hasty exit gracefully when you're nude and every ounce of tension has been driven out of you by three or four hours of intermittent, head-board-banging sex.

"Mojo," Tucker said when I got to the threshold of his bedroom. I heard him crash the receiver back onto the charger. "Where do you think you're going?"

I stopped, turned. Actually, I hadn't thought that far. I'd just wanted to get away. Now I remembered I didn't have a car; I'd ridden with Tucker. I didn't even have my purse, because I'd left it in the Volvo, which was still parked in Greer's driveway.

"To find my clothes?" I said.

He threw back the tangled covers, sat up. "I'll get them," he replied, sounding resigned.

I took a short shower while he was gone, and when I came out of the bathroom, wrapped in a towel, my dress and bra were lying on the bed, the dress carefully folded, my sandals beside them. The panties were missing in action, evidently.

I put on what I had and followed the smell of cooking food into the kitchen.

Tucker stood at the stove, barefoot, wearing only his jeans and stirring something in a saucepan. "Chicken pot pie," he said, giving me a sidelong glance that made me remember certain peak moments in our lovemaking and blush a little. "The frozen variety. The microwave is broken, so I'm reduced to using the stove."

I wanted to say I wasn't hungry, but the truth was, I was ravenous. Hungry enough to eat chunks of chicken pot pie warmed up in a saucepan, actually. It didn't occur to me to ask why he didn't use the regular oven—I had reason to know he was the innovative type.

I came as far as the table, but didn't sit down.

"Why did you tell Allison you were with me?"

"Because she needs to know."

"Why? Why does she need to know?" I could put myself in Allison's place all too easily, I found. She had two children by Tucker. They'd been lovers, and built a life together.

Tucker stopped stirring the mess of crust and veggies and chicken chunks and turned to look at me. "The divorce was Allison's idea. I was a long time getting over it. Then I met you. Now, because she's scared and she's grieving, she thinks she wants me back. *I* want her to know it isn't going to happen, Moje."

I pulled back a chair, fell into it. "Where are my panties?" I asked.

Tucker grinned. "Damned if I know," he said. "I searched the garage, but they're gone."

I blushed, imagining some meter reader, or the kid who mowed Tucker's little patch of lawn, finding them behind a dusty box.

Tucker's grin broadened. "You won't need them anyway," he told me.

"Braggart," I said.

He took the food off the burner, scraped heaps of the stuff onto two plates and got out a couple of forks.

The concoction looked bad, but it tasted all right. We ate in silence for a while.

"I'm glad I'm not the only one who is grocery challenged," I said, because I was starting to feel really embarrassed about the way I'd carried on, serving myself up like a meal in the backseat of his *car,* for pity's sake. And when I'm embarrassed, I chatter.

"I was going to make scrambled eggs," Tucker said, his green eyes twinkling, "but I was afraid one of them might hatch."

"Thank you," I said, "for that image."

He set down his fork. Reached out to caress my cheek, the gesture so gentle that it made my throat hurt. "As soon as school lets out," he said, "Allison's taking the kids to Tulsa for a month, to visit her folks. Then I can move back here. By the time they get home, Allison should have regained some of her perspective, and Daisy and Danny will have calmed down, too."

I closed my eyes, opened them again. Tried to smile. "Or not," I said.

Tucker closed his hand over mine. Squeezed. "I know things seem pretty impossible right now," he said quietly. "But I—care about you, Moje. Have a little faith, will you?"

He *cared* about me.

Had he been about to say he loved me?

If he had, I would have bolted, and he probably knew it.

"You still care about Allison, too," I said.

"And you still care about Nick," Tucker replied.

"I do not," I protested. "Nick and I had been divorced for a long time when he was killed. I was so over him."

"Until he came back and haunted you. I saw your face when he did the final fade-out, Moje, and I know you miss him."

I wanted to say it wasn't so, but it was. I just hadn't realized that until Tucker brought it up.

"It's okay," Tucker said, and he sounded as though he meant it.

"He was a lying, cheating bastard," I said.

"He also saved your life," Tucker answered. "And you must have loved him a lot if you married him, especially considering all the secrets you were keeping."

I pushed my plate away. Pulled it back again. Took another forkful of chicken à la weird.

"I'm coming to your place tomorrow night," Tucker said. "And we're going to make love again. We've got some catching up to do."

Sitting there pantyless, I felt myself moisten at the prospect. "We can't," I said. "Because of the kids."

"Kids?"

"Gillian and Justin."

Tucker's eyes narrowed thoughtfully. "Who is Justin?"

"Didn't I mention him?"

Tucker shook his head.

"He was killed six years ago, waiting to cross the street after a concert. Drive-by shooting."

I saw Tucker go into cop mode, knew he was riffling through mental files. Before he'd worked for the DEA he'd been a homicide cop with Scottsdale PD. Although Justin had died in downtown Phoenix, the departments traded information all the time.

"Last name?" he asked.

"Braydaven," I said.

He nodded. "I remember that," he said. "When the trial began, his mother tried to bring a pistol into the courtroom. Phoenix didn't charge her, but a judge ordered therapy."

"I have a feeling it didn't work," I said sadly.

"Why?"

"Because Justin's still here," I answered. "If he wanted his killer found, like I think Gillian does, it would be more clear-cut. But the guy who shot him is in the pen." A wave of sadness came over me, because there were lost children in the world, and *between* worlds, too. I wanted to hammer at the doors of heaven and demand to know who was in charge. "He told me he's waiting for his dog," I choked out. "Pepper's old, and Justin's afraid the poor thing will get lost between here and the after-life, but I think that's only part of it. His mother is holding him back somehow."

"How?"

"I don't know—maybe it's the intensity of her grief. I want to go and talk to her, but what do I say? 'Stop mourning your son'?"

Tucker reached over, pulled me onto his lap. Pressed my head against his shoulder. There was nothing sexual about it, but his tenderness over-whelmed me in ways his lovemaking never could have. I felt swamped with sorrow and consolation, clogged with tears, and not just in my sinus pas-sages, either. In my whole body, and even my soul ached.

"Stay," he said quietly. "I'll call Allison, and the kids can get by without me for one night."

I shook my head. As much as I would have loved to lie in Tucker's arms until morning, he had re-sponsibilities, and so did I. My sister's husband was dead. She was on the edge, between that and the blackmail, and I wanted to be nearby in case she needed me. "Greer," I said, trying to explain.

"Jolie's with her," Tucker said.

"Jolie doesn't understand," I told him. I knew I

should get off his lap, stop acting like a baby and make him take me home. But it felt too good, having his arms around me, strong and protective. Plus, I loved the smell of his T-shirt.

"What doesn't she understand?" Tucker persisted.

"How scared Greer is. She didn't see her in that bus station...."

Tucker eased me back a little way, so he could look into my eyes. "You've lost me," he said. "What bus station, Moje?"

I'd never told Tucker the complete story of my past. He knew I was really Mary Josephine Mayhugh, that I'd seen my parents murdered when I was only five years old and that I'd been kidnapped soon afterward by a neighbor, Doris Blanchard, who promptly changed her name to Lillian. And mine to Mojo, though I'd come up with the "Sheepshanks" part on my own.

I explained how Lillian and I had met Greer in Boise. I *didn't* say she'd been hooking, nor did I mention what I'd recently learned—that she borrowed an alias from an actress on the late show. He'd ask what her real name was, and I didn't know.

Suddenly it bugged me that *I didn't know.* All these years my adopted sister had simply been "Greer" to me. Now I wondered who the hell she really was, and what she'd done that made her run away at such a young age, and turned her into a viable target for blackmail.

There was always the possibility, of course, that Greer hadn't done anything wrong. Maybe she was the victim of someone *else's* evil deed.

While all this was running through my mind, Tucker absorbed what I'd told him about how I'd met Greer in the first place.

Because I was distracted, he caught me off guard when he asked, "What's Greer's real name?"

There it was. Cop mode.

I stiffened.

Tucker chucked my chin. "Bad question?" he asked.

"Bad question," I confirmed.

"You don't want to answer?"

"I don't *know* the answer."

I could see by the look in his eyes that he believed me, and I got all emotional again. I wasn't used to people believing me, mainly because so much of my life had been a lie. I'd lied about my name, and what I hadn't remembered about my past. So many things.

Maybe that was why I understood Greer's need to keep secrets.

"I'd better take you home," Tucker said with a wicked light in his eyes. "Because it's getting to me, knowing you're not wearing underpants."

I laughed, but it came out sounding sniffly.

He kissed me. Lightly. No tongue. If there'd been tongue, I'd have been in trouble, because I was even more aware of my missing underpants than Tucker was.

"Tomorrow night," he reiterated.

"What about the kids?" I was referring to Gillian and Justin, but then Daisy and Danny came to mind, too.

"Maybe they won't be around," Tucker said, nuzzling my neck.

I jumped to my feet. Much more nuzzling and we'd be back in bed. "Thanks for the chicken stuff," I said.

He grinned up at me. "Just the chicken stuff?" he drawled.

"Hey," I protested. "You had fun, too."

He laughed, but it was a dry sound, with something broken in it. "It shouldn't be this hard, Moje," he said. "I'd give just about anything to wake up next to you in the morning."

I leaned down, kissed his forehead. "Put on some clothes, Detective Darroch. The party's over."

CHAPTER SIX

TUCKER DROPPED ME OFF at Greer's guesthouse on his way back to Allison's.

I tried not to think about what might happen when he got there, but I couldn't help it. Earlier, in his bed and—gulp—the *backseat of his car,* I'd been fiercely, ferociously female, queen of the Amazon warriors, engaged on every level of my being, not just the physical. Giving as good as I got. (And believe me, it *was* good.) Now I felt subdued, even a little shy. Intellectually, I understood that Tucker was protecting his children, and even that I wouldn't have wanted him at all if he'd been willing to turn his back on them. It was a primal responsibility, and I knew that.

I had a solid Dr. Phil take on the whole situation.

My heart, however, was 180 out from sensible. Being intimate with Tucker invariably opened a vast vacuum inside me, an emotional black hole, powerful enough to suck in entire star systems, swallow them whole, without so much as a burp. And that terrified me.

It was fine to want another person.

It *wasn't* fine to need them the way I was starting to need Tucker. I'd been in less danger looking down the barrel of a killer's gun.

"I think we should see other people," I told him after he'd checked under the bed and behind the shower door for the kind of psychos I'd recently begun to attract.

Tucker had been about to kiss me good-night when I said those fateful words. I'd felt so raw, so exposed, that I threw out the announcement as a defensive barrier. A bunker I could duck behind, however after the fact.

He stopped in mid head tilt and his eyes searched my face, grave and wary. "Coward," he said, being nothing if not direct.

I entered a forlorn guilty plea.

Tucker rested his hands lightly on the sides of my waist. The awareness of my missing panties reasserted itself. "You're a big girl, Moje," he said quietly. "If you want to play the dating game, that's your choice."

I swallowed. "I can't afford to need you, Tuck," I said. I was being truthful that night. Maybe it was the sex. I didn't have the energy for the usual diversion tactics and camouflage techniques.

"Why not?" he asked, though not unkindly. As I said, Tucker was the direct type. In or out of bed, he didn't take prisoners. He came, he saw, he conquered—not necessarily in that order.

"You *know* why not," I answered. "You have kids. You're still entangled with Allison, sex or no sex. Getting involved with you is the same as spilling my guts on the 101 and letting cars run over them."

Tucker winced at the image. Being a cop, he'd probably seen things like that in real life. "Too late," he said. "You're *already* involved, Moje."

I gnawed at my lower lip.

He caught it gently between his thumb and forefinger. "Stop it," he said. I wasn't sure if he was talking about my bad habit of chewing on myself or the sudden angst over our nonrelationship. Probably it was both.

"Go home, Tucker," I said, putting a slight emphasis on the word *home*.

"Give this a chance," he argued. "Don't wimp out on me. Something big is happening here."

"Exactly my point," I answered, but I didn't bite my lip. Sometimes you have to be content with the tiniest bit of progress. "It's *too* big."

"And you'd rather find a safe guy? One who didn't make you feel too much? Care too much? *Want* too much?" The challenge was softly spoken, but there was steel behind it.

"Right now," I said, because it was apparently my night for involuntary candor, "I'm leaning toward no guy at all. It doesn't get any safer than that."

"Give it a shot," Tucker answered, stroking my

cheek lightly with the backs of his knuckles. With some men the gesture might have had an element of threat. With Tucker it was tender enough to pick at the tight stitches in my soul. "Try another guy. Try No Guy. It won't be enough. And when you realize that, I'll be waiting."

I trembled, closed my eyes. There were so many things I wanted to say, but they wouldn't coalesce into words.

Tucker touched his mouth to mine, breath-light. "I'll be waiting," he repeated hoarsely.

I didn't open my eyes again until I heard the door close behind him.

"He's seriously into you," a voice said. "What I don't get is why you won't go for it."

I started a little and turned my head. Justin Braydaven stood practically at my elbow, looking confused and sympathetic. "I wish you wouldn't do that," I said, peeved.

"Do what?" Justin asked innocently.

"Just *appear* like that," I snapped. "Out of nowhere!"

"I can't help it," Justin said, shrugging a little. "I think 'Mojo Sheepshanks,' and picture you in my mind, and zap, here I am. It's sort of like on the *Star Trek* reruns, when Captain Kirk or Mork or somebody steps into that big cylinder thing and teleports."

"The character's name," I said, irritated, "was *Spock,* not Mork. Doesn't anybody have a firm grasp on TV trivia anymore?"

Justin grinned. "I don't think it's much of an issue here in the great In-Between," he said. "Chill out, will you? You're just pissed off because you want the cop like crazy and you're scared to take what he's offering."

"Have you been spying on me?"

"Oops," Justin said with an insouciant grin.

I wanted to slap him, but one, he was a kid, two, he was dead and three, he was right. That's what really chapped my hide—he was *right*. I *did* want what Tucker was offering, and supersized. "You'd better not have been watching us," I said. As if there was a thing I could do about it either way, but when you live by your wits the way I do, you have to bluff a lot.

"Relax," Justin replied. "I'm not into peep shows. Way uncool. I just got here a couple of minutes ago. I've been hanging out with Pepper all evening." A shadow of sadness crossed his face, and I realized that, as young as Justin had been when he died, he must have been a heartbreaker. And bright, too. It made me wonder yet again about the general management of the universe. Why did good kids like Justin die, while their killers survived? "My mom has this little shrine on the mantel in the living room," he went on. "Pictures of me. The badges I earned in Scouts. Votive candles. It's kind of creepy."

I softened. Completely forgot about the Tucker drama, at least for the time being. "She misses you, Justin. Losing a child has to be the worst thing that can happen to a person." *Oh, Gillian,* I thought. Danny and Daisy came to mind then, which inevitably looped the mental tape right back to Tucker.

"Pepper doesn't want to leave my mom alone. That's why he won't come with me."

Everything inside me ached and tears filled my eyes.

Justin went on glumly, "He's in a lot of pain. Arthritis. Hip dis—dis—"

"Dysplasia?" My heart crept out from behind the barrier I'd erected earlier to protect myself from Tucker, and rushed to the dog. They're loyal in ways a human being could never understand, dogs are. They'll hold on literally until their last breath, no matter how much they're suffering, caught in the twisting vines of somebody's love.

"You've got to talk to her," Justin said, his eyes pleading. "I've tried, but she can't hear me."

Paying a visit to Justin's mother was on the long list of last things I wanted to do. I was up to my butt in hassles—Greer had just lost her husband, she was being blackmailed and she was a semisuspect in a murder.

For all I know, he's lying dead in the desert somewhere...

And then there was Gillian. I had to help her— the knowledge grew more urgent with every breath I drew—and I didn't have the first idea how to go about it. Why had she come to me, of all people, and not to our famous local psychic, the one who inspired *Medium?*

All that was missing in my current life scenario was somebody who wanted to kill me, in the most painful way possible, and I figured they'd be along anytime now.

I pulled in some air, let it out in a noisy gust. "Justin," I said evenly, "have you seen the Light? Is that what this is about?"

"Sort of," he answered, looking understandably confused. "There's this…space. Sometimes it's up ahead. Sometimes it's to the side, or I can feel the heat of it behind me. It's like a doorway or something and I'm supposed to go through it, I know that. And I'm strong enough to do it now. But I can't leave Pepper. I can't." His eyes said a lot more. They begged me to help. "When I was fourteen I had mono. I was in bed for six weeks. Pepper didn't leave me, except when he needed to go outside. Mom had to bring his food and water to my room."

I laid a hand on his shoulder. He felt warm; if I hadn't known better, I would have sworn he was alive. "I'll stop by your mother's place tomorrow," I promised, resigned.

The tension in the boy's face eased a little. "Thanks," he said. And then he blipped out—most likely because he'd thought of Pepper and been teleported.

I locked up, brushed my teeth, washed my face and swapped out my sundress and bra for a T-shirt

Tucker had forgotten at my apartment, back when we first met and things weren't so complicated. I lugged it everywhere I went, because it smelled like him.

I got into bed, waited a few minutes for Gillian to show up and switched out the lamp when she didn't.

I closed my eyes, not expecting to sleep, praying not to dream if I did, and when I opened them again, it was morning.

There were no dead people in the room, and no psychos.

So far, so good.

I showered, put on a tailored black pantsuit and subtle makeup and corralled my hair into something resembling a French twist. When I went to see Mrs. Braydaven, I wanted to look businesslike. Practical.

Sane.

I was off to a good start, until I got to the kitchen and found Alex Pennington sitting at the table, reading yesterday's copy of the *Arizona Republic.*

I suppose he was good-looking—salt-and-pepper hair, nice physique, square jaw—but I was distracted by the bullet holes strafed across his chest. So far, the ghosts of my acquaintance—Nick, my childhood cat, Chester, Gillian and Justin—hadn't sported the wounds of their demise.

I stopped, staring.

Calmly Alex closed the newspaper and laid it

aside. I don't know about you, but I don't think I could have been that casual, with blood and powder burns staining my clothes.

"What are you doing here?" I asked. It was becoming a routine question with me. I probably sounded cool and collected, even reasonable, but inside I was squealing like a little girl caught in a lawn sprinkler in her favorite party dress, and I had to clutch the door frame on both sides just to stay upright.

"My name's on the deed, after all," he said mildly, but the old dislike was there, in his eyes.

"It was," I answered, wondering even as I spoke where I got the moxie, "but now you're dead. D-e-a-d, dead."

"I can spell," he informed me, shifting a little in his chair as though he might get up and come toward me.

I knew I'd lose it if he did.

I tried again. "Why are you here?" I asked, terrified of the answer.

"Because of Greer. They're going to blame her for killing me. She didn't do it."

I gave a deep sigh, and it felt a lot like relief. Had I thought, on some level, all my protests to Jolie aside, that Greer *had* been the one to shoot her husband?

"Who did?" I managed, that being the obvious next step.

Alex studied me, long and hard. We'd never been buddies, and I suppose he was reluctant to trust me. "That doesn't matter."

"It will to the police," I replied.

"Suppose I'd rather keep my suspicions to myself?"

"Then they'll probably find a way to hang it on Greer. Or maybe Beverly." My eyes went so wide, so suddenly, that they hurt. "*Was* it Beverly?"

Alex chuckled, and the sound was bitter, unkind. Even scornful. "As much as Bev would have loved to reduce me to a chunk of Swiss cheese, she hasn't been sober enough to draw a bead on a boxcar in over twenty years."

"You have to give me a name, Alex."

His straight shoulders slumped a little, and he stared down at the floor for several pulsing seconds. When he looked at me again, the expression in his eyes was bleak. "I can't be sure—all I have is a suspicion or two. I was abducted in the underground garage at my office—I do remember that—knocked over the head from behind. Probably thrown into the trunk of a car. When I woke up, my hands were taped behind my back and there was a bag or something over my head, so I couldn't see. Somebody dragged me to my feet, and the next thing I knew, I was shot. Unless I miss my guess, the ballistics people will trace the slugs they dug out of my chest to a gun registered to Greer."

Greer had owned a *gun?* Add that to the growing list of things I didn't know about my foster sister.

Alex must have read the question in my face, because he answered as surely as if I'd asked it out loud. With a rueful little smile and a shake of his head, he said, "Yes—45 caliber automatic, hollow-point bullets. If you think the entrance wounds are bad, you should see my back."

"Spare me," I said. It wasn't that I wasn't sym-pathetic—Alex's story was horrible, and it chilled me to the marrow. I just wasn't up for gore, espe-cially before breakfast. I hoped he wouldn't leave stains—or worse—on the back of the chair he was sitting in.

"Greer was always paranoid," Alex said. "She's being blackmailed, you know."

"I know," I said with a partial nod. "She won't tell me who's putting the squeeze on her, or what she did to put herself in this position."

Alex arched an eyebrow. "And you call yourself a detective? She's from a little town in Montana—a place called Shiloh. Start there."

"Can't you just tell me, since you're obviously a few steps ahead?"

"Honey, I'm *miles* ahead. Aeons. Light-years. Six months after Greer and I were married, my accoun-tant clued me in that she was taking out credit cards in my name and maxing them out with cash ad-vances. Obviously she was paying somebody off."

"Why didn't you stop her? Put your foot down? Go to the police?"

Another bitter smile. "I loved her," he said. "I didn't want her arrested—or killed. I made discreet arrangements—money wired offshore, and all that—to pay the blackmailer off permanently. Half a million in cash. For a long time nothing happened. I thought it was over. Then Greer started acting out again—hocking jewelry, running up credit cards, even hitting up friends of mine for loans. The bastards tried to abduct her just last week, if you'll remember, and broke her arm in the process. If Jolie hadn't rescued her, she'd be six feet under by now."

I didn't miss the derision couched in the phrase "if you'll remember," but I didn't comment on it, either. I was sick to my stomach, and not just because there was a dead man in my kitchen. I'd known Greer was in mortal danger, but Alex's words had driven the fact home in a new way.

"You never found out who the blackmailer was?"

Alex shook his head. "Somebody in Shiloh, and more than one person, I think, unless they hired a thug to do their dirty work and muscle Greer into that van. I went to Montana a couple of times—trust me, that place is strange—trying to find out, and I've had some of the highest-priced private security firms in the business on the case. Nothing. Whoever this is, they're pretty professional."

Bile scalded the back of my throat. "If you dealt with all these security firms, why didn't you hire bodyguards for Greer?" I made myself glance at the bullet holes. "Or for yourself?"

"I did. Until the money ran out."

"You're broke?"

"I've wired something like three million dollars

into various numbered accounts in the Cayman Islands. By the time my estate is settled, Greer will have to move in over Bad-Ass Bert's, with you. She could earn her keep as a cocktail waitress, if you ever decide to open the bar for business. And Bev isn't going to be in much better financial straits."

I stared at him, speechless. I could deal with a lot of things—I'd proven that. Much as I loved her, rooming with Greer on a long-term basis didn't happen to be one of them.

"I hope I don't sound cold," Alex said coldly.

I wanted to shut my eyes, but I was afraid to. Afraid Alex would be standing directly in front of me when I opened them. "Are you going to haunt me until all this is over?" I asked, my voice a lot smaller than I would have liked.

Alex grinned. "I wish I could. I think it would be entertaining, if a bit tiresome at times." He glanced at his Rolex. "Alas, I'm due back at the train station in less than half an hour. Now that I've done the right thing, they'll punch my ticket and I can catch the midnight express to glory."

I gulped. Nick, my dead ex-husband, had mentioned a train station, too, while *he* was haunting me. "No shit?" I murmured. In moments like that one, it's hard to be eloquent. "There's really a depot?"

"Yeah," Alex said. "By the way, your ex figuratively wrote your name on the men's-room wall.

'If you need help, haunt Mojo.' You can pretty much expect a steady stream of ghosts and ghoulies from now on."

"Great," I said. "I need the numbers for those Cayman Island accounts, if you have them."

"On my computer," he said. "In a file marked 'Tropical Vacation.' The password is *Surgeon-Guy*." With that, Alex stood, and I was no longer afraid he was going to touch me. Much as I wanted him to leave, I needed to know who'd killed him, for Greer's sake. I had to have a name—*something*—to give Tucker. It was his case, and I was more than willing to hand over the information and stay out of it.

I'd get into Alex's computer first chance I got.

"Tell me," I insisted. "Who did it, Alex? Who murdered you? You said it yourself—there's someone you suspect."

Alex gave the dearly departed equivalent of a sigh, all motion and no breath. He shoved a hand through his expensively trimmed hair. "My son, Jack," he said after a long time. If a ghost can be haunted, Alex Pennington surely was. His eyes were shadowed with despair, and seemed to sink deeper into his head. "We ran a real estate development firm together—it was just a tax shelter to me, but to Jack it was everything. He was unhappy, to say the least, when he found out the current cash flow problem was likely to be permanent."

"So he shot you? Your own son?"

"I'm not sure—it's only a theory. Jack was angry. There was life insurance. He needs the money to sustain his lifestyle."

"I'm sorry," I said, and I meant it. It's bad enough to die violently, obviously, but when the killer might be someone you love and trust, it has to be—well— *murder.* "But if Jack killed you, then he should be the one to take the fall for it, not Greer."

"Jack's never taken responsibility for anything in his life. That's the problem." Alex chuckled, and like the grins that had gone before it, the sound was sour as vomit. "I actually thought he loved me, though. Somewhere, deep down inside. I was wrong." He paused, looked me squarely in the eye. "Jack's dangerous, Mojo. And he's smart. Do a little digging, though, and you'll get the goods on him."

"You loved her," I said, marveling. "Greer, I mean. But there's one thing I don't understand. If you cared enough to bankrupt yourself trying to keep her safe, why did you cheat on her?"

Alex was beginning to fade, cell by cell. I knew when he vanished, it would be permanent. "Because I was starved," he said quietly. "I gave until I literally bled. I needed something—*anything*—back. And Greer didn't have it to give. I'm—I was—a surgeon, not a shrink, but if I had to hazard a diagnosis, I'd say she's a borderline sociopath."

More fading.

"She can't be." Was I in denial? My analysis of

Alex Pennington's character had been off the mark; maybe I was wrong about Greer, too.

No.

"I know you want to help her, Mojo. I do, too, obviously. But she's damaged, and if I were you, I'd watch my back. Greer talks a good game, but if it's her or you, she'll throw you to the wolves. Remember that."

I took a step toward him. "Alex, don't—"

He was gone. Fade-out complete.

"Shit," I said, rubbing my eyes so hard that my mascara probably smeared. I was going to have to do a touch-up job before I went to see Justin's mother.

I stood there for a long time, hating my life. Then I went to the phone. My palm made the receiver slippery. I thumbed in the speed-dial number for Tucker's cell phone.

"Darroch," he said. His voice was clipped, and I knew he was into something heavy, and not alone. If that hadn't been the case, he'd have seen my number on his caller ID panel and probably made some comment about my missing panties.

"I think I know who killed Alex," I blurted.

"Whoa," Tucker rasped. "How?"

"Never mind how. 'Who?' is the pertinent question."

"Oh, I've got about a hundred of those. Who, then?"

"Jack Pennington. Alex's son. He probably used a .45 registered to Greer, but that part's conjecture."

"And you came by this information how, as if I didn't know?" He definitely didn't sound like the Tucker who'd gone down on me in the backseat of an SUV in the shadowy privacy of his garage and subsequently brought me to one soul-shattering orgasm after another. Just one more reason for keeping the black hole buttoned up tight.

Tucker could compartmentalize; I couldn't.

"Alex told me," I said miserably. I would share what I'd learned about Greer later, when he was more receptive. As in that night, after the headboard of my bed had pounded through the stucco on the wall behind it.

"Well, hell," Tucker retorted dryly, "how could the D.A. ask for anything more?"

"Look," I said, "I don't know what your problem is, but take it out on somebody else, okay?" I was about to hang up when he sighed.

"Moje, wait," he said.

"You're with Allison," I said.

"I'm at *work*," he answered. "Some of us have jobs, you know."

I broke the connection with a jab of my thumb.

The phone rang almost immediately.

I looked at the ID panel, on the off chance the caller was somebody I wanted to talk to.

Nope. Tucker Darroch.

I marched into the bathroom and reapplied my mascara.

I knew he'd try my cell phone next, but it was

still charging. He'd get my voice mail, and be frustrated.

Modern technology, annoying as it was, was not without its compensations.

After leaving the guesthouse, I debated stopping by the mansion on the other side of the pool to look in on Greer. Nothing Alex had said had changed the fact that she was my sister, but when I saw Jolie's Pathfinder parked out front, I used that as an excuse to skip the visit.

At the moment I needed to focus on one problem at a time.

I drove to Justin's house, after swinging by McDonald's for a sausage biscuit, consumed en route.

I probably should have called first—after all, I was a stranger to Mrs. Braydaven, and she worked out of her house. She would have pegged me for a crazy if I had, though, and told me to take a flying leap. Since she was probably going to do that anyway, I figured it might as well be in person instead of over the phone.

I climbed the front steps, drew a deep breath and pressed the doorbell.

The door creaked open, but the glass security door remained fastened. Mrs. Braydaven peered at me, Pepper at her side. It was the grizzled old dog that gave me the courage to stand my ground, instead of murmuring some excuse about having the wrong address and bolting for the Volvo.

"Mrs. Braydaven," I began bravely, trying to

look as if I wasn't selling anything, taking a survey, stumping for votes or trying to convert the heathen, "my name is Mojo Sheepshanks, and I'm—"

I'm *what?*

A ghost whisperer?

A detective?

A concerned bystander?

"I'm here about Justin," I finished lamely.

She'd been a pretty woman once, I saw, through the thick glass of the security door. The deep lines in her face testified to years of grief, and considerable anger. Her hair was gray, and the cut was so bad, I figured she must have done it herself. Blindfolded.

"Justin is dead," she said after a long silence, during which I fully expected her to slam the door in my face. "Are you a social worker? A cop? Some kind of church lady?"

"None of the above," I said gently. "Let me come in. Please."

She didn't open the door. The dog looked up at her and whimpered.

"What do you want?" she demanded after another extended silence.

"Do you believe in an afterlife, Mrs. Braydaven?"

Definite mistake. Such questions are usually followed by a religious tract and a hasty spiel about the Last Days, complete with lakes of fire and rivers of blood. Her face hardened, and she started to shut the door.

"The dog's name is Pepper," I said quickly. "Justin had a bad case of mono when he was fourteen, Pepper stayed with him night and day. You had to bring kibble and water to Justin's room."

Mrs. Braydaven's eyes widened slightly. She stopped closing the door. Stared at me in furious confusion. I could almost read her thoughts.

I couldn't have gotten that information off the Internet; it hadn't been made public. While she was probably about a furlong short of convinced, I'd caught her interest.

She let me in without a word. Turned and led the way into the living room. The shrine Justin had mentioned flickered eerily on the mantel over the fireplace, and the tabletops gleamed. The tile floor was spotless, and there was no clutter, anywhere. Obviously, when Mrs. Braydaven wasn't mourning or doing credit card billings in her home office, she cleaned. Frenetically.

"I saw you on TV," she said. "You're that little girl who was kidnapped down in Cactus Bend, after your parents were murdered."

I wasn't a little girl by anybody's standards, of course. Semantics. I merely nodded.

"It must have been awful," Mrs. Braydaven said.

Our separate tragedies gave us common ground. "It was," I agreed softly. My gaze drifted to the candlelight dancing on the mantel, amid framed photographs of Justin, taken at various stages of his boyhood. The Scout badges were displayed on a velvet backing, protected by glass. "But no worse than losing your only child."

Tears filled Mrs. Braydaven's eyes. "Sit down," she said.

I sat. Pepper laid his muzzle on my lap, and I stroked his graying head with a light hand.

"Would you like some bottled water, or maybe a cup of coffee?" Mrs. Braydaven asked. I knew she needed a moment alone, out of sight in her kitchen, maybe to force back the tears, maybe just to catch her breath.

"Water would be nice, thanks," I replied. When she was gone, I looked down into Pepper's limpid brown eyes. "I'll do my best," I whispered.

CHAPTER SEVEN

IT'S PECULIAR, HOW YOU CAN avoid the truth all your life, not because you're a liar, but because it's just too painful, and then suddenly find yourself in a position where nothing else will work.

Mrs. Braydaven handed me a bottle of cold water, then took a seat in one of her living-room chairs, near where I was sitting, but not too close. Pepper still rested his head in my lap.

I realized the blinds were drawn, and felt a craving for sunlight.

"I've seen Justin," I said bluntly.

I couldn't read her expression. "Ms. Sheep-shire—"

"Sheep*shanks*," I corrected politely. "Please call me Mojo, Mrs. Braydaven."

"Angela," she said with a distracted nod. "My name is Angela." She leaned slightly forward in her chair, studying the dog, then raised her gaze to my face. She looked skeptical—no surprise there—but not frightened. "What do you mean, you've seen Justin? He was killed six years ago."

"I know," I said carefully. "In a drive-by shooting, after a concert."

"That's public information," Angela said. "Anyone could find that out in five minutes, just by going online and running a search."

I glanced down at the dog, stroked his head again, very lightly, trying to convey by touch what I couldn't say aloud—that it was okay to let go and follow Justin.

In the instant after I looked up again, Justin appeared, standing behind his mother's chair. Watching me with an expression of desperate hope.

I made eye contact without thinking, and Angela turned to see what I was looking at. I knew by the sag in her shoulders that she didn't see Justin, but she might have sensed his presence, because she gave just the tiniest shiver, not afraid, but suddenly alert.

"But I couldn't have known about the mono," I said.

"You might if you knew some of his friends, or one of his middle-school teachers."

"Remind her how she still filled a Christmas stocking for me every year," Justin put in, "even after I was too old to believe in Santa. When I was seven she put a little compass in the toe, because we'd moved over the summer and I was going to a new school for second grade and I was scared of getting lost."

I repeated the pertinent information. Getting lost seemed to be a theme with Justin.

Angela Braydaven's eyes widened, then narrowed. "Why are you here?" she asked. Her hands lay, fidgety, in her lap.

"Because of Justin. He—he asked me to come." I looked nervously at the shrine over the fireplace, briefly at Justin and then back to Angela. She seemed tense now, as though she might be wishing she had a phone handy, so she could dial 911, or calculating her chances of escape before I went berserk and struck her down with a lamp or something.

"That's impossible," she said. "He's dead."

"Not really."

Angela flushed with anger. "I saw his body. I buried him. If this is some kind of con…"

I shook my head. "I don't want anything from you, Mrs. Braydaven. I'm just here because Justin asked me to tell you—"

"That I love her," Justin said quickly, stretching his arms far from his sides. "This much. All the way to forever and back."

I put the water bottle—still unopened—down on a coaster on the coffee table and mimicked the gesture. "He loves you this much," I said. "All the way to forever and back."

Angela began to cry, softly, silently, and with a desolation that made me want to weep, too.

"And then she'd always say back," Justin went on with an eagerness that tore at my heart, "'I love you *twice* that much.'"

I choked up a little, repeating that part.

Angela cried harder, and then she asked essentially the same question Helen Erland had when I'd told her I could see Gillian. "Why isn't he in heaven? He was such a good boy."

"He's waiting for Pepper," I said, my eyes wet. So much for the artfully applied mascara.

"Pepper?" Angela echoed.

"The dog wants to die," I said. "He's old, and he's in a lot of pain. But he's hanging on because—because you need him so much."

Angela sat in silence for a few long moments. Then she spoke to the dog. "Pepper," she said gently. "Come."

He lifted his muzzle off my lap and walked stiffly over to her, tail wagging slowly. Even that seemed to be an effort.

Angela Braydaven took his head between her hands and looked deep into his eyes. "If you have to go," she told him quietly, "it's all right. I'll be fine on my own, I promise."

Now Justin was crying, too, and so was I.

Angela caressed the faithful old dog's ears for a while, then eased him back a little so she could stand. Without looking at me—I might not even have been there—she made a slow, complete turn. "Justin, are you here?"

"Tell her I am," Justin urged.

"Yes," I said. "He's here."

Angela spread her arms wide. "I love you this much," she said. "All the way to forever and back."

"Tell her I love her twice that much," Justin said. I did.

Angela nodded, as though resolving something within herself, turned, went to the mantel, took the votive candles in her hands, one by one, and blew out the flames. Stood with her back to the room, spine straight, staring at the assembled memorial to her son.

I rose, patted Pepper on the head once more and left the house as quietly as I could. Justin stayed behind. He couldn't speak to Angela, but it didn't matter. There are goodbyes that run too deep for words, and this was one of them.

"WHAT HAPPENED to you?" Jolie demanded when I got back to Greer's place and let myself into the main house. She was dressed for work, purse and cell phone in hand. "You've got mascara all over your face. And what's with the loan-officer getup?"

"Never mind," I said. "How's Greer?"

"Not good," Jolie replied. "And I can't sit with her today or tonight, Moje. Sweetie's probably digested my new couch by now, and I *do* have a job." Sweetie was Jolie's dog, a mixed-breed pound fugitive roughly the size of a Shetland pony and possessed of a profound dislike for yours truly.

I swiped self-consciously at my cheeks with the backs of my hands and sniffled, still making the emotional shift from the Braydaven visit to Greer Central. "Chill," I said. "I'll take it from here."

Take it where? That was the question of the hour.

To Shiloh, Montana?

It was, as Alex had maintained, the logical place to start. I guess I knew, even then, that Greer wasn't going to be forthcoming with any helpful details, and, besides, if she really was a suspect in Alex's murder, she wouldn't be allowed to leave Arizona. There was still the funeral to get through, too, and I couldn't leave Gillian.

What I needed, I thought, pushing back my bangs, was a *paying* client. I get cynical when I'm stressed.

"Where is Greer?" I asked, trying to sound like a person who could cope.

"On the patio, crying," Jolie said. "The erstwhile Mrs. Pennington called first thing this morning. She wants to make all the funeral arrangements. I say, let her. But Greer's in a state. In fact, I think she's working herself into a nervous breakdown."

I nodded grimly. Squared my shoulders and headed for the patio.

I hadn't even gotten all the way across the entry hall, though, when Jolie stopped me with a tersely whispered, "Wait a second!"

I stopped, turned.

Jolie took a few steps toward me. "Something else has happened," she said, eyeing me with suspicious concern. "You look as though all the blood's been drained out of you and replaced with skim milk."

I swallowed, already rifling through my personal issues, trying to decide what to share and what to keep to myself. Jolie knew I saw ghosts, and she was a believer, due to a direct experience with Nick in the kitchen at my apartment, not to mention my dead cat, Chester, but it wasn't something we talked about a lot. "I saw Alex Pennington this morning," I said, sotto voce. "He believes his son, Jack, killed him, using a gun that belongs to Greer."

For a moment I expected Jolie's two jillion shining mahogany braids to stand out from her head as though electrified, shooting blue sparks. *"What?"*

"Don't make me repeat it, Jolie," I said. "It was hard enough to say the first time."

By then, Jolie was practically nose-to-nose with me. "What *else* did he say?"

"That he died broke," I said. "And that he knew about the blackmail." I left out the part about Shiloh, Montana, and diagnosis: borderline sociopath.

Greer was self-absorbed. She was definitely high maintenance. But she *wasn't* a sociopath, borderline or otherwise.

"There's no money?" Jolie asked.

"No money," I confirmed. "He went through a chunk of it trying to get Greer out of the jam she's in. Had some tied up in real estate investments, overseen by *Jack* Pennington. There may or may not be a life insurance policy—Jack is going to collect on one—but according to Alex, Greer'll be a bag lady when the fiscal dust settles."

Jolie took a few minutes to absorb the implications. "Sistah," she said, "is *not* coming to live with Sweetie and me!"

"If Tucker can't prove Jack Pennington shot Alex, Greer may wind up in the state penitentiary," I said pointedly. "Let's get past *that* before we start arguing about who has to take her in."

"Mojo?" Greer's voice sounded small, tentative and very nearby. "Is that you?"

"I'm out of here," Jolie said, and booked it for the front door.

"It's me," I called back to Greer as cheerfully as I could. It was only about ten o'clock, but I already felt wrung out and used up—relaying I-love-you-this-much messages between a dead boy and his mother will do that to a person. And don't even get me started on the dying dog.

Greer appeared in one of the three eighteen-foot arched doorways trisecting the entry hall, the dining room behind her. She wore jeans, a T-shirt with one sleeve cut away to accommodate her cast, and the kind of plastic flip-flops Walgreens sells for $1.99.

I hadn't seen her dressed like that in years, and frankly, the sight took me straight back to the bus-station coffee shop in Boise, where, with Lillian, I'd first met Greer. She'd worn her hair in a blue Mohawk then—a look that definitely wouldn't fly in Scottsdale—and she'd had piercings, too. But some element of her appearance, besides the wardrobe, was the same.

I decided it was the look of pure terror in her eyes.

I heard Alex's voice again. *But if I had to hazard a diagnosis, I'd say she's a borderline sociopath.*

He'd been wrong about that. He *had* to have been wrong. Was there a *Damn Fool's Guide to Identifying the Sociopaths in Your Life?* I was pretty sure there wasn't, but I had skimmed a convincing book once, wherein the author maintained that one out of every four people qualified.

It shed a new light on neighborhood poker games and garden clubs. Not to mention Brownie troops and church socials.

I jumped off that thought train and rolled down the metaphorical bank beside the tracks, dizzy when I landed.

"You okay?" I asked Greer, because nothing more sensible came to me right away, and it was my turn to talk.

"How can I be 'okay'?" Greer demanded, flailing her one good arm. "My husband is dead. And the police probably think *I* killed him."

I'm not proud of it, but I wondered in that moment if I'd have to spend my recently acquired nest egg on defense lawyers for Greer. If what Alex had said about her financial condition was true, and I had no reason to think it wasn't, she wouldn't be able to raise the money.

Then I decided I was getting ahead of myself.

Greer *wasn't* the killer.

Jack Pennington was.

Probably.

All I had to do was make sure somebody—preferably Tucker—proved it.

"You haven't been formally charged with anything, Greer," I reminded her, approaching and taking her by the elbow to steer her back out to the patio. She and I needed to talk about Shiloh, Montana, and about the blackmail, whether she liked it or not. "The police question everybody when someone is murdered, especially those closest to the victim."

Greer's eyes were awash in tears.

I guided her through the dining room, then the kitchen and then to the umbrella-covered table where she'd been sitting, according to Jolie, when I got back from Angela Braydaven's place.

"Do you own a gun, Greer?" I asked, once I'd sat her down and taken a chair for myself.

She swallowed. "You sound like the police," she accused. She paused, squinted at me. "What happened to your face?"

"I've been crying," I said. "Stop stalling. *Do you own a gun?*"

"Is it over Tucker Darroch?" Greer persisted, still stuck on the mascara stains. "I *told* you you shouldn't get involved with a married man."

"He's divorced," I said, rising above the temptation to point out to Greer that Alex had still been married to Beverly when she'd snagged him. "Answer my question."

"A .45," she said grudgingly. "Automatic."

"Do you have it?" I know, I know, it sounds like

a dumb question, since if said lethal weapon had been found, the police would hold it as evidence, but I needed to know what she'd say.

"It disappeared weeks ago," Greer said. "And I reported it missing as soon as I knew it was gone."

I could ask Tucker later if the gun had been found, examined by the lab and stashed in some evidence room. And if Greer had filed a report when it disappeared. "How come it never came up in conversation that you had a .45?" I inquired.

Greer hesitated, bit her lower lip. "It was my gun, wasn't it?" she whispered, skirting my question yet again. "Alex was shot with *my gun*. My fingerprints will be all over it. The *real* killer probably wore gloves—"

"Take a breath, Greer. I know you didn't kill Alex, and I'll find a way to prove it. Right now, you have to tell me about Shiloh."

She looked as though I'd punched her in the stomach. "Shiloh," she repeated woodenly, and that fevered, hunted glint was back in her eyes.

"Your old hometown," I said, and though I was going for casual, I probably sounded accusatory. "I can find out everything I need to know about the place in five minutes, just by logging on to the Internet, but I'd rather hear it from you first."

Greer rocked in her chair, huddled in on herself, trying to disappear. "Who told you?"

"That's beside the point," I said. "What happened in Shiloh?"

"N-nothing."

I started to get up. "Okay, fair enough. I'll just check out Google awhile."

"Don't," Greer pleaded.

I hovered between the chair seat and my full height, with my knees bent. "One more time, Greer," I said. "What happened in Shiloh?"

She sighed.

I sat, even though I wasn't sure I'd won the little standoff. Between last night's sex marathon, Alex's visit to my kitchen and the interlude with Justin, his mom and Pepper, my legs were noodly. "You told me you did something terrible," I reminded her. "What was it?"

"They'll kill me if I tell."

This job takes a lot of patience. Sometimes a lot more than I happen to have on hand. I managed to refrain from getting Greer by the throat. "Who is 'they'?"

"I don't know."

"You must have some idea," I insisted.

"You should wash your face," Greer said. "It can't be good for your skin, all that smudged mascara."

"Greer."

"I really don't *know*, okay? Someone must have seen—or stumbled across something—"

"Tell me what you did."

The phone rang, and since the receiver was sitting in the middle of the patio table, Greer reached for it.

I stopped her by grabbing her wrist. "Let voice mail pick up," I said.

"It could be the blackmailers," Greer said, and she looked so frightened, so frantic, that I let go of her so she could take the call. "Greer Pennington," she chimed, as though it were an ordinary day, and Alex might stroll in with an offering of conciliatory jewelry at any moment.

"Put it on speaker," I said, expecting resistance.

Greer surprised me by thumbing the speaker button immediately.

"This is Jack Pennington," the caller said flatly, and a chill went through me. The voice of a probable murderer, and not just *any* cold-blooded killer, either. The man might well have rubbed out his own *father,* over money. "The police won't release Dad's body right away, so we'll have to move the funeral up a week. Not that that will matter to you, since you'll probably be in jail."

Greer opened her mouth, but no words came out, just a barely audible croak. It was literally all I could do not to turn the tables on Jack Pennington, and tell him I had reason to think *he'd* been the one to empty the magazine of an automatic pistol into Alex's chest. I didn't want to give him the options of hiding evidence, skipping town, or shutting me up for good, along with Greer and possibly even Jolie.

"Greer?" Jack demanded. "Are you there?"

"I didn't kill your father," Greer said.

He laughed, the bastard. He actually *laughed.* "Of course you did, Greer," he said. "Or did you hire your sister the detective to do it? That would amount to the same thing, you know. You'd still be charged with murder one."

Another chill whispered against my nape. It was ludicrous to be afraid—I *hadn't* killed Alex, though God knows I'd wanted to, more than once. But I *was* afraid. What if Jack found a way to frame me for the shooting? Fingerprints or none, the police probably didn't think Greer could have strong-armed Alex out into the desert and sprayed him with hollow-points, especially with one arm in a cast.

I couldn't have strong-armed him, either, *The Damn Fool's Guide to Self-Defense for Women* notwithstanding. But I could have jumped him in the parking garage beneath his office building, thunking him on the head with something hard, like the butt of a pistol, bound his hands with duct tape and put a bag over his head. It would have been a struggle, but I could have hoisted his inert form into the trunk of a car, driven him out into the desert, slipped on a pair of gloves and let him have it with the .45.

Motive?

Revenge, possibly. I'd done Alex's medical billings for a long time, and he'd fired me recently, when he found out I'd been snooping, at Greer's behest, into his extramarital escapades. On top of that, he'd accused me, in front of television cameras no less, of murdering my own parents. Even though the actual perpetrators had been arrested and charged, with trials pending, there were probably a lot of people out there who still believed I'd somehow picked up the gun, held it in a five-year-old's hands and fired the fatal shots.

"Don't call here again, Jack," I heard Greer say, and realized I'd been woolgathering when I should have been listening. "And I *will* be at the funeral. Alex was *my husband.*"

"You were setting him up—" Jack began, but Greer ended the call, slammed the receiver down.

"About Shiloh," I said, calmer now that I'd had a few moments to recover from my brief foray into raging paranoia.

"I'm going to throw up!" Greer cried, and dashed into the house before I could stop her.

By the time I caught up with her, she was behind the locked door of the powder room off the kitchen, hurling.

I raised a fist to pound on the door, but lowered it to my side.

Greer wasn't going to tell me about Shiloh, which meant I'd have to find out on my own, probably with her working against me the whole time.

I wanted to go straight out to the guesthouse, get my stuff, load it all into the Volvo and wheel it back to Bad-Ass Bert's. Live in my own apartment again, where I belonged.

But I couldn't abandon Greer. In a lot of ways

she was as helpless as Gillian. I knew she was hedging, but the vomiting was for real. She could have faked the sounds, but the smell would be hard to duplicate. What if she was seriously ill? What if she needed an ambulance?

An ambulance.

Brilliance strikes at the most unexpected times.

"Greer," I called forcefully, "if you don't open this door, I'm going to call an *ambulance*. The paramedics will break it down."

More spewing. Then "Go away!"

"I'll do it, Greer."

"No—" gag "—you *won't*."

"I'm heading to the phone right now—9-1-1. I am calling 911—"

"Stop!" The knob jiggled, and the door opened a little way.

Seeing Greer on her knees in front of the commode, looking wretched, I almost called my own bluff and summoned the medicos. She immediately started the barf-o-thon again, and I held her hair, washed her face when the spasms subsided, flushed and sprayed.

I'm a sympathy barfer. By the time I'd handled that situation, I was on the verge of retching myself.

"I have a migraine," Greer moaned, and I believed her.

"I'm calling your doctor," I said.

"No," she protested. "I just need to take some medicine and lie down."

I helped her upstairs to the sumptuous suite she'd once shared with Alex. Got her settled in the enormous round bed, brought her bottled water and her pills.

"Pull the drapes," Greer groaned after gingerly swallowing a tablet and a sip of the water. "The light hurts my eyes."

I complied. "I still think I should call your doctor—or take you to the emergency room."

Greer shook her head. "Please, Mojo," she whispered. "Just leave me alone. Let me sleep...."

Given her state of mind, and the trouble she was in, I was afraid to leave the migraine pills where she could get them. I dropped the small brown bottle into the pocket of my pantsuit jacket, took the phone receiver from the base on the bedside table and laid it near her hand. "I'll be in the guesthouse," I said quietly. "Call if you need anything."

Greer merely nodded, her eyes already closed.

"I'll look in on you in a little while."

She nodded again.

I crept out, closing the bedroom door softly behind me.

Paused a moment or two in the hallway, grappling with my conscience. I wasn't going to get a better chance to search the place for any clues to the Shiloh secret, but what if Greer needed me, called the guesthouse and got no answer? The mansion was seriously big; she'd have no way of knowing I was within shouting distance.

Provided she had the strength to shout, after all that throwing up.

I dashed out to my place, hoping there wouldn't be any ghosts in residence—though I *was* getting a little concerned that Gillian hadn't put in an appearance since she'd popped out of Helen's double-wide the evening before.

One thing at a time, I told myself. *The Damn Fool's Guide to Maintaining Sanity.* I toyed briefly with the idea of writing that one myself, despite a glaring lack of credentials.

The guesthouse was empty. Snatching up my phone, I hotfooted it back to Greer's.

She and Alex shared a "study" on the ground floor of Casa Pennington—a swank layout with a pair of matched antique desks, probably looted from some hacienda in Mexico, leather chairs and a wall of oak filing cabinets.

There were twin computers, one on each desk, and I headed for Alex's first, tapped in with the password he'd given me and found the file containing the bank account numbers we'd discussed. There were four of them, and I copied the numbers carefully onto a piece of monogrammed notepaper, folded it and tucked it into my pocket. I shifted to Greer's computer with some reluctance—I figured there might be evidence against Jack Pennington on Alex's hard drive, and I wanted to get to it before the police confiscated the whole works as part of their investigation. The trouble was, I didn't know

how much time I had before Greer miraculously recovered from her migraine and caught me snooping.

She'd stored her password, just as I'd hoped,
and I went straight to her e-mail, with only a mild
pang of guilt, and scanned the senders' names for
potential blackmailers.

Jolie's was there.

So was mine.

There were the usual generous offers from
multi-level marketing companies and Internet
porn providers.

And that was it.

The phone rang. For a second I didn't realize it
wasn't the one I'd stuck in my pocket out in the
guesthouse, on top of Greer's pill bottle. Nor was
it the main line into the house, since it was muffled.
No, the cheery little jingle came from the top
drawer of the desk I was sitting at.

I opened it, found a cell phone—the throwaway
variety, probably, though it had a camera function.
I stared in disbelief at the little panel where the
caller's picture showed. Skull and crossbones.

I wasted another moment pondering that, then
flipped the phone open and uttered an uncertain
"Hello?"

Instant freeze from the other end. I mean, I
actually *felt* it, like a shivery wind coming off an ice
floe. It raised goose bumps on my forearms.

"Who is this?" someone demanded. The voice

might have been altered, but I wasn't sure of that. Could be the person smoked unfiltered cigarettes two at a time.

"Mojo Sheepshanks," I said. "My sister is ill, so I'm answering her phones."

"She gave you *this* phone?"

Man? Woman? Creature from the Black Lagoon? I couldn't tell from the rough, raspy voice. I tensed, and the skull and crossbones in the picture panel suddenly seemed a lot more than tasteless. It was full-on sinister.

"Not really," I said, trying to sound sweetly stupid, and therefore harmless. "It rang and I tracked the sound to her desk drawer." I paused, frowned. "Who's calling, please?"

"Stupid bitch," the caller said, though whether he/she/it was addressing me or a companion was anybody's guess.

"I beg your pardon?" I said, not so sweetly.

"Tell Molly she's a dead woman."

Molly? Who the hell was Molly?

Before I could ask, the caller hung up.

I immediately hit star sixty-nine. Blocked, of course.

I stared at the phone, the innocuous e-mails on Greer's computer screen forgotten. Checked for stored numbers.

Nothing.

Pushed Redial.

Nothing again.

Pulled the battery, found the serial number on the little label behind it. I practically needed a microscope, even with my twenty-twenty vision, but I finally figured it out and copied the digits onto a piece of notepaper. I had no idea, at that point, what value the information might have. It just seemed, frankly, like something a smart detective would do.

I had, alas, more questions than answers. I scrolled through the photo files, but found zip.

Frowning, I sat back in the cushy office chair, staring at the phone in my hand. The caller had threatened Greer's life, and I had a sick feeling that he/she/it meant every word. Had I just spoken to her blackmailer, or Jack Pennington, disguising his voice? Or did Greer have other enemies I knew nothing about?

What was with the skull and crossbones?

I had learned one thing, though.

Greer's name had once been Molly.

CHAPTER EIGHT

I PUT THE DISPOSABLE cell phone back into the drawer, but it preyed on my mind as I signed out of Greer's e-mail to run a search for Shiloh, Montana. She had a regular cell, a sleek, high-tech prototype, not yet available to the scruffy masses, that did everything from reminding her of appointments to downloading first-run movies. Why would she own a cheap alternative, probably purchased online or in some discount store?

I wanted to shake her awake and ask her about the phone and about her past life as Molly, but what good would that do? She'd only stonewall me, as she'd been doing ever since I arrived.

I thought about calling Tucker for some input, but discarded the idea almost immediately. He had, as he liked to remind me, A Job, and no part of it involved helping me with cases, especially during working hours.

For a homicide cop, that's 24/7, but he was planning on knocking on my door when he got off work, and I was planning on letting him in. I'd show him the cell phone then, give him the bank account numbers Alex had steered me to and tell him what Alex had said about the blackmail situation. I might or might not tell him about the Molly angle—I hadn't decided yet.

Meanwhile, I'd bide my time.

There were a surprising number of Web links for Shiloh, Montana. I started with the chamber of commerce, mostly because it was first on the list, but also because I didn't have a map handy and I wanted to pinpoint the place.

It was in the western part of the state, population "3000 and Growing," nestled on the "gloriously timbered shores of spectacular Flathead Lake," and offering "incomparable" opportunities for fishing, hunting, boating, swimming, et cetera. There was the requisite Native American casino—a point in the town's favor, from my perspective, since I've rarely encountered a slot machine I can't loot—along with grocery stores, bars, restaurants and a couple of "family motels," meaning, I supposed, no vibrating beds, dirty movies and hourly rates.

I printed the chamber material and went back to the Google list.

Next I found the Web page for the Shiloh *Bugle*.

Cute, I thought. A major battle in the Civil War had been fought at Shiloh, Tennessee, and the "bugle" part was probably a reference to that, meant to conjure images of the cavalry riding over the hill at top gallop. Never mind the topographical dis-

tance between Flathead Lake and the Union-Con-
federacy action—I guess even towns can be
wannabes.

I scanned the articles in the archives.

As far as I could tell, no one had ever been
murdered in Shiloh. There had been no kidnap-
pings, no heists at the Farmer's and Cattleman's
Bank, the only institution of its type in the town.
Zip. The biggest news in a decade, apparently, was
Miss Rainbow Trout of 2003 having to step down
before her year was up because of "family respon-
sibilities." As in, I thought cynically, she'd probably
started one, necessitating a hasty wedding.

Glumly I logged off the *Bugle* site. I was going
to have to start from scratch and go to Shiloh in
person if I wanted to find out who was blackmailing Greer—and I had to know. Surely I could pick
up some kind of thread there, and follow it to the
truth.

I opened the desk drawer and peeked in at the
cell phone again, frowning.

It hadn't moved.

The phone in my pocket rang.

Phones are handy. No doubt about it. But they
always ring when I'm busy doing something else.

Expecting an upstairs-downstairs call from
Greer, I didn't stop to check the caller ID panel. I
just thumbed it and said a quiet—make that resigned—hello.

"We had an appointment," Beverly Pennington

said tersely. "Carlotta made lobster salad, and you didn't show up. You didn't even *call*. Am I supposed to be impressed by that, Ms. Sheepshanks?"

Bitch, I thought. There were a lot of people I would have liked to impress, but she wasn't one of them.

"I figured you were busy, what with the police being there to tell you your ex-husband had been murdered," I said in a crisp professional tone. "Under the circumstances, calling you seemed like an unnecessary intrusion."

Beverly was quiet. I wondered if she was crying. If she'd still loved Alex Pennington, hoped he might have overlooked the small problem of all-out alcoholism and come back to her one day.

I softened a little. Waited silently for her to recover. Her turn to talk, not mine.

"The bastard would have left me penniless," she said presently, and with venom, "if I hadn't had the good sense to pay up the life insurance policies out of my divorce settlement."

So much for treading lightly around the delicate subject of mourning the father of her children. I considered warning her that her son Jack might be about to erase her from the planet to collect a few bucks, but that would have been defamation—if not definition—of character. In any case, Alex had been wrong about the financial situation wife #1 would be in following his sudden and tragic demise. I hoped he'd been wrong about some other things, too—like Greer being a sociopath.

Greer talks a good game, I heard him say, *but if it's her or you, she'll throw you to the wolves.*

Jack was the dangerous one, I reminded myself.

"Be careful, Mrs. Pennington," I said—carefully.

I didn't need to see her face to know she was frowning. I heard it in her voice.

"Of what?" she asked, nonplussed.

Of your son. "Just be careful."

Another thoughtful and clearly unfriendly pause. Then, "I would still like to discuss hiring you to do some...work for me. When can we meet?"

"I'm tied up today," I answered moderately, unsettled and at the same time curious as hell. What could this woman possibly want from me, besides a means of sticking it to Greer somehow? There were plenty of established P.I.'s listed in the Yellow Pages. Why call me? "How about tomorrow afternoon?"

"Two o'clock," Beverly said. "You have the address?"

I confirmed that I did, and we hung up.

I jammed the phone back into my jacket pocket.

The trouble with being a detective is that you always have to be thinking about what to do next.

A noise in the entryway, just outside the study, sparked a fizzy little burst of alarm in the pit of my stomach.

It was probably Greer, feeling better and wanting something to eat, or some company.

Tell Molly she's a dead woman.

Or it could be whoever had called on the throw-away cell phone, expecting to get Greer.

I stiffened in my chair. Listened.

Carmen, Greer's housekeeper, appeared in the archway, smiling.

"Hello, Mojo," she said, her speech heavily accented in a Spanish direction. "Where is Mrs. Pennington, please?"

Hallelujah, I thought. With Carmen to look after Greer, I could hit the street, get some gumshoeing done. "Upstairs," I said. "She has a migraine." I remembered that Greer had said her housekeeper was on vacation. "I thought you were out of town."

"My husband, he call me in San Miguel," Carmen said, no longer smiling. Her dark eyes glistened with emotion. "He say Dr. Alex is killed. I hurry back for Mrs. Pennington." The housekeeper was a small, compact woman, her black hair tidily braided and wound into a knot at the back of her head. She'd been working for Greer and Alex for about a year, by my best estimate, and though she'd served me a number of meals and appeared at my elbow a thousand times with a pitcher of iced tea while Greer and I dished on the patio, I didn't know her well. Now I studied her carefully. She wore a pink polyester uniform and sensible shoes and carried a purse the size of a duffel bag.

"Mrs. Pennington is sick?" she asked, plainly worried.

I wondered how badly she needed this job, and

how long it would be before Greer couldn't pay her salary any longer.

"She's been throwing up a lot," I said. "Is that new?"

Carmen blinked. "She was fine when I leave for San Miguel." There was a defensive note in the woman's voice; clearly, she wouldn't have gone on vacation if Greer had been ill when she left. "Upset because the doctor, he move out of the house. But only that."

More wondering on my part. Did Carmen know Greer was being blackmailed? And if so, could she be persuaded to share the details?

I fished. "There wasn't any other sort of—problem?"

Carmen set the mongo purse on top of one of the oak filing cabinets against the far wall of the study. "What do you mean?"

Was she stalling, hedging—the way Greer had done every time I tried to get the skinny on the blackmail? Or was she sincerely confused? I couldn't tell.

I took the skull-and-crossbones cell phone out of the desk drawer and rose to cross the room, holding it out to her, balanced on one palm.

"Have you ever seen this before?"

Carmen peered at the instrument, as if reluctant to touch it, and crossed herself hastily when she spotted the pirate sign in the photo panel. She shook her head. Up close, I could see wariness in her eyes. My internal lie-o-meter lit up.

"It's disposable," I said, playing it by ear. "The kind of phone drug dealers like, because the calls are hard, if not impossible, to trace."

Carmen gasped. "Drug dealers?"

"Criminals of all kinds," I said wisely, though I didn't really know what I was talking about. Nothing new there, either. You have to wing it a lot in my line of work. "Kidnappers." I paused for dramatic effect, then leaned in a little and whispered, *"Blackmailers."*

Carmen crossed herself again. Her eyes went wide and she leaned back. She looked over her shoulder, then confided, with a nod at the cell, "Phone come in mail one day last month. Mrs. Pennington, she very frightened when she see it. Go off by herself."

"But she didn't mention who might have sent it?"

Carmen shook her head, probably wishing she hadn't spilled any information at all. As I said, I didn't know her, which meant she didn't know *me,* either. Her loyalties lay with Greer, of course, and I *had* figured out that she wasn't given to idle gossip. If I hoped to get anything else out of her, I would have to convince her that the boss lady was in grave peril first.

"Mrs. Pennington," I said, "is being blackmailed. And today—just a little while ago, in fact—somebody called on this phone and threatened her life."

"Madre de Dios," Carmen whispered, staring at me. "You call police?"

"Not yet," I answered. "I want to handle this very carefully, because whoever these people are, I think they mean business. I have a—contact at the sheriff's department."

Oh, Tucker and I had made *contact,* all right.

I felt suddenly pantyless, even though I was wearing bikini briefs fresh from my underwear drawer in the guesthouse bedroom.

"I'll talk to Detective Darroch when I see him tonight," I added, hoping I sounded moderate. I'd be doing a lot more than *seeing* Tucker, come eventide, if he had his way. And I knew he would, because where he was concerned, I was downright easy. "Right now, Carmen, if you know anything else about this, please tell me."

"I don't know about blackmailing," she said, and my gut told me she was lying. She glanced at the printouts on Shiloh, the numbers scrawled on a sheet of notepaper.

I saw her bristle.

"Greer has been understandably upset over her husband's death," I said. Would that I'd had time to hide the evidence of my snooping, but I hadn't. "She's scared half out of her mind, Carmen. Too scared to tell me anything, so I can help."

Carmen weighed my words, studying me with what appeared to be mingled suspicion and a growing concern for Greer's safety. Her glance strayed again to the printouts. For all she knew, *I* was the one blackmailing Greer.

We were at an impasse.

Lots of questions, not very many answers.

I remembered Greer's prescription painkillers and checked the label for a physician's name. Alex Pennington, M.D.

Interesting, but not unusual. A lot of doctors prescribe medicine for their families, and for themselves. Still, it occurred to me that Alex *might* have given Greer something lethal, trying to solve one of his many problems the no-muss, no-fuss way. That problem being Greer.

She'd run him into bankruptcy, after all, contributing to Jack Pennington's alleged decision to hijack him and then gun him down in the desert. And who knew what else had happened between them?

I popped the lid on the pill bottle and shook one out, hoping I could persuade Jolie, a forensics expert, to run a tox report on it. Surely she still had access to lab facilities. Most likely, though, the stuff was just what the label said it was: migraine medication.

I handed the bottle to Carmen. "I have to leave," I said, dropping the tiny white pill into my jacket pocket and hoping the seams were good. Then I produced a business card, newly printed with "Sheepshanks, Sheepshanks and Sheepshanks—Private Investigations" and my phone numbers. "Could you stay with Mrs. Pennington, Carmen? Overnight?"

Carmen took the card, glanced down at it, considered the question briefly—it was safe to assume

she had a life outside the walls of Casa Pennington—then nodded, the set of her face conveying
resolve rather than resignation.

"Call me if there are any problems," I said. "And
keep the doors locked. Look through the peephole
before you let anybody in."

Carmen started looking scared again.

I waited for her to cross herself, but she didn't.

I headed for the door, eager to get out before
another phone rang, precipitating another crisis.
"And Carmen?"

She stared at me bleakly.

"Do you know Dr. Pennington's son, Jack?"

She nodded, still speechless.

"Does he have a key to this house?" I asked.

Another nod.

"Have the locks changed. Today. And get a new
security code for the alarm system, too."

At this, Carmen actually paled. I hoped she
wouldn't grab her big purse, rush to her car and boogie
for home as soon as I was gone. "Mr. Jack—?"

"Could be dangerous," I said.

She followed me to the front door, in order to
lock it behind me, and that gave me a chance to ask
one more question.

"Do you know where Mrs. Pennington keeps
her gun?"

"It was stolen, this gun," Carmen answered very
quietly, after gulping once. "She kept it in a wall
safe, in her closet."

I figured it was time to let the poor woman off the hook. As it was, she'd probably try to barricade the door with the entryway breakfront as soon as it closed behind me. "Try not to worry," I said. "I don't mean to alarm you, but you can never be too careful."

I slipped out, stood in the brick-paved portico for a few moments.

I didn't like leaving Greer, even in Carmen's care. It froze my blood to know that Jack Pennington had a key to the front door, and almost certainly knew the alarm code. Come to that, he could let himself into the guesthouse, too, if he wanted to.

It was time to shop for that Glock I'd been wanting.

It was definitely time.

GUNS ARE PLENTIFUL in Arizona, and a lot of unlikely people pack heat—soccer moms, TV talk-show hosts and even preachers. It's that kind of state; the Old West is still part of the collective psyche. There's no helmet law to keep motorcyclists from bashing their brains out on roads, and when it comes to daylight saving time, just forget it. When the rest of the country springs forward or falls back, Arizonans don't adjust their watches.

I drove to a shop in Cave Creek, the kind of joint where they sell postcards, tacky souvenir fridge magnets, mugs and ashtrays, T-shirts, mineral specimens and plastic rabbits with antlers.

Oh, and serious firepower, too, though that's often a sideline.

"I want a Glock," I told the clerk, who looked as though he might belong to one of those radical patriot groups who gather around pool tables and in detached garages amid rusted-out pickup trucks, where they smoke, drink beer and plot the overthrow of the United States government.

Bubba, who was missing several teeth, needed to wash his hair and had a coiled snake and the words Don't Tread On Me tattooed on his right forearm, straightened behind the grimy souvenir counter and looked me over. I saw recognition register. When guys like Bubba actually think, it startles the rest of their body, and causes a visible chain reaction—twitching, restless fingers, shifty eyes and some foot shuffling.

"I've seen you around Bad-Ass Bert's," Bubba said. "And on TV, too."

Media fame can be a burden. I dug in my purse for my wallet.

"Shame about ole Bert biting the dust the way he did," Bubba went on when I didn't speak. "I heard he left the bar to you in his will. You gonna open it up for business anytime soon?"

"Probably," I said. The way my P.I. career was going, I'd need the income, but the truth is, it made me sad to think of setting foot inside the saloon again. Russell, the basset hound, wouldn't be around, and neither would Bert. Besides, I'd had some traumatic experiences there.

"Why a Glock?" Bubba asked conversationally.

Because Kay Scarpetta carries one in Patricia Cornwell's books didn't seem like a good answer. Nor could I admit to the other reason—that my boyfriend, the cop, owned two.

I leaned in, even though it was a rash move, considering Bubba practiced poor oral hygiene and needed a more reliable deodorant product than he was currently using. "Gun of choice for private investigators everywhere," I said seriously.

"I saw in the papers where you were a dick," Bubba said, bending, presumably to bring some of his wares out from under the counter for my inspection.

I let the dick remark pass, even though it was rife with possibilities for sarcastic comebacks.

"You know how to shoot one of these things?" Bubba inquired after laying two battered plastic cases on top of the counter.

I planned on getting Jolie to teach me, or maybe Tucker. There might even be a *Damn Fool's Guide* on the subject. Suffice it to say, if I had to do anything technical, like release the safety or slam in a cartridge magazine to qualify to buy the gun, I'd be leaving Bubba's unarmed.

"Yes," I lied. "Of course I do."

Bubba opened the cases. The Glocks gleamed inside, one black, compact, with a short barrel, one shiny steel, with a long one.

I went with black, because it looked like Tucker's gun and would be easier to carry in my purse. Plus, black goes with everything.

"Bullets?" Bubba asked mildly.

"Lots of them. Whatever fits. And definitely hollow-point."

Bubba whistled. "They'll do some damage, them hollow-points," he said, smiling conspiratorially.

"How much?" I asked, wallet in hand.

"Well, these here guns are secondhand," Bubba mused. Then he named a price that made me catch my breath. Glocks, alas, are not cheap.

I imagined Jack Pennington possibly abducting and then gunning down his own father in the desert. I'd never met him, but he was active in the community, and I'd seen his picture in the paper a lot.

He might come after Greer—or me, since I intended to dig around in his background a little.

I thought about the caller on Greer's throwaway cell phone.

And I wrote a hefty check.

I wanted to ask if I needed a permit, but that would have revealed my ignorance to a degree even Bubba might notice. At the time, all I wanted was a way to save myself if I woke up some night and found somebody standing over my bed in a ski mask, so I didn't worry about the legalities.

Back in the car, I stuck the Glock under the front seat, still in its case, and sat there in the gravel parking lot, shaking and sweating a little.

Then I got a grip. If Jolie could manage a gun, so could I. No problem.

I'd no sooner gotten that grip when I lost it again,

flashed back in time to an August night in my childhood, when both my parents were shot to death at
close range. I was five when it happened, but now, at
twenty-eight, I could smell the coppery scent of blood,
see it lying in crimson pools, reflecting the light.

My stomach seized with a painful wrench.

Good thing it had already ground the sausage
biscuit down to nothing.

I drew deep breaths until the memories began
to subside.

My cell phone rang, and this time I was glad of
the interruption. "Mojo Sheepshanks," I said.

The caller was Helen Erland. "You can get in to
see Vince anytime this afternoon," she said dully.
"Just show up at the jail. His lawyer's already made
the arrangements."

"That's good," I said, blessing the unknown
public defender. "Are you okay?" I could have
chewed off my tongue after I uttered that question.
Of course she wasn't okay. Her daughter was dead,
and her husband, who might have been innocent but
might also have been Gillian's killer, was in jail.

Still, I was heartened, because I knew I'd be able
to tell if Vince Erland was guilty if I could look him
in the eye, just the way I always knew when a slot
machine was about to pay off.

That's why they called me Mojo.

"Oh, I'm just dandy," Helen said, and hung up
on me.

The phone immediately rang again.

This time it was Tucker.

"Hey," I said, still feeling a little shaky.

"Hey," he replied. "What are you doing?"

"Shopping," I told him, torn between hoping he'd say he couldn't make it to my place that night and hoping he'd offer to pick up dinner on the way. "What are *you* doing?"

He lowered his voice, so he probably wasn't alone. "Anticipating," he said.

Heat suffused my body, which had been stone-cold and clammy only moments before, and I got a little damp. "Did you check out the Jack Pennington lead?"

Tucker sighed.

"Just asking," I said cheerfully.

"He's clean, Moje. Pennington's never had so much as a parking ticket."

I felt discouraged, but the prospect of hot sex with Tucker did a lot to raise my spirits. "That doesn't mean he's not a murderer," I pointed out.

"Can we not talk business?" Tucker asked.

"We can talk about dinner," I offered. "What are you bringing?"

He laughed. "I'm in charge of dinner?"

"Unless you want me to cook," I said.

"Scary thought," he answered. "How about Chinese takeout?"

"Works for me."

"Moje?"

He sounded so serious that I was scared he'd

been planning to break bad news over the chow mein and kung pao chicken, and had just now decided not to wait. I expected him to say something like "Allison and I have decided to try again" or "I've just been diagnosed with a terminal disease."

"What?" I asked, barely whispering.

"Don't wear underpants," Tucker replied.

CHAPTER NINE

AFTER I LEFT BUBBA'S, I headed for downtown Phoenix and the jail. Parking was a bitch, but I finally found a spot, locked up the car, went inside and introduced myself at the reception desk, all the while keeping a sharp eye out for Tucker. He was bound to find out I'd been to visit Vince Erland, but I wanted it to be after the fact, when he couldn't interfere, not before, when he could hustle me out of there.

Getting in was remarkably easy. I was almost disappointed, since I'd been all geared up for a bureaucratic hassle of some kind. I was sure they'd say the public defender hadn't called, the paperwork was lost, the prisoner had been carried off by visitors from another planet.

Instead, I was handed a clip-on pass, herded through a metal detector and shown to the visitors' area.

It was right out of a TV movie. Thick glass wall, with a chair and a phone on either side. Graffiti scratched into the counter.

I sat down and waited.

When Vince Erland arrived, wearing the regulation orange jail outfit, I sized him up. He was tall and super-skinny, with a bad complexion and greasy hair, reminiscent of Bubba. His mouse-brown tresses were thinning on top, but the rest of it was long, and pulled back into a ponytail. His eyes were a cold, smoky gray.

He sat down, reached for the phone receiver and said, "I wondered what somebody named Mojo Sheepshanks would look like." His gaze wandered lazily over me. "Now I know."

"I'm here to ask some questions about the day Gillian died," I said.

"Yeah," he answered, leaning so far back in his chair that I half expected him to slide out of it. "Helen told me she hired you."

"What happened, Mr. Erland?"

"Vince," he said, as if we'd met in a bar and he was about to ask me to dance.

Something burned in the back of my throat. "Vince, then," I replied, sitting up very straight. Then I waited.

"I picked Gilly up after her dance class," he said. "We couldn't afford the lessons, and after all, the kid was stone-deaf, but Helen insisted she could *feel* the music...."

"Go on," I said evenly when his voice fell away.

"She wanted a damn dog. It was all she talked about—waving her hands around all the time. So I promised her I'd look into it. That's all I said—that

I'd look into it. I figured she'd forget the whole thing eventually. Hell, I've been out of work for six months, and Helen barely makes enough to keep us going."

Everything inside me soured. Vince Erland might be telling the truth, but even if he hadn't killed Gillian, he was a son of a bitch. "You know sign language?" I asked.

"No," he answered. "But the kid managed to get her point across just the same."

"She wanted a dog," I recapped, to get him back on track.

"We stopped off for milk and beer, and I broke it to her that there wasn't going to be any dog. She took off—I thought she'd gone to the bathroom or something, or decided to walk home. I looked all over the store, and then I drove back to the trailer, expecting to pick her up along the way and give her what-for for skipping out like that. There's all kinds of creeps out there." He cocked a thumb to indicate the outside world, which was ironic in itself, since he was sitting in creep-central. "They'd as soon kill you as look at you."

My skin crawled, but I managed to project sympathetic detachment. "You didn't call the police or alert the store manager when you realized Gillian was gone?"

Erland went a muddy color that clashed with his jail clothes. "The cops are making a big deal out of that," he said. "The kid was always flying off the handle, taking off—look at her crossways, and she'd be over to Chelsea's or God knows where else. I thought she'd gone home, or maybe to find Helen. I didn't get worried till I got home and called around a little. Nobody'd seen her, it turned out, so I called the police. Next thing I know, I'm on my way downtown for 'questioning.' Then it's some bullshit about parking tickets. My lawyer's going to get me out of here, though. They're running out of excuses to hold me, and mark my words, lady, they haven't got *shit* for evidence."

I wondered what Helen Erland had seen in this man.

Had he killed Gillian?

The mojo failed me. I didn't know.

He was a jerk, that was obvious. But that didn't mean he'd murder a child.

"Helen told me you saw the kid's ghost," he said. He sleazed upward in his chair, leaned forward and thumped the glass hard with a middle finger. "Listen up," he went on. "Here's the only reason I agreed to talk to you. Stay away from my wife. She's got problems enough without a bunch of hocus-pocus, I-see-dead-people crap. You got that, Mojo Sheepshit?"

As if *that* was original. I'd heard it on the playground as a kid, and from a couple of Nick's girlfriends, too. I replaced the phone receiver, proud of my restraint, stood up and left.

I was no closer to finding Gillian's killer than I'd ever been. But I knew this much: Vince Erland was still in the running.

THE GLOCK AND I HEADED back north, this time to Scottsdale.

I parked in the lot of an indoor target range, got out my cell phone and called Helen at the convenience store.

"You upset Vince," she scolded, once she knew I was the one calling.

"Murder investigations are always upsetting," I said.

"You're fired," Helen told me.

I sighed. She could fire me—no great loss, since I wasn't getting paid—but I wasn't leaving the case alone until I knew who'd ended Gillian's life that day after the dance rehearsal class. "A little professional advice?" I ventured.

"What?" Helen snapped.

"Get a divorce," I answered. And then I hung up.

I did some deep breathing to restore my equilibrium, and then, leaving the Glock in its case under the seat, I went inside the range to ask about shooting lessons. The stakes had gone up; I'd just made another enemy—Vince Erland.

The muffled pop of bullets somewhere out back was clearly audible from the reception area.

A side door opened, and a man came through it.

He was good-looking, dark haired and leanly fit. He wore khakis and a navy blue polo shirt that matched his eyes. I pegged him right away for either a former FBI agent or an ex-cop, which says something for my instincts. Turned out he was both, though I didn't find that out until later.

"I want to learn to shoot," I said, and then blushed, because the way he looked at me made me feel strangely self-conscious. I'd had the presence of mind to leave the guesthouse phone in the car this time, but I wished I'd changed out of the pantsuit.

"You came to the right place," he replied, and even though he ran his gaze over me much as Erland had at the jail, the feeling was remarkably different. It wasn't attraction, really—I was gone on Tucker, for better or worse—but I knew I *could* be attracted to this guy if I let my guard down for an instant. "Do you own a firearm?"

I don't know what made me lie. Maybe it was habit. Maybe it was common sense—if the Glock under my car seat was illegal, I wanted Tucker to be the one to tell me, not some stranger who might feel bound to call the cops first and ask questions later.

"Not yet," I said. "I thought I should learn how to handle a gun before I bought one."

"Good thinking." He smiled. A long counter stood between us. He put out a hand. "Max Summervale," he said.

"Mojo Sheepshanks," I replied as we shook.

A charge jolted up my arm.

Max squinted, still grinning. "I've seen you somewhere," he said.

"I was on TV a while back," I answered, hoping he'd let it go at that.

"You're an actress?"

"A private detective," I said after shaking my head once, hoping he wouldn't ask me to elaborate on how that could get me on the news.

He didn't. But Max was a long time letting go of my hand, and for some reason, I didn't pull free. "I'll need to see some ID," he told me, "and you'll have to fill out a form. Just a formality. We have guns and ammo inside, and I'll be your instructor."

"Can I shoot today, though?" I asked.

"Tomorrow," Max said. "Provided your background check comes back okay, of course. I'm sure it will."

I nodded, a little disappointed. It wasn't as though I had time on my hands; I had detecting to do, and a hot date with Tucker that night. I'd need to keep a finger on the pulse of the Greer situation, Helen Erland had just fired me and Beverly Pennington was expecting me at two the next afternoon.

For a person who wasn't earning a living, I was pretty busy.

"Okay," I said. I filled out the form, showed Max my driver's license and made an appointment for my first shooting lesson at nine o'clock the next morning.

I left the building, got back in my car.

It was too early to bolt for the guesthouse. If I did, I'd end up pacing, waiting for Tucker and, as I said, I had Things To Do. What I *didn't* have was a plan—just a sense of restlessness, underlain with a hamster-wheel urgency.

So I went to Bad-Ass Bert's, steeled myself and let myself into the downstairs bar.

Sawdust floors.

Pool tables.

A dark, silent jukebox.

The hot-dog cooker on top of the makeshift bar. It had been Bert's pride and joy, that bar. A few barrels, with boards nailed on top, bought at a sale in Tombstone. According to Bert, the likes of Wyatt Earp and Doc Holliday had stood before it, swilling whiskey.

I missed Bert.

Touched the bar stool where Russell the basset hound used to sit. I missed the dog even more than Bert, but I was never going to see either of them again. They were in Witness Protection, along with Bert's girlfriend, Sheila, after testifying in some drug trial, behind closed doors. The details had never been made public, and while Tucker knew the scoop, thanks to his stint with the DEA, he wasn't telling.

I looked around the place. I could sell it—the building was old, but the real estate was prime, right on the main street of Cave Creek. To look at the town itself, you'd have thought it was low income, but there were mansions in them there hills.

The thing to do was let the bar go. If I didn't, the taxes alone would eat me alive, and I knew even less about running a bar than being a private detective, which ought to tell you something.

I lifted my eyes to the rough, weathered board ceiling. My apartment was up there—nothing special, but *mine.*

The plain fact was I *couldn't* give the place up—not the apartment, not the bar. I couldn't really explain why, except to say I wasn't through with it yet. Selling Bad-Ass Bert's would have been like leaving a theater before I'd seen the end of a movie.

I would get the liquor license transferred from Bert's name to mine, I decided. Reopen the joint and call it Mojo's. Run my P.I. business out of the bar.

None of that would be easy to do, I knew, but it made me feel better just to decide. I perched on Russell's old stool, propped an elbow on top of the bar and imagined myself serving up brewskies to a lot of pool-playing bikers.

It daunted me, but not as much as going back to medical coding and billing, or applying for a receptionist's job somewhere. I wasn't making any money as a detective, and my cash stash, though in excess of three hundred thousand dollars and drawing serious interest, could disappear overnight if I had to use it to pay for a criminal defense lawyer for Greer.

I needed an income.

I got out Bert's phone book and my cell phone and called the State Liquor Board, first thing. For a fee, I could transfer the license and be selling beer, wine and whiskey within ten days. I scribbled down the Web site address the clerk gave me, where I could download the form.

Buoyed by the unexpected lack of resistance, I called a sign company next. Ordered a blue neon tube spelling Mojo's in cursive, and read the numbers off my ATM card into the phone.

When that was done, I rooted around in Bert's cupboards—*my* cupboards, now—and found a ring binder I'd seen my friend consult many times in the past. It was Bert's supplier list. I carried that out to the car, tossed it on the passenger seat and relocked the doors.

Then I went up the stairs and let myself into the apartment.

This time I wasn't scared.

I stripped off the pantsuit, took denim shorts, a bra and a skimpy top—but no underpants—from the dresser in my bedroom, stripped, adjusted the shower spray and stepped over the edge of my old-fashioned bathtub, pulling the curtain firmly. *Take note, psychos and serial killers,* I thought, *Mojo is* back.

After the shower I dressed and, feeling refreshed, went into the kitchen and brewed myself a cup of coffee. While the pot was perking away, I called Tucker's cell from the kitchen.

"Darroch," he said.

"Check your caller ID once in a while," I replied. "Ask me where I am."

"Okay," Tucker said. "Where are you?"

"My place."

"And this is supposed to be news?"

"My place," I repeated. "Soon to be known as Mojo's."

"You're in the apartment? *Alone?*"

I straightened my spine. "I will be until you get here," I said, feeling ever so slightly defensive. If Tucker had had his way, I'd live in a steel vault someplace, and wear full body armor. Sans underpants, of course.

"Damn," he said.

"It's as safe as anywhere else," I argued. "The locks have been changed and all unauthorized entrances have been sealed." I remembered, with a shudder, the way a killer had gotten in, not all that long ago.

"I don't suppose I can talk you out of this," Tucker said.

"Nope," I said.

There was a long pause. Then, "You still want Chinese?"

"I want you," I said. "The kung pao chicken is a bonus."

He laughed. It was a weary sound, indicating better than anything he could have said that he knew a lot of things I didn't, and they weighed on him, but hearing it was good, just the same.

"I'll be there around five-thirty," he said. A guarded note came into his voice. "I can call ahead for the takeout, but I have to stop by Allison's for a few minutes on the way."

"Something wrong at home?" I asked as casually as I could.

"I don't know," Tucker replied. "Allison called a little while ago, and she said it was important."

I didn't argue. After all, a lot of guys wouldn't have mentioned the pit stop at all. Tucker had been straightforward.

I had to trust him—or let him go. And I wasn't any more ready to let go of Tucker than I was the bar downstairs, or my apartment. The best I could manage at the moment was not to cling like a scared climber on a steep wall of rock.

"See you when you get here," I said as lightly as I could.

"Moje?"

"What?"

"It's no big deal, my stopping by Allison's. She probably just needs a form signed or something."

"Did I say it was a big deal?" *You sleep there. Couldn't it wait?*

"You didn't have to. I can hear it in your voice."

I closed my eyes for a moment. "Okay," I said weakly.

We said goodbye, hung up.

I decided to check my collection of *Damn Fool's Guides* for one on keeping it together, even though I knew I wouldn't find it. I settled for *Time Management,* but it didn't hold my interest for very long, and I shoved it back onto the shelf with all its companion volumes.

I went into the kitchen. The coffee was still brewing, so I wandered into the living room—

and stopped in my tracks because Gillian was sitting on the couch.

"Where have you been?" I mouthed, exaggerating each word.

She watched me the way she might have watched a mime at a street fair or in a park, then leaned forward and wrote in the layer of dust on top of my coffee table.

"MOM."

I went to the couch, sat down beside her, slipped an arm around her tiny shoulders. She felt cold, but solid, and wiggled free to write another word in the dust.

"DOG."

At this, she smiled.

"Maybe," I said, thinking of Vince Erland, the promise he'd made to this little girl, one he'd never intended to keep. The chances were good he'd done a lot worse, too.

She smiled more broadly. "DOG," she wrote again, this time with a confident flourish.

I thought about Justin and Pepper, and wondered if the dog and the boy had crossed over yet. As if in answer to the thought, Justin appeared, alone.

I started. You don't get used to things like that.

"Still here," I said, on a long breath.

Justin nodded. "Pepper's gone, though."

Tears filled my eyes. "When?"

"About an hour ago," Justin said.

"I thought you were going with him."

"I can't. You need me." He nodded toward Gillian. "And so does the kid." He paused, looked around. "Different place. What happened to the fancy guesthouse with the plasma TV?"

"I'm sort of in between," I said.

"Tell me about it," Justin replied.

"You should have gone with Pepper," I said, though the truth was, I was glad he'd be around for a little while longer, although if he and Gillian were still hanging out when Tucker showed up, it would put a serious crimp in our plans to swing naked from the chandeliers.

Not that I *had* an actual chandelier. Apartments over shit-hole biker bars don't usually come with that kind of extra.

"He's okay," Justin assured me. Then, in apparent anticipation of my next question, he added, "Mom is, too."

Turning his attention to Gillian, he began to sign.

She beamed at him, happier than I'd ever seen her, and signed back.

"We're going to Burger King," Justin explained when the conversation was over.

"Why?" I asked. "You can't eat, can you?"

"Happy memories," Justin said. "And I like the way it smells." He waggled his eyebrows at me. "Besides, you're expecting company, aren't you?"

I blushed, profoundly uncomfortable with the amount of information Justin was privy to concerning my personal life.

He grinned, apparently reading my mind. Which was even more disturbing than his knowing so much about my plans for the evening. "It shows in your aura," he said confidentially. "No visuals, or anything like that. Just a strong glow."

"If you're spying on me, Justin—"

"I'm not spying," he insisted. "I told you, it's the *aura*."

"It had better be," I warned, though he must have known there would be nothing I could do about it if he was lying.

He signed to Gillian.

Gillian signed back.

And they both vanished.

I was a little jangled by the whole appearance/disappearance thing. Some of my earlier confidence ebbed away.

I put on some flip-flops—I'd been barefoot since my shower—and went down to the Volvo. Got my new used Glock out from under the front seat and carried it upstairs practically at arm's length, half afraid I'd make some wrong move and it would go off in the case.

The coffee was ready when I got back.

I set the gun case in the middle of my kitchen table and stared at it for a while. When it didn't explode, I figured it was safe to keep it in the apartment until morning, when I would motor over to the indoor target range and become a sharpshooter.

My computer beckoned, and I spent some time

downloading the application to transfer Bert's liquor license into my name. After that, I switched on the TV. When in doubt, do something constructive.

The early news was on, and I was noticeably absent.

It was all good.

I'd just switched to a rerun of *Judge Judy,* and was already half dozing, when a really weird thing happened.

I mean *really* weird.

Judge Judy did a fade-out. I yawned, expecting a commercial, and stretched out on the couch with a contented little sigh.

In the next moment I was sitting bolt upright, staring aghast at my rent-to-own TV.

On the screen I saw Gillian, in living color, dressed for the recital rehearsal, still wearing both dance slippers. There was no sound.

Gillian smiled up at someone off camera, nodded and extended her hand.

I shot to my feet, electrified. I knew I was seeing the child just before she was murdered—her death might have been minutes away. An instinct compelled me to examine the back of the TV for an extra wire, check the DVD player for a disc, but an even stronger one kept me riveted to the screen, even though I was terrified of what I might see.

Had the killer had an accomplice?

What kind of sicko would *take pictures*...

Bile scalded the back of my throat.

Gillian was walking beside someone, along a familiar sidewalk, one hand upraised, no doubt clasped in the killer's, signing cheerfully with the other. I stared hard, but I couldn't see any detail of the other person—not an arm or a leg or even a hand.

There was a clue here, I knew that subliminally, but I was so riveted, so horrified, that I couldn't catch hold of it. I wanted to turn away before I saw something I would never get out of my mind, but doing that would have amounted to betraying Gillian.

Tears stung my eyes.

My stomach roiled.

I watched, mute, as Gillian walked between two buildings, then over dry ground littered with old beer bottles and rusted things, smiling, curious.

Trusting.

Then the screen suddenly went blank again, and Judge Judy was back, with her lace-collared judicial robe and her attitude. I stood there, blinking, paralyzed.

What the hell had just happened?

Who had held the video camera?

A couple of minutes must have passed before I could move. I went to the TV, looked for a wire at the back. Nothing. Same with the DVD player— there was an old copy of *Smokey and the Bandit* in the disc holder.

I straightened, shivering.

Looked around. Somebody had piped the clip

in, somehow, from somewhere. They'd wanted me to see it.

But how had they done it?

And how had they known I would be in the apartment to see the piece, instead of in Greer's guesthouse, where I'd been staying for days?

A shiver trickled down my spine, then shinnied back up again.

What the hell was going on?

I spent the next forty-five minutes scouring the place for electronic bugs, hidden cameras, anything. There was nothing.

Finally I hunkered down on the couch again, drawing my knees up, wrapping my arms around my legs. And I brooded.

But I think I knew even then that what I'd seen hadn't come through a wire, or by means of some electronic techno-magic. Oh, no. This was another kind of thing entirely, and there were no *Damn Fool's Guide*s to explain it.

I was still sitting there, staring, when I heard a knock at the apartment door and knew Tucker had arrived.

I felt both relief—when he was around, I was safe—and sorrow, because I knew even *he* wouldn't believe it if I told him I'd seen the prelude to Gillian's murder on my TV screen.

"Coming," I called halfheartedly, heading for the door. My legs felt wooden, and I was stiff. Cold. "Tucker?"

"Yo," he said.

I opened the door.

He was holding a cluster of take-out bags in one hand and a leash in the other. At the end of the leash was a small black-and-white dog with pointy ears, one of which tipped forward at a rakish angle.

"Meet Dave," Tucker said, apparently referring to the dog.

Dave gave a hopeful little yelp of greeting and looked up at me with one blue eye and one brown one.

I stepped back to admit them both.

Tucker frowned as he handed me the take-out bags and reached back to shut the door. "What's up?" he said. "You look—if you'll excuse the expression—like you've seen a ghost."

"I had a headache earlier," I fibbed. "I'm better now."

I hadn't had a headache, and I wasn't "better," either.

Tucker unclipped the leash, and Dave went sniffing into my living room. "Aren't you going to ask about the dog?"

"What about the dog?" I asked dutifully.

Dave lifted a leg against a bookshelf and let fly.

"See that," Tucker said. "He already feels at home."

I gave him a look, carried the takeout into the kitchen, dumped it on the table and started tearing paper towels off the roll to wipe up the piddle.

"Somebody dumped him at Allison's front gate,"

Tucker went on, watching me closely and some-
what thoughtfully, as if he knew something was up
with me but couldn't quite get hold of what it was.
"That's why she asked me to come by. She checked
him over and gave him his shots, but she can't keep
him because she's shutting down the practice while
she and the kids visit her folks." He spread his
hands, as if he'd just brought stone tablets down
from Mount Sinai to a waiting world. "You need a
dog. Dave needs a home. It's fate."

CHAPTER TEN

RIGHT ABOUT NOW, you're probably thinking I broke down and told Tucker all about seeing the prologue to Gillian's murder on my TV screen—and about my visit to Vince Erland at the county jail.

I did neither. I needed to make sense of both experiences within myself before I could share them, and I was a long way from doing that. I'm big on processing, and that's a private thing.

So we ate Chinese food in my kitchen and drank coffee.

Dave scored some of the chicken, then curled up in the corner of the room, yawned and went to sleep. He had the air of an exhausted traveler, home at last after crossing mountains and valleys and windswept prairies.

All to get to me, the human Mecca.

I looked askance at Tucker, because I couldn't look askance at the *dog,* now snoring contentedly, with his bent ear almost touching his nose.

Tucker followed my glance and grinned. "Falling in love?" he asked.

I narrowed my eyes at him. "No," I said. I'd loved my cat, Chester, and he was gone. I'd loved Russell, the basset hound—ditto. I'd even begun to love Justin's dog, Pepper, for heaven's sake, and where was *that* going to get me?

I flat-out couldn't afford to love Dave, too.

"Liar," Tucker said, looking smug.

"You've got a lot of nerve," I said. "Bringing that dog here, expecting me to take him in."

"It's required in my line of work," Tucker answered. "A lot of nerve, I mean. And you've been wanting a dog ever since Russell went into Witness Protection."

He was right, of course, but I didn't have to admit it.

My conscience, napping during the Dave exchange, yawned, stretched and shook itself awake. Focused on the gun I'd bought that day.

I'd buried the Glock, still in its case, under the crumpled take-out bags piled on the table, hoping it wouldn't catch Tucker's eye before I was ready to break the news that I now owned a lethal weapon. I wasn't sure how he'd react—he might be relieved, but he was more likely to give me the speech about how easy it would be for an assailant to get hold of the gun and use it against me. The standard discourse on tragic accidents would follow, complete with verifiable statistics.

Tucker, like many cops, believed ordinary citizens were better off without guns. It wasn't that I disagreed with him—in fact, I was sure he was right—but I wasn't an ordinary citizen. I was a detective, and a psycho magnet.

I had enemies.

I could feel them, a dark pressure in the atmosphere around me.

It made me shiver, dimmed the light flowing in through the kitchen window.

I looked at Dave again. He'd be a lousy guard dog, small as he was, but he'd make good company, I supposed. I'd just have to be extra careful not to start caring about him too much.

He slept on.

Tucker and I finished our meal in silence, and when he would have cleaned up the bags and cartons, thus uncovering the Glock, I suggested sex instead.

We retired to the bedroom, got naked and spent the next couple of hours alternately rattling the walls and lying stuporous in each other's arms.

I was just mellow enough to tell Tucker about the Glock and my assessment of Vince Erland and my appointment at the target range the next morning, not to mention the blackmailer's call I'd inadvertently taken at Greer's, when the phone on my bedside table broke the blissful, honey-warm silence with a shrill *bling*.

I scrambled over Tucker's bare torso to grab it.

He looked at me curiously, and one side of his mouth kicked up in a little grin.

"Hello?" I said.

"What are you doing at the apartment?" Jolie demanded. "The locks have been changed at Greer's, and nobody answers the door."

Tucker set me astraddle his hips. Eased inside me, the stroke long and slow and deep.

I fought to keep my voice normal. "C-Carmen's with her."

Tucker watched my face as he began to move beneath me, his hands cupping my backside, guiding me along the length of him in a maddening rhythm. My nipples hardened, and he raised his head far enough to take one into his mouth.

I gasped, my control shattered. Jolie was ranting, but I couldn't make sense of the words, and I didn't dare answer. So I thumbed the end button and tossed the receiver aside, groaning hoarsely as the first of several sharp orgasms slashed through me.

The phone immediately rang again.

I ignored it.

Tucker took me over the edge, and soon followed.

"That was a dirty trick," I told him some fifteen minutes later when I'd recovered my power of speech. "Jolie's probably on her way over here right now, thinking something awful's happened to me."

Tucker eased out of my arms, sat up, grabbed his jeans off the floor and pulled them on. "Hey," he said. "You were naked and lying across my chest. What was I supposed to do?"

Male logic.

A car door slammed hard in the parking lot below the apartment.

Footsteps pounded on the outside stairs.

Dave, who hadn't made a sound while Tucker and I were raising the roof off the bedroom, started up with a yappy bark, his toenails tapping on the bare floor as he headed from the kitchen toward the front.

A fist thundered against the door.

"She's here," Tucker said, grinning as he tugged a T-shirt on over his head.

I got out of bed, too, and had all my clothes on while Tucker was still pulling on his boots.

Blushing, I dashed for the door, practically tripping over Dave in the process, and wrenched it open.

Jolie stood on the mat, glaring at me. Her gaze rose, and I knew Tucker must be standing right behind me. In the next instant she was back to drilling a stare into my face.

"We're in the middle of a family crisis and you were *having sex?*"

"We weren't..." I protested weakly, stepping back, as an afterthought, to admit her.

"Hi, Jolie," Tucker said, with a grin hiding in his voice. "Come on in. There might be some kung pao left."

Jolie softened a little in spite of herself. Tucker had that effect on people of the female persuasion. She grumbled a "hello" and looked down at Dave, who was peering around my right knee and no longer barking.

Tucker receded.

Jolie bent to pat Dave on the head.

"Is Greer all right?" I asked.

"What do you care?" Jolie retorted, straightening and pinning me with another scorching look. "I called all over looking for you. I couldn't get you on your cell phone, or at the guesthouse. Who'd have thought you'd be *here,* where you were *almost murdered,* bouncing on a mattress with the boyfriend?"

"Can we get past that?" I asked, getting annoyed. "Carmen was at Greer's when I left. I asked her to have the locks changed, and she must have gotten right on it."

Jolie followed me into the living room, Dave keeping pace. He was an odd, wiry little dog, with a spring in his walk that made his bent ear jiggle.

"Sit down," I said to Jolie, gesturing toward the couch.

My sister seemed calmer, now that I'd told her I'd ordered the lock change at Greer's myself. I'd probably put such a scare into Carmen, telling her about the threat against her boss's life, that she was afraid to open the door.

"Did you see Carmen's car?" I asked. "When you were at Greer's, I mean?"

"No," Jolie said, "but her husband usually drops her off in the morning and picks her up at night."

"You tried calling the main house?"

Jolie skewered me with another glance. "Of *course* I did."

"Greer wasn't feeling well when I left. She's probably ignoring the phone *and* the doorbell."

"I still don't like it," Jolie said.

"We'll go over there in a few minutes," I assured her. "And break in if we have to."

Tucker was in the kitchen, and I heard the takeout bags rustling.

Then a clipped, quietly thunderous *"Mojo."*

I stiffened and rolled my eyes toward the ceiling. He'd found the Glock.

Jolie took a seat, but perched on the very edge of the sofa cushions, fairly bristling with restrained energy. Raised a curious look to my face.

Tucker appeared in the doorway, holding the pistol. He did not look like the same man I'd been in bed with only a few minutes before. "Were you planning to tell me about this?" he asked evenly, his expression stony, his jaw hard.

Jolie gave a low whistle of admiration, probably for the gun, but possibly for the way Tucker looked holding it.

"Yes," I said.

"When?"

I blushed. The correct answer was "After we had sex," but I couldn't say that in front of Jolie, even though she was obviously up to speed on that subject. "Tonight," I said, still sounding meeker than I would have liked.

"Where did you get it?"

"Good question," Jolie put in.

"At a souvenir shop," I answered. Dave leaned heavily against my leg, and I was grateful for his support—if that was what it was.

"A *souvenir shop*," Tucker marveled. "Not from the back of a car behind some liquor store? Or maybe at a yard sale?"

"There is," I said loftily, "no reason to be sarcastic. And I start shooting lessons tomorrow morning. Nine o'clock. The guy at the target range ran a background check and everything."

A muscle in Tucker's cheek bunched. "What's the name of this 'souvenir shop'?" he inquired mildly. Before I could answer, he was at my desk, copying the serial number off the Glock onto a scrap of lined yellow legal paper.

I was reminded of the pirate phone, which was still in the pocket of my pantsuit jacket, along with the offshore bank routing numbers, the pill I'd taken from Greer's prescription bottle and the digits I'd scribbled down off the battery of the throwaway. At the time, I hadn't planned on taking the phone itself—there was always a chance the blackmailers would call again, and Greer had to be the one to answer. Distracted by my conversation with Carmen, I'd forgotten, and automatically dropped it into my pocket.

I gave Tucker the shop name. Glanced at Jolie. "There's more," I said, addressing both of them.

They looked at me balefully.

"Great," Tucker said, drawing out the word.

I took charge. After all, it was my apartment.

"Sit down, Tucker," I said.

He complied, but he was in no particular hurry to do it.

I went into the bathroom, snatched my jacket off the top of the hamper, where I'd tossed it before my shower, and returned to center stage. Also known as the living room.

"I was doing some—sleuthing—at Greer's this morning," I said, "and one of her desk drawers rang. I opened it, and found this inside." I flourished the throwaway. Jolie swiped it right out of my hand and studied the device.

"So?" she asked.

"So I answered, that's what, and the person on the other end was surprised to get me instead of Greer. Whoever it was asked me to pass a message on to her—that she's a dead woman. And they referred to her as 'Molly.'"

Jolie gaped at me.

Tucker got up from my desk chair, strode across the room and grabbed the cell phone, frowning. "There are messages on this thing," he said.

The pit of my stomach opened like a trapdoor.

The blackmailers must have called while I was showering, or eating Chinese takeout with Tucker, or—well, you get the picture. When Tucker and I made love, we also made noise. A lot of it.

A bomb could have gone off at the bottom of the outside stairs and we might not have heard it. Forget the muffled ring of a cell phone in another room.

Tucker keyed in a sequence on the keypad. "PIN number," he said.

Jolie gave it.

It's that easy to guess a PIN number, if you know a person very well at all. They use their birthday, the last four digits of their Social Security number, even their street address.

Tucker followed through, and patched right into Greer's voice mail.

Listened, his face darkening.

"Damn," he said when he'd finished.

Jolie held out one hand for the phone, and he gave it to her. She replayed the messages, and her beautiful coffee-dark skin took on an ashen hue as she listened.

"More death threats?" I asked Tucker.

"Yes," he said. "Straight out of Quentin Tarantino's worst nightmares."

I closed my eyes, swayed slightly.

Jolie caught hold of my hand and pulled me down to sit beside her on the couch. She looked sick, and considering that she was a crime-scene technician by profession, and before that she'd worked in a sophisticated forensics lab, weighing vital organs and picking bone fragments out of brains, her reactions gave me pause.

Numbly she handed me the phone.

Tucker shook his head. "Don't," he rasped.

I had to listen. If I was going to help Greer, or even try to protect her, I needed to know everything there was to know about the situation.

I sat through it, shivering.

And then I ran into the bathroom and sat on the edge of my tub, in case the gagging escalated to something a lot messier.

When I had the reflex under control, I splashed my face with cold water, straightened my shoulders and returned to the living room.

Tucker was on his cell phone, talking in terse undertones.

"Who's he calling?" I asked Jolie, who was pacing, jingling her car keys in one hand. I was still a little rattled, or I might have worked it out on my own.

"The Feds," she said impatiently. "Greer's over there *alone,* Moje."

My heart lurched.

Tucker ended the first call and made a second, to 911.

I couldn't bear to think about what we might find when we got to Greer's, so I went with the next-worst worst case scenario. I pictured government agents swarming over the main house, simultaneously invading peaceful Shiloh, Montana, and I was alarmed. While I knew the FBI *might* protect Greer—since the advent of terrorism, they'd been hard up for manpower—I was still scared to death. The blackmailers weren't just blackmailers anymore—they were ruthless extortionists. And they might get to my sister before the good guys did. Considering the things they had planned for her, I couldn't let that happen.

Except, they might *already* have gotten to her.

I snatched the Glock off the coffee table, where Tucker had laid it down, and he immediately took it from me, slipped it into the waistband of his jeans. He was still on the line with the emergency dispatcher as he, Jolie, Dave and I all rushed down the outside stairs.

We piled into Tucker's SUV and laid rubber getting out of there.

Tucker snapped his phone shut. Pulled a light-bubble from the floorboard beneath his feet and reached out the driver's window to attach it to the roof of the vehicle.

He didn't say anything, but I knew what he had to be thinking—that I should have told him about the throwaway cell phone and the threat on Greer's life immediately, not when I got around to it. I was thinking the same thing. My mind was so busy, in fact, that I completely spaced Vince Erland and the bank accounts in the Cayman Islands.

Jolie fumed silently in the back, where she and Dave were sharing a seat belt. She exuded fury, most of which seemed to be directed at me.

It wasn't the time to remind her that she'd known Greer was being blackmailed as long as I had. It was just that there was a lot of other stuff going on when we found out, and Greer had refused to tell us anything. Refused to call in the police, too, no doubt because of the blackmailers' graphic threats of reprisal if she did.

She'd been terrified—and with good reason.

When I'd taken the call on the throwaway that morning instead of Greer, the creeps had probably panicked, thinking she'd decided to call their bluff. As long as she'd paid them, and kept the police out of the equation, they'd had no reason to slaughter the golden goose. Now, figuring the goose had squawked, they'd stretch her neck on the chopping block and sharpen the ax blade.

I began to rock in the front seat of Tucker's SUV, willing him to drive faster. We were zipping through traffic as it was, weaving in and out, and though most drivers had the good sense to get out of the way, there were a few who remained oblivious to a swirling red light in their rearview mirrors.

Two squad cars were parked in Greer's driveway when we arrived, behind an unfamiliar convertible Jag, gold, with the top down. One police car bore the county insignia, and one was Scottsdale PD. Light bars flashed blue and then red and then blue again. The colors splashed dizzyingly against the garage. The front doors of the house gaped open, and light spilled golden into the portico.

Leaving Dave in the SUV, Tucker, Jolie and I hit the ground running.

Tucker got there first, and Jolie and I wedged

through behind him, then almost crashed into his back because he stopped so suddenly.

A body lay in the center of the entryway, arms and legs askew.

I knew immediately that it wasn't Greer or Carmen, but I didn't have time to be relieved.

One of the deputies turned, acknowledged Tucker with a nod. "According to his ID," the man said, "his name was Jack Pennington. That's his Jag parked out front."

My knees sagged. I glanced at his face—a younger version of Alex's—but Greer was uppermost in my thoughts, so I bolted for the stairs, Jolie beside me.

Tucker caught us each by an arm and easily held us back.

For some reason, neither of us struggled.

"My sister," I managed.

"There's nobody else in the house," someone said.

"Oh, my God," I whispered. I was about to add, "They've got her" when Tucker shut me up with a subtle motion of his elbow.

"Are you sure?" Jolie asked. She'd had a lot more experience with the police than I had, of course. She was looking at Jack Pennington's body as she spoke, and I knew she was cataloging details, noticing things I probably wouldn't have registered. All I knew was he was dead. "Did you check the guesthouse?"

"Not yet" came the slightly terse answer. "We haven't been here that long, and our first priority was to look for the shooter and any other victims, then keep the scene secure." The man's gray eyes rolled back and forth between Jolie and me, like pinballs bouncing off plastic flippers in a grudge game. "Do either of you live here? Do you know this man?"

I swallowed. "I've been staying in the guesthouse. The property belongs to our sister—Greer Pennington."

A deep shudder went through me. Where *was* Greer? Where was Carmen? Had one of them shot Greer's stepson and then fled the scene? Or had the extortionists done it? Perhaps they'd come for Greer, and Pennington had been there, or arrived in the middle of some scuffle?

I put a hand to my mouth.

The cop was still studying Jolie and me.

"I've met Jack before," Jolie said, in belated answer to his question.

"Maybe you'd better sit down," he said. "Both of you."

I was rooted to the spot, but Jolie took my hand and pulled me toward the living room, and Tucker gave me a little shove from behind.

More cops came.

Then the crime-scene techs, closely followed by the medical examiner's people.

Tucker brought Dave in from the SUV and Jolie and the dog and I repaired to the kitchen. Jolie gave

Dave some fancy lunch meat from the fridge, and filled a bowl with water for him.

And we waited.

The entire house was searched again, along with the guesthouse and the grounds. Tucker reported, in a brief pass-through, that Greer's car was still in the garage.

And then I ran into an acquaintance—Detective Andrew Crowley, Scottsdale PD, homicide division. We'd gotten to know each other during my last big adventure and, frankly, even though he was a nice enough guy, I'd hoped I'd never see him again.

Crowley was middle-aged, mild mannered and smart as hell. He entered the kitchen by way of the dining room, looking rumpled. "Why is it, Ms. Sheepshanks," he drawled, "that every other time I set foot on a crime scene, you happen to be there?"

Dave, slumbering at my feet, rose far enough out of his doggy dreams to give a halfhearted growl.

"Just my good luck, I guess," I said.

Crowley nodded to Jolie, scraped back a chair and sat down at the table where Jolie and I had been keeping a mostly silent vigil for at least an hour. He looked tired, but affable.

"Mrs. Pennington," Jolie said after giving me a shut-your-smart-mouth look, "is our sister. This is her place. We've been worried about her lately, and Mojo has been staying in her guesthouse."

"Were you here when Mrs. Pennington's stepson was shot?" Crowley asked. He already knew the answer, of course. The uniforms, or possibly Tucker, would have briefed him when he arrived. His tactic was an old standard—ask a lot of questions and hope somebody trips up.

"No," I said.

Crowley looked to Jolie for confirmation—as if I wasn't credible, or something. I was vaguely insulted.

"No," Jolie said. "I came by earlier to look in on Greer and nobody answered the door. I tried my key, but the locks had been changed." Here, she glanced at me, thereby opening a whole new can of worms. If I hadn't thought Crowley would notice, I'd have kicked her under the table.

Crowley turned to me again, one eyebrow slightly raised. He'd caught Jolie's look, and interpreted it correctly. He knew *I* knew about the changed locks, and probably that I wished Jolie hadn't brought the subject up at all. Not that it wouldn't have come out eventually, of course.

I was shaken.

I was scared—make that petrified—for Greer and for Carmen, too.

Crowley would want to know why I'd asked Carmen to call a locksmith right away. And I'd have to tell him about the throwaway phone and the calls from the blackmailers-turned-extortionists. I would rather have consulted the Feds first, or better yet, Tucker. But I wasn't going to get the chance.

I willed Tucker to come through the kitchen door and intervene somehow, but he didn't.

"Ms. Sheepshanks?" Crowley prompted when I was silent too long. "The locks?"

"I asked Carmen—the housekeeper—to have them changed."

"Why?"

I considered my reply, probably a bit too carefully. I knew by the sudden flicker in Crowley's eyes that he expected me to lie, and he was extra watchful as he waited. Then inspiration struck. "Alex Pennington was murdered," I reminded him. "I think it's understandable that I'd be concerned for Greer's safety—especially considering that she was assaulted recently." *Oh,* I imagined myself adding, *and Dr. Pennington's ghost appeared in my kitchen and told me he was pretty sure he'd been killed by his own son. You might want to look into that.*

Crowley sighed and his eyes ranged over the tidy countertops in Greer's kitchen, came to rest on the coffeemaker.

Jolie got up, without being asked, and started a pot brewing.

"You know, of course," Crowley went on, "that Mrs. Pennington is a person of interest in that case."

"She didn't do it," I said, with a certainty that obviously intrigued Crowley.

He leaned a little way forward in his chair. "Dr. Pennington filed for divorce only a few days before he died," he told me. "I understand he was repeatedly unfaithful. Mrs. Pennington was upset that her marriage was ending, wasn't she?"

"Yes," I said, shaken because I hadn't known papers had actually been filed. "But that doesn't mean she killed him."

"Right now," Crowley admitted, "I'm thinking Greer Pennington shot her stepson. Maybe they had a confrontation of some kind. Maybe things got out of hand. Maybe Mrs. Pennington panicked when she realized what she'd done—and ran." He paused. "And *maybe,* Ms. Sheepshanks, you know where she's hiding."

Sorrow welled up inside me. Greer had a broken arm. She'd been ill with a migraine, vomiting, doped up because of the pain. *Was* she hiding, guilty of killing Jack? Or was she tied up in the trunk of someone's car, on her way to the slow, isolated and very grisly death the extortionists had promised, via voice mail?

"I wish I did," I said. I don't know how Crowley read me then, but if he was as good as his reputation, he believed me. I'd never said anything I meant more than that. Under the circumstances, I would have been *relieved* if Greer had been found huddled in a closet somewhere in the house, covered in Pennington's blood, the weapon still in her hands.

Jolie finished starting the coffee, set three crockery mugs on the counter in readiness and came back to the table. "If Greer killed Jack Pennington," she said, sitting down, "it was self-defense."

"Why do you say that?" Crowley asked.

I was wondering the same thing. Jolie and I had never discussed Greer's stepson, and I hadn't had a chance to tell her about Alex's ghostly visit to the guesthouse. But perhaps Greer had confided something in her—some fear of Jack—or she'd witnessed an argument between the two.

"He hated Greer," Jolie said.

I moistened my lips, which suddenly felt dry to the point of cracking open. I waited for her to go on—and so did Crowley.

Jolie blinked a couple of times. I tried to catch her eye, but she wouldn't look at me. "Greer was being blackmailed," she said. "She would never tell me or Mojo who it was—most likely, she doesn't know—or what this person had on her. I think it might have been Jack Pennington."

Inwardly I reeled. If Pennington *had* been the one blackmailing Greer, it might mean she was safe, now that he was dead. Sure, he probably had partners, but he had to have been the ringleader— he was the one with the personal stake in getting rid of the woman who was draining away his inheritance *and* he was collecting the loot for himself at the same time. It was ingenious, really. He wouldn't even have to pay taxes.

And now the police would dig into every corner of Pennington's life, looking for clues to his killer's identity. That would have his cohorts in crime running for cover, wouldn't it?

"Why, specifically, do you think that, Ms.—?" Crowley asked, looking at Jolie again.

"Travers," Jolie said. "Jolie Travers." She drew a deep breath, huffed it out. "I heard them arguing—Jack Pennington and Greer, I mean—at Christmas. I was right here in this kitchen, helping Carmen clean up after dinner so she could go home and be with her own family, and they were on the back patio. Alex had given Greer a diamond bracelet as a present, and Jack was furious. He said it was extravagant, and accused her of playing his father for a fool."

I stared at Jolie in undisguised surprise. She'd never mentioned the incident to me before, and I wondered why. I'd been confined to my apartment over the holidays, brought low by a flu bug.

And since when did Jack Pennington spend Christmas with his father and the second wife?

"How did Mrs. Pennington react?" Crowley asked.

Jolie looked at me then, and I saw acute misery in her eyes. Then she turned to Crowley, facing him squarely, her shoulders straight and rigid. "She laughed at him," Jolie said.

"And?" Crowley pressed, very gently. There *was* an "and." I'd sensed it, too, dangling unspoken at the end of Jolie's last sentence.

"Greer said she could convince Alex of anything, and if Jack messed with her again, she'd tell his father he'd been coming on to her. Alex would have believed it, too. He was still crazy about Greer then, even though he was running around with other women—crazy enough to pay a hundred thousand dollars for a bracelet. He probably would have cut Jack out of his will."

Crowley sat back in his chair, pondering. "Interesting," he mused.

"Yeah," I agreed, scowling at Jolie to let her know how I felt. She could have told me all this. She *should* have told me. "*Very* interesting."

CHAPTER ELEVEN

CROWLEY KEPT JOLIE AND ME corralled in Greer's kitchen until the wee small hours, drinking coffee and presenting the same questions over and over again, the words varying slightly, like little actors changing costumes in the dark wings of the conversation. Meanwhile, Jack Pennington's body was being measured, photographed, examined, speculated over and finally bagged for shipment to the Maricopa County medical examiner's office in Phoenix.

I knew two things for sure. Pennington had been shot to death—there'd been a lot of blood, and one of the cops had mentioned searching the house for the shooter—and Greer was missing, as was Carmen.

I believed my sister had been abducted by the same people who had been blackmailing her—since Tucker had let slip that her car was still in the garage—and might be dead herself, along with her housekeeper. I still believed Jack could have been behind the whole scam, but maybe I'd been mistaken. Or maybe something had gone wrong and the others, whoever they were, had decided to cut him out at the last minute. The cops had a different take on the situation, if Crowley's general attitude was anything to go by—they thought Greer had pulled the trigger during an argument, and subsequently headed for the proverbial hills.

I suspect Jolie was leaning that way, too—in the cop direction, I mean—maybe because as horrible as it was to think Greer might have taken a life, it was better than thinking she'd died, or was dying, in any of the unspeakable ways described in the voice mail messages Tucker, Jolie and I had heard earlier.

By now, Tucker had surely turned the throwaway cell phone over to his superiors as evidence. The blackmailers-turned-extortionists had to know their terms had been violated—the police were definitely Involved, up to their badges.

Damage control. At this point, that was the best I could hope for.

It was nearly dawn when the gruesome party broke up.

Tucker took Jolie, Dave and me back to my place. I couldn't stay at the guesthouse—I was too freaked out. Jolie, grimly distracted and moving like a sleepwalker, got into her Pathfinder and drove home to her little rental in Phoenix to get ready for work and see what furniture Sweetie might have eaten in her absence. Tucker came upstairs with me, checked the place out for psychos and, finding it clear, left the dog and me on our own while he went to a nearby supermarket to buy kibble and presumably the makings of breakfast. My fridge contained a box of baking soda, a package of AA batteries and a block of moldy cheese.

I was pacing the kitchen, waiting for the coffee to brew and trying to give birth to an idea that had been churning in the back of my head throughout the night, when the telephone rang. I pounced on it without checking caller ID, terrified and hopeful at the same time.

Let it be Greer, I prayed. *Let her be safe.*

"Where is Tucker?" Allison Darroch demanded, skipping right over "hello."

I sighed. "He's not here," I said, feeling bruised.

"But he spent the night with you." It was an accusation, and it hit me wrong.

"He spent the night bagging a body," I countered. Okay, I was a little testy, but I was, after all, up to my butt in hungry alligators, and their jaws were snapping. "If you have questions for Tucker, ask *him.*" I was about to hang up when she stopped me.

"Wait," she said, quickly and with some urgency.

I waited, thinking all the while that it would have been smarter to follow my first instinct and end the call. But I'd heard something in Allison's voice, in that single word, that snagged my attention. Fear? Despair? I wasn't sure.

"What?" I prodded, still terse, when she didn't speak.

"You said Tucker was working, and I'm not

going to ask how you know that. But, please—who was killed? Not another child?"

"Not another child," I confirmed, almost gently. I wasn't a mother, but I could imagine how frightened Allison must be for her own children, after what had happened to Gillian. The tragedy had struck too close to home. I also noted the subtle indication that if Allison was fearful, it meant she believed Vince Erland might not have been Gillian's killer. For a moment I wished we weren't natural adversaries, so I could talk to her about it. After meeting Erland, I didn't know what to think.

She started to cry. "I need to talk to Tucker, and he's not answering his cell phone," she said.

"I'll tell him," I replied.

Allison sniffled. "Okay."

We hung up.

I turned away from the phone, an old-fashioned wall unit, after setting the receiver back in its hook, and found myself face-to-face with the idea that had been eluding me.

Justin was standing in the middle of my kitchen, watching me.

I barely flinched, which meant I was getting used to impromptu visits from dead people. Was that good or bad?

I was too antsy to decide, at least at the moment.

"I need your help," I said.

Justin looked pleased, in a broken, weary sort of way. Pepper had already gone on, and I knew Justin would follow soon. Just what I needed—another person to miss.

"Great," he said, rubbing his palms together. "What do you want me to do?"

"Find my sister," I answered, moving past him into the living room to go through the few photographs I owned. I kept them in a shoe box, since there weren't enough to justify an album, let alone frames, and they were all outdated. Lillian hadn't allowed a lot of pictures while I was growing up, since we were on the run the whole time, but there were a few. I'd burned Nick's and my wedding photos, which is another story.

I riffled through snapshots until I found what I was looking for—a strip of three black and whites, taken in a mall photo booth: Greer, Jolie and me, with our heads together, grinning like fools.

I felt a pang, looking at those youthful faces. Stared at them for a long moment before handing the strip to Justin.

Justin studied the images, a range of emotions moving across his face like cloud shadows dappling sunny ground.

A deep dread spread over me, and I felt sick, even a little dizzy. But I didn't take time to question Justin; I wanted him on his way, ASAP. Tucker would be back any minute with the kibble for Dave and whatever he'd bought for our breakfast, and even though he knew I talked to dead people on a fairly regular basis, I wasn't really keen on having a conversation with someone he couldn't see or hear while he was around.

"Nice dog," Justin said, bending to pat Dave, who licked his hand. It was comforting to know Justin was visible to him—it made me feel a touch less crazy.

"Thanks," I replied. I pointed Greer out in the picture. She was young, only eighteen or nineteen years old, blond and smiling brightly, though, like the photo-me, she had a watchful, hunted look in her eyes. Of the three of us, Jolie was the only real person, confident in her identity—Greer and I were impostors, expecting to be caught out at any moment. "Her name is Greer Pennington," I said. "Can you focus on her or something, and zap yourself to where she is?"

Justin pondered Greer's image. "It's harder with pictures," he said. "And thinking 'Greer Pennington' isn't working for me."

Down in the parking lot, a car door slammed.

Tucker was back.

"Justin," I said urgently, "please—just try."

Justin nodded.

I thanked him again.

Tucker was coming up the outside stairway. Dave began to bark out happy, tentative little yips, and headed for the door, toenails skittering on the bare floor.

Justin handed back the photo, and I touched his arm. He was dead and no one could harm him, but he was still a child. What if he teleported himself into some grisly scene? "It might—it might be bad," I said, compelled to warn him. "The place where Greer is, I mean."

He nodded, squinched his eyes shut and blipped out.

I went to the door to let Tucker in. He was lugging a twenty-five-pound bag of dog food under one arm, and he carried a fast-food bag in his free hand. He gave me a tired smile and then a peck on the forehead as he entered.

"You need to call Allison," I told him. "She said she tried your cell phone a few times, but you didn't answer."

He stiffened, turned his head to look back. I knew he was worried—I saw it in his eyes—though he tried to hide it. He was tired and he needed a shower and shave, and watching him, I felt something dangerously close to love. "The battery's been acting up," he said. "I need a new one."

"You can call from the kitchen," I said, nodding him in that direction.

I stayed in the living room, determined not to listen in. But it was a small place, and I couldn't help hearing him set the dog food bag down and grab the telephone receiver off the hook.

Because I was all ears, I retreated to the bedroom, got a clean sundress from the closet, then showered, half expecting Tucker to be gone when I was finished.

Instead, he'd finished his phone call, set the fast-food breakfast out on plates and poured us each a cup of coffee. Dave was crunching away on his kibble, but it was the Glock that drew my attention.

Tucker had confiscated it the night before, but now it was sitting in the middle of the table, where a normal person might have kept salt and pepper shakers. I looked at it, looked away, re-membering I was scheduled for a nine-o'clock shooting lesson with Max Summervale. I was sure Beverly Pennington would want to cancel our meeting at two that afternoon, given that her son had been shot to death the night before, but I meant to call her anyway, if only to leave a mes-sage of condolence with some visiting relative or a member of her staff. She'd been peeved when I hadn't gotten in touch the day Alex's body was found, and while a dead son was different from a dead ex-husband, I wasn't going to make the same mistake twice.

"Everything okay at home?" I asked. If I'd had the energy, I would have been proud of the modera-tion in my tone and manner.

"Allison's dad's having some kind of surgery tomorrow morning," Tucker answered. "She has to fly back to Tulsa right away, and since she'll be at the hospital around the clock for a few days, she isn't taking the kids. Chelsea will watch them after school, until I get off work."

I smoothed the skirt of my sundress primly, like

somebody at a garden tea party, and sat down. Reached for my breakfast sandwich, one of those croissant things with enough trans fats in them to clog a mule's arteries, let alone those of an ordinary human being. "I've met Chelsea," I remarked, because that was the first thing that came into my muddled head. I was actually thinking about Justin, wondering if he'd already zeroed in on Greer, and Tucker's mention of Allison's father's surgery didn't register immediately. In fact, a few moments passed before I even put Chelsea's name and image together. "She's Helen Erland's neighbor, and she used to sit with Gillian sometimes."

Tucker nodded absently, munching on his sandwich. His body might have been sitting at my kitchen table, but his mind was obviously somewhere else.

My brain finally began to work. *Surgery,* it said. *Bad thing.*

"I hope Allison's father will be all right," I said.

Tucker's gaze connected with mine. "It's probably his heart," he said. "There's been some talk about a bypass."

"I'm sorry," I said.

That's when Tucker surprised me. "I think it's time Daisy and Danny got to know you a little better," he told me. "How about coming by the house for supper tonight? Around seven?"

"Allison's place?" I asked. I'd been on the property once, when Tucker and I took Russell to

Allison's veterinary clinic for emergency care, but I hadn't gone inside the house.

A muscle ticked in Tucker's cheek, but the expression in his eyes, though bleak, indicated a clear conscience. "That's where they live," he said.

"I don't know," I murmured. "It's—well—kind of intrusive, isn't it?"

"They need to get used to the idea, Moje."

"The idea of what?" I was edgy and because of that, I probably sounded abrupt.

"You," Tucker said. "The divorce. That life changes, and that's okay."

I wasn't the other woman—Tucker's divorce was final when I met him—but I felt guilty just the same, and it was a good bet that Allison had conditioned the twins to see me as the villain of the piece, the sole Reason Daddy Lived Somewhere Else.

Tears scalded my eyes.

Tucker reached across the table and took my chin in one hand. "No pressure, Moje," he said hoarsely. "If you don't feel ready, I'll deal with it."

My thoughts were still jumbled, but the gist of it was, I could go on orbiting the fringes of Tucker's life like some negligible planetoid or stray moon, fighting the pull of gravity, or I could be somebody real to Danny and Daisy—and to myself. In some ways, even though I'd worked hard to raise Mojo Sheepshanks from the wreckage of Mary Josephine Mayhugh's brief existence, I felt insubstantial, as invisible as Justin or Gillian or the dead greeter at Wal-Mart.

Tucker grinned gently at my expression. "You're thinking too much again," he said.

I wanted to smile back, but I couldn't quite make the grade. "I guess it's no big deal," I admitted. "It's not as if I'll be their new stepmother or anything."

Tucker didn't say a word. He laid his sandwich down, though. Looked away, taking a sudden interest in the calendar tacked to one of the cupboard doors.

I figured it would be a good time to change the subject.

"Maybe you ought to get some sleep," I said quietly. "I have an appointment, but you can crash here if you want."

He turned back to me, but his gaze dropped to the Glock before rising to meet mine. "No rest for the wicked," he said, his voice a little gruff. "I didn't get a chance to run the stats on this gun. If it's illegal, I'm going to have to confiscate it—permanently." He pushed back his chair, stood and set the pistol on top of the refrigerator. "In the meantime, hands off."

As if I couldn't get to it if I wanted to. I did an internal eye roll. "Whatever," I said.

He came to stand directly in front of my chair and leaned down so we were practically eyeball to eyeball. "I *mean* it," he said. "If the serial number checks out, I'll teach you to shoot. If it doesn't, I don't want your fingerprints all over the thing."

Something just in back of my stomach twitched,

and paranoia hormones flooded my system. I hadn't
fired the Glock, but I'd certainly handled it.

"Promise," Tucker insisted, still leaning, although now it was more mouth to mouth than
eyeball to eyeball. His breath made my lips tingle.

I promised, albeit reluctantly.

He kissed me lightly, then straightened, but he
was still within easy range.

I fought a strong temptation to unzip his jeans
and delay his departure for a while.

He stepped back. Smiled down at me. "Don't
touch the gun," he said.

I grinned up at him. "Is it loaded?" I asked.

"For bear," he said. And then he kissed the top
of my head, cleared the remains of his breakfast
from the table and left.

I waited until I heard him descending the outside
stairs before following to lock the door behind him
and put the chain on.

Then I just stood there for a while, uncertain
what to do next.

I decided Dave ought to have a walk, and found
the leash. Went through the whole process of un-
locking and unchaining the door again.

By the time Dave and I got back to the apartment, it was almost time for my shooting lesson at
the range. I decided the sundress probably hadn't
been the best choice, and swapped it out for black
jeans and a lightweight turtleneck of the same
somber hue. All I needed to complete the cat-

burglar look, I thought, assessing my reflection in the mirror over my bureau, was a stocking cap.

I'd been hoping Justin would come back with the ghost report on Greer's whereabouts, but he didn't show, and neither did Gillian. I filled a water bowl for Dave, made sure he had plenty of kibble, spread some newspapers on the floor and vacated the premises.

MAX SUMMERVALE was waiting with a smile when I showed up at the indoor target range in Scottsdale. I automatically checked his ring finger, which was bare and as tanned as the rest of his body. Not that you can always go by that, because married guys can be tricky. My dead ex-husband, Nick, for example, had taken his wedding band off about a week after we got back from our honeymoon, claiming he was afraid of catching it on something and peeling the skin off like carrot parings.

As if you could do that tapping at a computer keyboard or punching in numbers on a cell phone, which was about as close to physical labor as he ever got. Nick was a wheeler-dealer real estate kind of guy, and he always worked in a suit and tie.

God, I was naive back then.

"Ready to shoot?" Max asked, picking up a pair of safety goggles and a set of orange-and-black earphone-style hearing protectors.

Suddenly I flashed on Jack Pennington, sprawled dead on the floor of Greer's entry hall, and I must have gone a little pale or something, because Max tilted his head slightly to peer at me.

"Are you all right?" he asked.

"Fine," I said, injecting a shade more perkiness into my tone than firing at a paper figure of a man really warranted.

"It's not unusual to be a little nervous the first time," he said, and his hand rested lightly, unobtrusively and very briefly against the small of my back. When I stiffened, he untouched me pretty fast. "Shooting, I mean."

I looked at Max and noticed a faint blush along the upper part of his neck and his lower jaw. He was capable of embarrassment, then. Probably not the sly type. I decided I liked him.

"Lead on," I said.

"Are you interested in target shooting as a hobby?" he asked, opening the door to a kind of locker room, with a long panel of glass, hopefully bulletproof, separating it from the actual range. Beyond it was a row of aisles, with the requisite paper target at the end of each one. There were a few shooters popping away at them, the sound muffled but unmistakable.

"Self-protection," I said. "I don't have time for hobbies."

Max opened a door, waited for me to pass through ahead of him. "I believe you mentioned yesterday that you don't own a firearm."

I do, I imagined myself confessing, *but it's on*

top of my refrigerator at the moment, and I prom-
ised my boyfriend the homicide cop that I wouldn't
touch it until he made sure it was legal. I bought it
from a guy in a souvenir shop, you see.

"No," I said, surprised to find that the lie, small
as it was, bothered me a little. Maybe I was losing
my touch.

Skepticism flickered in Max's dark blue eyes. "I
see," he said.

I willed myself not to blush, but it was too late.
I tried to get past the uncomfortable moment by
changing the subject. "How did you wind up in this
business? Teaching people to shoot, I mean."

He grinned, closed the door behind us. A pistol
waited on a counter a few feet away, looking cold,
black and ominous. "Not everybody needs lessons,"
he said. "A lot of cops come in to practice—com-
petitive shooters, too." He paused, sighed. "I've
been around guns all my life. My dad was a state
patrolman, and he had me popping cans and bottles
off sawhorses as soon as I was big enough to hold
a revolver. Once I'd graduated from college, I went
into the army and served with the military police.
From there, it was the FBI."

Tucker had been DEA until very recently, so it
wasn't as if I'd never met a federal agent before, but
I was impressed in spite of myself. Max was an *im-*
pressive man, exquisitely fit, self-possessed, obviously intelligent. Not to mention good-looking.

"You don't seem old enough to be retired," I said. I'd pegged him at thirty-five, tops.

"I was injured," he told me, handing over the ear protectors and goggles.

The words jarred me. *Everybody has a history,* I reminded myself, putting on the gear and forcing myself to step up to the waist-high counter where the pistol lay. Seeing it up close and personal made my heartbeat accelerate, and not in a pleasant way. The Glock hadn't affected me, beyond what tension one might expect to feel when handling a deadly weapon, but this one brought back a rush of vivid and horrific memories. It was like the semiautomatic used to murder my parents.

I trembled a little.

Max moved in behind me, put his arms loosely around me and guided my hands to the pistol. A sensation like static electricity rushed through my body with such intensity that I almost expected my hair to stand up. Was it the gun? Or was it Max's close physical proximity?

"This is easy," Max said, close to my temple. "Relax."

I trembled a little more. "Okay," I said shakily. It's hard to describe, but I felt as though I might literally be expelled from my own skin, like a grape squeezed hard, and never find my way back in.

He chuckled, and the sound vibrated through me, through all the passageways hollowed out by the electricity and the strange sense of coming untethered from that place where my essence and my physical being connected. "Easy," he repeated.

He showed me how to make the paper target move, using a button on the floor under the counter. It was creepy, the way the man shape rushed toward me when I stepped on the button, but I understood the reasoning behind it. Your average assailant won't stand still and politely wait for you to shoot him. He—or she—is a lot more likely to rush you instead.

If you're going to shoot, you'd better mean it.

I don't remember much about the first few minutes of that lesson; I know Max fired off a couple of shots before placing my finger on the trigger. I pulled, when the time came, and I was shocked by the way it made me feel. I'd expected revulsion, but I *liked* it, liked the kick of that pistol, the grim sense of power it gave me.

Max eventually stepped back, though I knew he was close by. Like Tucker, he seemed to take up more than his fair share of space in close quarters. I was more aware of Max than of the target, but I couldn't have admitted that to myself at the time.

He showed me how to reload, how to work the safety and then left me alone to practice.

I stepped on the floor button, made the paper man zoom forward, then backward. I riddled him with bullets, taking a primitive satisfaction in the *thwup-thwup-thwup* sound as I fired.

When target-man suddenly morphed into a

bloody, grinning specter, I knew I was seeing Jack Pennington. A soundless scream swelled in my throat when he glided rapidly toward me, as though he, like the target, was suspended from a roller in the low ceiling.

Sweat slickened my palms, and the pistol slipped out of my hands and clattered to the floor. Thank God it didn't go off on impact.

Jack was within inches of me, splattered in blood and gore, when Max hurried in, retrieved the pistol from the floor and set it back on the counter, then took me by the elbows and turned me around to face him.

"What is it?" he asked. "What's the matter?"

I couldn't speak for a moment. That scream was still stuck in my throat. Was the *thing* that had been Jack Pennington behind me, looming, ready to pounce? I was too scared to look. In fact, I'm not sure I wouldn't have sagged into a heap if Max hadn't been holding me up. I did manage to tear off my ear protectors and my goggles and fling them aside…just before I leaped right out of my body, rushing through total darkness at dizzying speed, then landing—*somewhere*—with an impact that should have left a crater.

I was conscious of being—well, *me*. I could see, though I didn't have eyes. I could feel, though I didn't have hands or feet or any of the anatomical parts that should have been there. I was pure energy, intensely focused, acutely aware and totally terrified.

Where was I?

In a dark room that smelled of cigarette smoke, cheap cosmetics and stale popcorn. A computer monitor provided the only light, the screen saver a dizzying spiral. As far as I could tell, there was no one around. I tried to move toward the computer, and the instant I made the effort I was flying backward through space again.

"Ms. Sheepshanks?" Max prodded anxiously as I slammed back into the body I had involuntarily abandoned seconds before. He towed me into the locker-room area, walking backward himself, sat me down on a bench, got me a paper cup filled with cold water from a nearby cooler, held it to my mouth.

My stomach pitched, and I was drenched in a cold sweat. For a moment I thought I was going to pass out. But after a few sips of water I began to feel minimally better.

"What just happened here?" Max asked.

I was wondering the same thing.

I couldn't tell him what I'd seen—Jack Pennington's ghost racing toward me on the target rollers—or about my impromptu out-of-body experience. He'd never have let me within a city block of the shooting range again if I had.

I pushed my hair back from my face. Managed an unconvincing smile, though I couldn't bring myself to look directly at Max. I was still shaking uncontrollably. "I might be coming down with something," I said to the row of lockers across from the bench. "Flu, maybe." *Or possibly I'm insane.*

Max went to refill the paper cup at the cooler, returned and handed it to me. Sat next to me, but not too close. "I know about your experience in Cactus Bend," he said quietly. Still disoriented, I wondered if he was referring to my parents' murder, when I was five, or the more recent nightmare in the same town, when I'd nearly been shot at close range. But I wasn't about to ask.

I was on overload as it was. I didn't need more information to process.

"Part of the background check?" I inquired between sips of cold water, proud of how calm and together I sounded. Slowly I was shrugging back into place inside myself—hooking up the nerve endings, blinking my eyes, tapping one foot just so I'd know I could still command my own physiology.

"Google," he said.

At last I was able to meet his eyes. He was smiling, but he looked concerned. "Do you check Google for all your clients?" I asked.

"Only the pretty ones," he replied. "If ever anybody had a good reason to learn to shoot, Ms. Sheepshanks, it's you."

I didn't know what to say to that. I was glad Max was there in my hour of need, but I still would have preferred Tucker. My shoulders sagged, and I came this close to bursting into noisy tears. It was the stress over Gillian, I told myself, exacerbated by my worry about Greer, and the all-nighter in her kitchen, Detective Crowley strafing me with questions the whole time.

Or the macabre apparition of Jack Pennington, rushing at me inside the shooting range. I was already trying to pretend the astral-travel thing hadn't happened at all.

Max patted my back. "You're not going to give up, are you?" he asked.

I shook my head. I wasn't going to give up on anything; I didn't know how. He meant the shooting, of course. I meant Tucker, and finding Greer, and helping Gillian, and making it as a private detective.

"Good," he said. His eyes twinkled. He had thick lashes, dark like his hair. "Say something, so I'll know you haven't been struck dumb."

"I'm involved with a guy named Tucker," I said. And I immediately felt stupid, because Max hadn't inquired about my dating status. There *was* an attraction, though it was probably all on my side, and I certainly didn't intend to pursue it.

"Damn," he replied. "I was afraid of that. Is it serious?"

I nodded. "Yeah," I admitted. "I think it is."

CHAPTER TWELVE

I CALLED Beverly Pennington on my cell phone once I'd left the shooting range and returned to my car. It wasn't a noble gesture; I wanted to get it over with, so I could get on with my nervous breakdown. Once I'd spoken to her, I planned to go back to the guesthouse for my toothbrush and the few articles of clothing I kept there. Home again, I'd fill a plastic storage bag with ice, lie down on my own bed with the bag on my head, and deal with that morning's quota of paranormal experiences. Sure, I was still a little nervous about the apartment, but after what had happened at Casa Pennington, I would have been even less comfortable there.

Beverly answered on the second ring, and she sounded remarkably composed for someone so recently bereaved. On top of that, I would have sworn she was sober. I recalled something Greer had said, about Alex footing the bill for his ex-wife to visit some pricey rehab center, but after my post-mortem conversation with the doc, I couldn't imagine him being that noble.

"I hope you're not calling to cancel," she said after I'd introduced myself.

I was stunned; for a moment I even wondered if the news about Jack had reached her yet. "Well, I assumed—"

"First rule of dealing with me, Ms. Sheepshanks," Beverly broke in briskly. "Never assume *anything*."

I stared through the windshield, almost expecting Jack's specter to rise from the hood and press itself in a bloody, grinning smear against the glass, which might just prompt me to spurt out of the old body again, like toothpaste from a tube. A shudder went through me. "It's just…" I faltered, started again. "It's just that your son—"

"Jack and I were not close," Beverly said, cutting me off. "I'll expect you at two o'clock, as planned."

"But don't you—I mean—"

"Be here at two," Beverly reiterated. "By then I'll have made the funeral arrangements." A pause followed. "Do you believe death comes in threes, Ms. Sheepshanks?" she asked.

I decided even a specter on the hood of my car would have been preferable to this ludicrous conversation. "Yes," I heard myself say, and it shook me, because I'd had every intention of saying no instead.

"Then we'd all better watch ourselves, hadn't we?" Beverly said. "Two down, one to go." This was followed by a goodbye, and the call was over.

It was a warm Arizona day, but I felt chilled sitting there in my car. *Two down, one to go.* Would the third death be Greer's? Or perhaps my own?

Or did poor little Gillian figure into the trio somewhere?

Methodically I put the cell phone away. But I was still hearing Beverly Pennington's voice in my head. And in the back of my mind I was seeing the spiral on that computer screen, in the dark room. The recollection made me nauseous—I wanted more than ever to hide out under the covers on my bed, but now that I knew the Pennington interview was still on, I'd have to delay hibernation.

Then we'd all better watch ourselves, hadn't we?

Had she just threatened me? And was she really so cool, calm and collected that she could dismiss her son's death—so soon after her ex-husband's—with what amounted to a breezy "oh, well"?

I put the Volvo in gear and pointed it toward Greer's place.

When I got there—I remembered nothing about the drive—I parked at the base of the driveway and stared up at the mansion.

It was so substantial, all stucco and red tile, its many windows gazing back at me like empty eyes. But it was a house of cards, I decided, already falling in on itself.

I might have gone inside to do more sleuthing, but the front door had been cordoned off with yellow crime-scene tape, and frankly I was relieved.

After the episodes at the shooting range, I wasn't sure I wouldn't bump into Bloody Jack if I set foot in the entryway, since he'd died there. Or blip myself into some other dark room. I knew if I told Jolie about that, she'd say I hadn't *really* left my body—I'd just disassociated, because I was under so much stress.

I considered buying into that theory myself, since it was a little less creepy than spontaneous astral projection, but I knew it had really happened. I'd *seen* that computer screen, glowing eerily in the gloom. And I'd known there was something important behind the twisting, snakelike spiral. A few taps at the keyboard...

Resolutely I shook off the creepy-crawlies and headed for the back gate, punched in the code on the keypad, and was glad Carmen hadn't changed it. Maybe, I reflected, remembering that the alarm hadn't been blaring when Tucker, Jolie and I arrived the night before to find the police already there, she'd gotten no farther than the main-house locks. Braced for the possibility that the guesthouse might have been taped off, I crossed the lawn.

No tape.

And my key worked.

I stepped inside, and immediately the tiny hairs on my forearms and the back of my neck stood up.

My first instinct was to turn and run, but I couldn't move. I just stood there, on the threshold, listening. Waiting.

I didn't see anyone, and I didn't hear anything.

There was a subtle weight to the air, though, and a negative charge, faint but unmistakable. Someone was there—or had been, very recently.

Nothing was out of place, at least in an obvious way, and yet things *had* been touched, shifted ever so slightly.

The police, I thought with a sudden surge of relief. Of course they'd searched the guesthouse the night before. That explained it.

What it didn't explain was the feeling that I wasn't alone.

I would have given a lot for that forbidden Glock right about then, though I was still far from an expert markswoman. I managed to communicate an order to my legs, and took a step back over the threshold. A splash of sunlight seared my eyes, temporarily dazzling me. I blinked, heard the sound of running feet—and felt someone bash into me, straight on.

I got the vague impression of a slender shape, dressed in dark clothes like mine, before I went down, conking my head on the door frame and then the high concrete edging of the flower bed.

I wasn't completely out, but everything went dark, and in the moment or two it took me to rally enough to sit up and look around, my assailant had vanished. I hadn't seen a car out front, so I decided he/she must have gone over the high stucco wall enclosing the massive backyard.

I got to my feet, gripped the door frame when darkness threatened again, then sprinted blindly for an antique Spanish bench set against the inside wall. I was pretty fit, but my physical prowess didn't extend to scrambling over eight-foot barriers. I climbed onto the back of the bench, as the intruder had done, given the scuff marks on the white-painted stucco, and vaulted to the other side.

I heard an engine start up—something gutsy, like a four-wheeler or a motorcycle—but I saw nothing but desert and, in the near distance, a side road and the golf course it bordered. Following the roaring sound of the getaway vehicle, whatever it was, I ran, staying close to the wall, ready to dodge one way or the other if it came at me.

Never think of worst-case scenarios. It seems to attract them.

A red four-wheeler zoomed around the curve in the wall, and except for noticing that the driver wore a visored helmet and a close-fitting black jumpsuit, I was too busy getting the hell out of the way to register any more details.

Fear-propelled, I realized that I had nowhere to go but up. I jumped on top of a squat barrel cactus, leaped for the top of the wall, still almost out of reach, and sort of perched there, clinging. The four-wheeler struck the wall with an earsplitting crash, and stucco dust billowed into the air in a cloud.

I don't know what made me do what I did then. It certainly wasn't courage.

From the top of the wall I launched myself at the driver of the four-wheeler and body slammed us both to the ground. The vehicle toppled onto its side while the driver and I struggled. Fear gave me strength, I guess. I managed to get on top, and tore off the helmet, flinging it aside.

Tiffany Oberlin stared up at me.

The woman who'd been with Nick the night of his fatal accident, and had sent me so many hateful e-mails.

Okay, so there was a notchlike scar through her left eyebrow, and her mouth sagged a little at one side, but she didn't look *that* bad.

"You have got to be kidding," I said, keeping her shoulders pinned with my knees. I was peripherally aware of several golf carts headed our way from the other side of the road.

Tiffany sputtered and tried to sit up.

The four-wheeler's engine sputtered, too, and then died.

"Did I *look* like I was kidding?" Tiffany spat.

"What's going on here?" a golfer asked, his cart being the first to arrive.

"Call the police," I said. "Now."

Tiffany struggled, tried to spit on me.

I pressed my knees harder into her shoulders.

"I hate you!" she said.

"No shit," I replied, gasping for breath.

"Let me *up!*"

"Not a chance," I answered.

"They'll be here in a few minutes," the golfer said, snapping his cell phone shut.

"I'd like to borrow that," I said with surprising moderation, given that I'd just tackled someone on a moving vehicle from the top of a stucco wall.

The golfer tossed me the phone.

I called Tucker.

"Sit tight," he said when I'd explained.

"Trust me," I answered, glaring down into Tiffany's flushed, filthy and furious face. "I will."

"We were arguing about you when the accident happened," Tiffany informed me.

"And that's my fault?" I asked. "I wasn't even there. Nick and I were divorced."

"You were all he ever wanted to talk about!"

I felt something squeeze inside my heart. *Nick,* I thought, despairing.

A patrol car zipped onto the road between the golf course and Greer's back wall. Two officers sprinted in our direction.

"This woman attacked me!" Tiffany told them when they each took me by an elbow and hauled me off her.

Fortunately I had a witness. The golfer explained that Tiffany had tried to turn me into a grease spot with her four-wheeler. The evidence—mainly the deep gouge in Greer's wall—supported me.

Tiffany was hoisted to her feet.

"Do you want to press charges?" one of the cops asked.

"Yes," I said. "But you might want to drop by the nearest psych ward before you throw her in the clink, because she's a few spins short of a jackpot."

By the time Tucker arrived the police had hand-cuffed Tiffany and taken her away. I thanked the golfer, gave back his cell phone and noodle-kneed my way around to the gate next to the garage.

Just how much, I wondered foggily, is one woman supposed to put up with in a single day?

Inside the guesthouse I slammed the door, threw the dead bolt and leaned against the panel, trying to catch my breath.

Was I seriously hurt? I didn't know, and the police had been too busy to ask, since Tiffany thought *I* should be the one under arrest, and raised hell before they finally managed to wrestle her into the back of the squad car. Except for a pounding in the side of my head, which I'd struck twice when the attacker knocked me down, I was numb.

I sagged to the floor with my back against the door, and sat there until Tucker arrived, knocking and yelling my name.

I pulled myself up, shakily, and let him in.

Tucker looked me over, then took me by the shoulders and eased me onto the couch.

By then, I was over being shocked by Tiffany's attack—and well into pissed off. I chattered out the story, the words tumbling over each other helter-skelter, landing in the wrong parts of sentences.

He sat on the coffee table, facing me, and began

checking me out as he listened. I flinched when he touched the side of my head and again when his hand came away bloody.

"You're going to the emergency room," he said.

"I don't want to," I protested, but it was already too late, because he was standing and I was being carried in his arms. "I have an appointment with Beverly Pennington at two o'clock and I can't possibly break it."

Tucker frowned, kicking the door shut behind us. "If they don't admit you, you might still make it," he said. "And what business do you have with your late brother-in-law's ex-wife?"

"Have you ever sat in a hospital waiting room?" I asked peevishly, ignoring his question, but Tucker didn't even slow down, let alone stop.

"It makes a difference when the cops bring you in," he told me.

"We need to stop at the apartment first," I said, feeling woozy again.

"Why?"

"Because Dave is home alone."

"Dave will be fine," Tucker said. "I don't get why this Tiffany broad blames you for the accident."

"It was traumatic," I said. "She had breast implants and they popped."

"She's crazy," Tucker decided.

"Brilliant deduction," I replied.

We reached his SUV, parked in the driveway

next to my Volvo. Like the gate, the driver's door was open. Tucker had been in too big a hurry to shut either one.

"How did you bang up your head?"

"Tiffany was inside the guesthouse when I came home," I said. I wasn't tracking very well, but I was determined to get the story out and make sense of the whole thing, no matter how many tries it took. "God knows what she was planning—probably she just wanted to scare me, but she must have panicked or something. She shoved past me and knocked me down, and I hit my head on the concrete edge around the flower bed."

"Ouch," Tucker said. He went to the passenger side and plunked me on the seat. I blushed, flashing briefly on another Tucker/SUV experience—one that had been a lot more fun. "You didn't recognize her at that point?"

I shook my head. "It happened too fast."

"But you went after her."

"It seemed like a good idea at the time."

"Right."

"I've got to know if Dave's all right. Tiffany might have gone there first."

"Is there a *Damn Fool's Guide* to making enemies? You seem to have a real gift for pissing people off."

It was time to change the subject. "Did you ever find my panties?" I asked.

Tucker's face was grim, but his mouth quirked up at one corner as he got behind the wheel and reached for the radio mic on the dashboard. He didn't bother to answer until he'd dispatched a deputy to the apartment to look in on Dave, adding, "The key's under the doormat" before replacing the receiver. Turning to me with a wry but worried look, he concluded, "You really shouldn't leave the key under the mat. It's the first place an intruder is going to look."

"I only put it there until I could think of a better place," I said, though I knew it was a lame excuse. Never hide a key under a mat, on top of a door frame, inside a mailbox, or in a plastic rock standing all by itself. *The Damn Fool's Guide to Home Security,* chapter one.

I rubbed my temples with the fingertips of both hands.

Tucker rolled his eyes. "Fasten your seat belt, Sherlock," he told me, already backing out. "And no, I never found your panties. Of course, I didn't exactly look for them."

I didn't answer.

"So where does the four-wheeler come in?" Tucker asked.

"I told you."

"You were babbling. Tell me again."

I sighed. Then I told him again.

Tucker was speeding, but I figured I must not be in grave danger of dying from my injuries, because he wasn't using the magnetic light he'd set on the roof of his SUV the night before.

I was having trouble keeping my thoughts in order, and dreading the hospital visit. With my cheapo insurance plan, I'd still be sitting in the E.R. waiting room when my hair started going gray.

Pretty soon the radio on the dashboard crackled. A Maricopa County sheriff's deputy reported that Dave was fine, and there were no signs of an intruder. The water dish had been empty, but he'd refilled it, and wiped up a puddle on the living-room floor.

Protect and serve.

Smiling a little, Tucker thanked the officer and overed and outed.

We arrived at a hospital in Scottsdale.

Tucker was right. It *does* make a difference when you're brought in by a cop. The medical personnel automatically assume you're a criminal and treat you accordingly.

But I was seen quickly after Tucker explained that I wasn't under arrest. I was poked, prodded, x-rayed and questioned. Antiseptic salve was applied to the cuts on my legs, no doubt sustained while Tiffany and I were rolling around on the prickly ground, and my good black jeans were a total loss.

I gulped down a couple of pain pills, signed the papers so my managed health care plan could be billed and Tucker took me back to the apartment in Cave Creek.

I was very glad to see Dave.

And I still had forty-five minutes before I was due at Beverly Pennington's.

I went into the bathroom and stood in front of the mirror over the sink, combing my hair gingerly, working around the knot rising from the head bumps, and tried to cover the abrasions on the side of my face with makeup. All in all, I looked like Frankenstein's bride wearing a thick layer of concealer.

Sighing, I peeled out of the jeans and turtleneck and put the sundress back on. It didn't look right with my boots, so I switched to sandals.

When I came out into the living room again, Tucker was still there, talking on his cell phone.

He muttered a goodbye and clicked it shut.

Dave licked some of the salve off my left leg.

"Tiffany's spending a night in the hospital before they book her," Tucker reported.

I nodded, feeling a little glum. I wasn't completely unsympathetic—Tiffany had been in love with Nick, and nobody knew better than I did how crazy that could make a person. "I guess I should have known something like this might happen," I said, "after all those nasty e-mails."

Tucker narrowed his eyes. "She's been threatening you all this time? And you didn't mention that to me? Or report it to the police?"

I sighed. "It was only a few snarly one-liners," I said. "And you know the law, Tuck. The police couldn't really *do* anything until she made a move."

"Why didn't you just block her messages?"

I smiled shakily. "They were pretty inventive," I admitted. "I figured if I ever wanted to write a thriller, I'd have lots of terrible ways to kill off characters."

Tucker rolled his eyes. "Well," he said, "she'll probably be charged with assault, or even attempted murder. You *are* pressing charges, right?"

I nodded. "I'm sort of going to miss the e-mails." I sighed.

Tucker waited a beat. A small muscle flexed in his cheek. "I don't suppose I could talk you into canceling your appointment with Beverly Pennington?"

"Not unless you arrest me," I replied.

"Don't tempt me," Tucker retorted. "I could run you in for unlawful possession of a firearm, among other things."

"It's not unlawful," I pointed out. "Not for sure, anyway."

Tucker grinned, folded his arms, in no apparent hurry to get back to making the highways and byways of Maricopa County safe for democracy. "How do you plan on getting to Mrs. Pennington's?" he asked, looking smug. "The Volvo is still at Greer's."

"You probably think I should have remembered that," I said, blushing a little, because I hadn't given the subject of transportation a single thought. I'd been busy being x-rayed, salved and peppered with cop questions from Tucker.

He chuckled, shook his head.

"I'll take a cab," I said, inspired.

Tucker sighed. "Just call and postpone," he said. "You don't know Beverly Pennington," I said. "That would be strike two with her, and I'm not getting a third swing."

"You might need your purse," Tucker suggested.

My purse was on the front seat of the Volvo, which, of course, was still parked in Greer's driveway. I was definitely batting a thousand.

"Help me out here," I said. "I'm trying to get started as a detective."

"So far, you're doing great," he told me with a note of sarcasm. But then he relented. "Okay, I'll take you as far as Greer's so you can pick up your car and the purse."

I smiled at him. "Thanks," I said, heading for the door. Dave trotted along behind, and I didn't have the heart to make him stay home.

Tucker collected the spare key from under the mat before we went down the stairs, and handed it to me. "Find a better hiding place," he said.

"Did I tell you I'm reopening Bad-Ass Bert's?" I asked, taking the key and, not having a pocket, putting it in my bra. "I'm calling it Mojo's, and I've already ordered the sign."

"You're going to run a biker bar?"

"Yeah. I need the income."

"You don't know anything about selling beer."

"I don't know anything about being a detective, either, but that hasn't stopped me so far."

Tucker laughed. "You've got me there," he admitted.

He drove Dave and me to the Volvo, and waited until we were both inside. "Don't forget," he called, in parting, through the open window of his SUV. "Dinner, my place, seven o'clock. Bring the dog."

"Can I postpone?" I asked.

"No," Tucker said, rolling his window up again before I could answer.

"He can be unreasonable," I confided to Dave, who was sitting in the passenger seat with his butt on top of my purse, excited to be hitting the road.

Tucker followed us halfway to Scottsdale, then veered off with a jaunty little toot of his horn.

Dave and I headed for Beverly's condo, and this time there were no squad cars choking the main driveway into the complex, as there had been on my first visit. Right about then, I questioned the wisdom of letting the dog come along for the ride. It wasn't hot yet, but I hadn't brought him any water, and I didn't want to leave the windows rolled down too far in case somebody stole him—or my car.

Fortunately a security guard approached as soon as I'd parked. I wasn't sure he was alive, since his color was odd and his uniform looked like something out of the original *Dragnet,* but asking him straight out would be dicey, so I smiled.

"Nice dog," the security guard said, smiling back.

"Would you mind keeping an eye on him for a little while?"

"I wouldn't mind at all" came the reply. "But if somebody tries to dognap him, I won't be able to do much about it. I've been dead since 1952."

"I wondered," I admitted, stealing a glance at my watch. Beverly Pennington was expecting me in five minutes. I'd have to make the interview concise. And I'd promised to stop by Scottsdale PD on my way home and sign a formal complaint against Tiffany Oberlin.

"Can I sit behind the wheel?" the dead guy asked hopefully. "That way, I could pretend I was driving. I wouldn't actually go anyplace, of course."

"Okay by me," I said, since Dave seemed to like him. I subscribe to the theory that animals are good judges of character.

I opened the Volvo door, and the security guard settled himself in the front seat, grinning from ear to ear, turning the steering wheel and making a *vroom-vroom* sound with his lips. He was sixty if he was a day, but he looked like a kid on a carnival ride, sitting there.

I headed for Beverly Pennington's front door. It was painted red, like every other door in the place, and had a big brass six on the front.

I pushed on the doorbell.

Mrs. Pennington opened it almost immediately,

but I didn't recognize her right away. She'd lost weight since I'd seen her last—we'd had a brief encounter at a local mall more than a year before, while I was shopping with Greer—and let her hair return to its natural gray. She wore beige linen pants with a matching tunic and a chunky gold necklace—very tasteful of course.

It crossed my mind that aliens might have abducted the original Beverly and replaced her with a robot.

She took in the concealer job on my face, and I knew she was having second thoughts about letting me in. In the end, though, she relented.

"Mojo Sheepshanks," I said, once inside the small entryway, putting out my hand.

Beverly Pennington ignored the gesture. "What happened to your head?" she asked, frowning.

"Small accident," I answered. "No big deal."

"Come in and sit down," she said, leading the way into a tile-floored living room with an adobe fireplace and big suede-upholstered chairs and couches.

I sat in one of the chairs, wondering why her eyes weren't puffy from crying over her dead son. She'd said on the telephone that they didn't get along, but it still seemed weird.

Beverly arranged herself on the couch, leaned forward and picked up a little crystal bell off the coffee table. She gave it a jingle, and a Mexican maid appeared. Carlotta of the lobster salad, I assumed. I realized I was hungry, since I'd had nothing since the breakfast sandwich Tucker had brought me that morning at the apartment, but this wasn't a lunch date.

"Iced tea, please," Beverly said to Carlotta. "And be sure to add mint leaves."

Carlotta nodded and vanished.

I waited, scanning the room. No family photos anywhere. No knickknacks. Certainly no votive candles flickering on the mantel in memorial to her dead son, à la Angela Braydaven. If I hadn't known better, I'd have thought the condo was one of those high-priced vacation rentals, elegant but anonymous.

The kind of place aliens might think would pass as normal.

Beverly caught me looking and smiled slightly, though not in a friendly way. "I understand from certain sources within the police department that you practically found Jack's body," she said.

I had to swallow before I could say anything. "I'm sorry," I said, acknowledging her son's untimely death, but not that I'd been among the first people to see his corpse lying on my sister's entryway floor.

"As I said on the telephone, Jack and I had—issues," she told me coolly. "He tried to scam me one too many times."

I thought of the numeral on Beverly's front door and figured somebody ought to add a couple more sixes. Issues or not, how could she be that cold?

Carlotta returned with two glasses of tea—nobody had bothered to ask if I wanted one—and set one down for each of us, on coasters, of course. I left mine untouched, since I don't eat or drink in the homes of people who may sprout horns, fur and hooves at any second.

When the housekeeper had gone, I got to the point. "What do you want, Mrs. Pennington?"

She smiled, took a sip of her tea and eyed me thoughtfully over the mint sprig jutting out of the glass. "I thought you'd never ask," she said.

I'd left my dog in the care of a dead security guard. My sister was missing, as was her house-keeper, I had a stop to make at the cop shop and I was getting nervous because I hadn't seen Gillian recently. I'd spent two hours at the emergency room, and I was due at Tucker's for supper at seven. Damn it, I had things to do.

"I just did," I said.

"I wasn't really planning to hire you," Beverly confessed, without a shred of remorse. "This is about your sister."

I started to get up.

"Sit down," Beverly said.

I did, but not because of the command in her voice. I sensed that something important was hap-pening, something I wasn't going to like but needed to know about just the same. I think on some level I'd understood that all along.

Beverly got up, went to a bureau against the living-room wall, opened a drawer and produced a manila envelope. Then she handed it to me. "I was planning to use this," she said, "but with Alex on a slab, it seems pointless."

My hands shook as I took the envelope, laid it in my lap.

Beverly backed off, fortunately. Sat down on the couch again, picked up her iced tea. I wondered if it was the electric variety, but she seemed sober. Had I imagined the drunken slur in her voice when we spoke on the telephone that first time? Maybe I had. At that moment I wasn't too sure about anything.

"Take it. Look at it at your leisure. It's of no use to me now."

I couldn't bring myself to open that envelope. Not in front of Beverly Pennington, anyway. "What is it?" I asked. I sounded uncertain, and I hated myself for it. I was pretty sure I could hate *her*, too, if I knew her better.

"Information," Beverly said. "Don't you want your iced tea?"

"I have to get back to my dog," I said. That time, I made it all the way to my feet. "Why give this to me?"

"You'll see," she said airily. Then she leaned forward, gave the little bell another tinkling shake.

Carlotta bustled in.

"Ms. Sheepshanks does not want her tea," Beverly informed her. "Please remove it."

I was already at the door, with my hand on the knob. I looked back at Carlotta, and for a moment it seemed she wanted to leave with me.

Our gazes met, held briefly. Then she bent, picked up my glass and left the room without a word.

I thought about Greer's reference to the rehab center, and Alex's assertion that Beverly hadn't been sober in twenty years. Now I wondered what the story really was, and if I'd ever know.

I decided to take a stab at it. "You sounded…ill when we spoke on the phone."

Beverly's smile was icy. "Drunk, you mean? I'm on medication, Ms. Sheepshanks, not that it's any of your affair. I've been under a lot of stress lately—or hadn't you heard?"

I didn't say goodbye—or anything else—to Mrs. Pennington. Figuring I'd pried enough, I just clutched the manila envelope to my side and booked it for my car.

The dead security guard reluctantly climbed out of the driver's side. "We didn't have cars like this in 1952," he said. "There isn't even a choke."

I stooped to make sure Dave was still okay, and he was. He'd nudged my purse aside and settled down for a snooze on the car seat.

I turned to the security guard again, planning to ask why he was hanging out in the parking lot of a Scottsdale condo-complex and gently steer him in the direction of the Light, but he was gone.

Feeling sad, I tossed Beverly Pennington's "information" into the backseat and climbed in. On the way to Scottsdale PD, I bought a cheeseburger for Dave and one for me, and we shared the fries.

Filing the report on Tiffany's attack was a tedious process, but I got it done.

I hurried back to my car, and Dave, and we were off. My cell phone rang when we were almost home, but it was in my purse and Dave was sitting on it, so I let voice mail pick up. When two more calls came in, in short order, I decided it was probably Tucker.

I pulled off onto the shoulder on Scottsdale Road, extracted the purse from under Dave and rummaged for the phone.

Tucker, all right.

I didn't listen to the messages. I just speed-dialed him.

"What?" I said.

"How did it go at Beverly Pennington's?" he asked.

"You called me three times and *that's* what you want to know?" I could have been dead. I could have been bludgeoned, poisoned, stabbed, run down by something diesel-powered, or shot. Did he bother to inquire about any of those possibilities? No.

Frankly, I was a little miffed.

"Her husband and her son are both dead," Tucker went on. "Your sister is missing. Beverly Pennington could be involved. So, *yes,* that's what I want to know."

"I'm fine, thank you. Just fine. Nobody's made an attempt on my life in, oh, three hours now." I swallowed. "I filed the complaint against Tiffany, and I feel rotten about it."

"She's a danger to herself and others," Tucker said.

A semi whizzed by, the driver blowing the air horn angrily.

I pulled farther onto the shoulder.

"She probably needs medication."

"That's for a doctor to decide," Tucker told me. "Tell me about Mrs. Pennington."

"Love makes people do strange things. And I think Tiffany really loved Nick."

"Mojo," Tucker said.

"She's weird," I told him, referring to Mrs. Pennington now and trusting Tucker to make the leap. "She gave me an envelope and when I asked what it was, she said I'd see. I'm scared to open it. There could be anthrax spores inside. Or plastic explosives."

"You're getting paranoid in your old age, Sherlock. Open it. If I hear a boom, I'll call the bomb squad."

"Gee, thanks. Except I'd be vaporized by then, wouldn't I, and so would Dave."

"Are your pain pills wearing off or something? You sound super-cranky."

"You'd be cranky, too, if you'd had a day like mine!"

"No argument there," Tucker said. "Go home. Take a couple of aspirin and a nap. Bring this mysterious envelope with you tonight, and we'll open it together."

It sounded like a plan, though I doubted I could

resist taking a peek before then. "Can I bring anything?" I asked, taking a stab at normal conversation. "For dinner, I mean?"

"Sure," Tucker answered. "As long as it isn't food."

CHAPTER THIRTEEN

NOBODY WAS LURKING in my apartment. Trust me, I checked, after retrieving the Glock from on top of the refrigerator. Granted, it wasn't loaded, and I didn't know how to remedy that, even though Bubba had sold me bullets and I had a shooting lesson under my belt, but I was counting on the intimidation factor.

While Dave lapped up water in the kitchen, I sat at the table, staring at the envelope Beverly Pennington had given me. My head ached. My legs stung, badly scratched. Call me a sap, but I felt genuinely sorry for Tiffany Oberlin. And the fact that I hadn't been to bed the night before finally caught up with me.

I repaired to the living room, stretched out on the couch and fell asleep.

When I awoke, it was dark, Dave was licking concealer off my face and the phone was ringing.

Blinking, I sat up. Flicked on the lamp on the nearest end table.

What time was it?

The phone stopped ringing, then started again. I stumbled into the kitchen to grab it off the hook. "Hullo?" I mumbled, still disoriented.

"You're late," Tucker said, though not unkindly. "Are you okay?"

"I'm not sure," I said blearily.

"Did you open the mysterious envelope?"

I shook my head, yawned loudly, then remembered he couldn't see me. "Not yet," I answered. "I sort of fell asleep. Did I miss dinner?"

"The kids have eaten. I'll throw another steak on the grill when I see the whites of your eyes. One for Dave, too."

The sensible thing would have been to beg off and stay home. I'd been wounded in action. I was rummy, not rested. And the idea of venturing onto Allison's turf, like some sneak thief, didn't appeal. But I wanted, even needed, to see Tucker.

"Okay," I said. "I'll be there in a few minutes."

"Bring the envelope," Tucker reminded me.

I nodded again, remembered again, yawned again. "Okay," I repeated, and hung up.

Next, I splashed my face with cold water at the bathroom sink, applied more concealer and did what I could with my hair, which wasn't much. I finally wound it into a gob on top of my head and secured it with a plastic squeeze clip.

Dave was up for a ride, already jumping at the front door when I joined him there, stuffing Beverly Pennington's envelope into my purse before taking

off the chain and turning the dead bolt. I'd considered bringing the Glock, too, but that seemed like
overkill. And, besides, Tucker would have his
handy, even though he was off duty.

Allison's big territorial, with the veterinary
office out back, was a little way out of town. When
I drove through the open gate I got heart palpita-
tions. I was on dangerous emotional ground, for
sure, but I couldn't turn back.

Tucker came outside to greet me when I pulled
into the driveway behind the house. He wasn't
wearing a chef's hat, but he did sport a barbecue
apron that said "Dad" on the front in big red letters
that looked like crayon. If my head hadn't been so
tender, I'd have laid it against the steering wheel in
utter defeat.

Daisy and Danny appeared behind Tucker, small
and blond and curious. They both summoned up
tentative, uncertain smiles—their friend had been
murdered, after all, and the world was no longer
such a safe place as they'd probably believed. I suspected those fragile smiles were more for Dave
than me, but I plastered an answering one on my
face anyhow, and forced myself to get out of the car.

Dave bounded after me, then past, rushing to
greet the twins.

Tucker put out a hand to me, and the gesture
touched me in an indefinable way.

"Hi," I said shyly.

Daisy and Danny were still playing with Dave,

but I knew they were watching when Tucker's hand closed tightly around mine for a moment, then rested on the small of my back.

"You remember Mojo?" he asked quietly, turning to his children.

"She was here with the sick basset hound," Danny said, nodding. "Mom fixed him."

"Mom's in Oklahoma," Daisy told me. "Grampa's heart is acting up."

Mine was, too, though I doubted I'd need a bypass in the near future. Hearts are tricky, tender things, prone to all manner of injury. "I'm sure he'll get better," I said. I wasn't sure of any such thing, of course. I was merely whistling in the dark.

"Mom can't fix Grampa if his heart attacks him," Danny said, looking worried. "She's not a people doctor."

The roots of the grass on Allison's lawn seemed to have grown up around my ankles, tangled, holding me fast to the spot where I stood.

"Come in," Tucker urged, giving me a tug in the direction of the house.

"Dad got you a present," Daisy said, looking puzzled but not resentful.

"A present?" I asked, surprised. Tucker was romantic in all the ways it really counted, but his gifts tended to come in fast-food bags.

We stepped into a large, pleasantly cluttered kitchen with red tile floors and granite countertops. There was a copper basket near the stove, shaped like a chicken and full of brown eggs, indicating a serious cook in residence. Pictures and school papers and a little chart with stars on it covered one side of the double-wide refrigerator.

Tucker smiled, releasing my hand now that there was less danger that I'd bolt for my car and zoom back down the driveway in the fabled cloud of dust, and handed me a wrapped package, tied with a ribbon.

"Open it!" Daisy and Danny chorused, jumping up and down. Dave got into the spirit of the thing, as dogs will, and did some jumping himself.

I accepted the package. Opened it slowly.

It was a book; I'd already guessed that by its size and shape. *The Damn Fool's Guide to Careers.*

Tucker grinned.

I gave him a look, then laughed. The message was clear. Forget being a private detective. Forget running a biker bar. Become Something Sensible in Ten Easy Steps.

If I hadn't known he meant well, I'd have hit him with the book.

Probably disappointed, Daisy and Danny immediately lost interest in the present. And me.

"Can we go camping with Chelsea and Janice?" Daisy wheedled, tugging at Tucker's arm. "Please?"

"No," Tucker said.

Danny remembered my presence. "Janice is making a real movie," he said solemnly. "I want to be in it. She said I could be Spider-Man."

"Go," Tucker told his children. "Play, or something, and take the dog with you."

"I'm not going to quit," I told him firmly when we were alone.

He set the book aside, pulled me into his arms and kissed me. "I know," he said against my mouth. "I just want you to keep your options open."

"How about that steak you promised?" I asked. "I'm starving."

He chuckled. "Coming right up," he said. Then he took my hand again and led me through a dining room, then a living room and out onto a patio. There was a pool, shaped like a horse's head and shining turquoise in the night, and distant lights twinkled in the dark desert. I had a strange, disjointed sense of being temporarily transported to some distant and sparsely populated planet.

A coyote howled, not too close but not too far away, either. The sound was poignant, bereft, full of yearning for the old days and ways, the time long before the first white settlers came to the area, and certainly before the developers began to gobble up the desert. The memory of ancient freedom was imprinted in Brother Coyote's nimble bones.

Alas. Still on Earth, then.

I sighed.

Tucker sat me down at a glass table and went to the fancy brick barbecue grill nearby to put a couple of steaks over the flames. And memory stirred in me, too, visceral and primitive, an echo of the desert dog's cry. The grill became a fire in a circle of stones, Tucker and I wore skins, and the house behind us was a cavern in the side of a dry red mountain.

"Who's taking care of the veterinary practice while Allison's away?" I asked, shaking off the clan-of-the-cave-bear mood. I still wanted to make a break for it, but I was settling down. Sort of.

"It's closed for the time being," Tucker answered. "Another doctor is covering for her, and her assistants have some time off."

"Oh," I said.

Tucker came back to the table, sat down. Held out a hand.

I knew what he wanted, and tunneled into my purse for Beverly Pennington's envelope. Handed it over.

Tucker held it for a moment, thoughtfully, as though preparing himself in some way, then opened it.

It contained several newspaper clippings—old ones—paper-clipped together with what appeared to be photocopies.

I relaxed a little. No explosion. Probably no anthrax spores, either.

So far, so good.

I scooted my chair a little closer to Tucker's so I could ogle the information Beverly Pennington wanted me to have. I saw right away that the clippings were from the Shiloh *Bugle,* tattered and yellowed at the edges.

My eyes widened when I saw the first headline,

and something quivered deep in my belly. I quickly identified it as dread.

Local Man In Critical Condition.

I picked up the clipping to get a closer look.

A chill went through me, a sort of prescience that meant my deeper mind was already cataloging data, adding things up, subtracting and multiplying. The conclusions might come to the surface immediately, days later, or not at all. That part was a crap-shoot.

Tucker got up to turn the steaks over on the grill. He'd seen the headline, too, of course, but he offered no comment. I was pretty sure he'd read the article, probably at a glance, and now he was digesting it.

I squinted at the report; there was plenty of light coming through the patio doors, but the print was small, old and a little smudged.

"Frederick Severn, 57, was rushed to a Kalispell hospital on Tuesday night, by ambulance, the victim of an apparent stroke. According to his wife, Alice, he fell ill while having supper on the Severn family farm, on Route 2, outside Shiloh. He has not regained consciousness...."

Tucker came back to the table, and I handed him the clipping and went on to the next, dated a few days later. The headline shouted Poisoning Suspected, but I could barely concentrate on the body of the article. I kept thinking that I'd been nine when Frederick Severn fell ill; it was the same year Lillian and I met Greer in that Boise bus depot.

What was I to make of all this?

Was Beverly Pennington trying to tell me that *Greer* had had something to do with Mr. Severn's illness?

I refocused on the article, but reading it was like wading through something gelatinous. My headache was suddenly a lot worse, and hungry as I was, I didn't think I'd be able to force down so much as a bite of that steak.

Tucker finally took the clipping out of my hand and read it aloud, in a quiet, matter-of-fact voice. What it all boiled down to was that, though Severn had survived, he was essentially a vegetable. Routine blood tests had revealed traces of a common garden insecticide in his system, and the elder of his two stepdaughters, Molly Stillwell, sixteen, who had run away from home soon after her stepfather was hospitalized, was being sought for questioning.

I did something terrible when I was young, I heard Greer saying that night in the guesthouse kitchen, when she'd come searching for the stolen tamale pie. *Someone knows.*

"Oh, God," I murmured.

"What?" Tucker asked.

I swallowed. "Did I happen to mention, in all the excitement, that Greer is being blackmailed?"

Tucker stiffened. "Yes," he said. "Last night, after we listened to the voice mails. But you were a little sketchy with the details—and you took your sweet time getting around to it. How long have you known?"

"Yikes," I said, stalling.

Tucker did not look appeased. He was leaning toward me, his eyes narrowed, his voice low and gruff. "'Yikes'? Two people are dead. Your sister *and* her housekeeper are officially off the radar. If you know more about this than you're telling me, spill it. *Now.*"

My steak was burning; I could smell it. Tucker didn't take it—or me—off the heat. I felt skewered by his gaze, like a shish kebab, and I was starting to char.

I swallowed again, hard. "I've known for a while," I admitted. "Jolie and I tried to get some answers, but Greer would never tell us anything. Alex said she'd almost emptied his bank accounts, paying somebody off. She'd taken out some credit cards in his name and maxed them, getting cash advances. He hired detectives and found out she'd lived in Shiloh, Montana, but if he knew more about it than that, he didn't say."

"You think she's Molly Stillwell, and she poisoned her stepfather," Tucker said.

"It's possible," I said glumly. "She told me she'd done something terrible, but that was all I could get out of her. And when I got that call on her cell phone, whoever was on the other end said, 'Tell *Molly* she's a dead woman.'"

"Lacing somebody's supper with bug killer would qualify as doing something terrible," Tucker said, forking the charred steak off the grill and onto a paper plate, then setting the works down on the patio stones for Dave.

I nodded, my throat tight. I was afraid to look at the two other clippings I hadn't examined yet— there are times when ignorance really *is* bliss. I forced myself.

There was a picture accompanying the third article, showing a slender, harried-looking woman in a cheap cotton dress, standing stalwartly beside a slack-jawed man in a wheelchair. The woman looked so much like Greer that it took me few extra moments to get past that, and read the headline.

Longtime Shiloh Family Enduring Hard Times.

Alice Severn had personally undertaken the care of her disabled husband, refusing to "park him in some institution," as she told the *Bugle* reporter. She prayed every day for her missing daughter's return and continued safety, and depended on her remaining daughter, Tessa, and stepson, Frederick "Rick" Severn Jr., for moral support. Members of her church had been "helpful," as had various community service organizations.

I wondered how long it had been before the casseroles and other donations had petered out—if Tessa had gone on to marry and live a normal adult life, or if she was still at home, helping to look after her stepfather. And what about Rick Severn?

The fourth and final article answered *that* question. Rick Severn had gone to prison three years after his father's poison-induced stroke, convicted of vehicular homicide. He'd been driving drunk, collided with a van on an icy Montana road the day after Thanksgiving and wiped out a family returning from a visit to Grandma's.

While I was absorbing all this, Tucker went into the house, came out with a fresh steak and plopped it on the grill. He set a salad in front of me, along with a bottle of Thousand Island dressing, my favorite.

"Eat," he said.

"I can't."

"Try."

I picked up the fork, stabbed a cherry tomato. "What do you make of all this, Tuck?" I asked, referring to the clippings.

"Beverly Pennington could be the blackmailer," Tucker answered, thinking out loud. "Though it doesn't seem likely that she'd risk prison by cluing you in."

"Alex told me he'd hired investigators to look into Greer's past. He might have given Beverly this stuff, or she could have swiped it from him at some point." I put down the fork, with the cherry tomato still speared on the tines, and gnawed at my lower lip. "I believed him, since he was dead and everything, but maybe he lied."

"Maybe," Tucker said with a note of glum wryness.

"He seemed—well—*sincere*," I said. "He thought Greer would be blamed for his murder, and he wanted to clear her."

Tucker upended the dressing bottle, squeezed Thousand Island all over my salad and put the fork back in my hand. "Eat, Sherlock," he said. "You're going to need your strength."

"I have to go to Shiloh," I said.

"Not," Tucker replied.

I wished I hadn't mentioned the embryonic plan, or even showed him the contents of that envelope. He'd try to stop me from going to Montana, for sure. At the very least, he'd pass the information on to the local authorities in Shiloh and probably to the Feds, too.

I wasn't sure Greer had been taken to Shiloh, but I knew I had to start there.

I began to eat salad. Tucker was right. I was going to need my strength.

I had one advantage. Allison was gone, and that meant Tucker couldn't tail me to Montana, because he'd have to leave his kids to do that.

And I had one *dis*advantage. Dave. I couldn't leave him with Jolie, because Sweetie might eat him. And I couldn't put him in a kennel, because then he might think I'd dumped him at the pound and wasn't coming back.

I'd have to take him with me, which ruled out flying; he was too big to fit under a seat, and I wasn't about to let him ride in the cargo hold.

At some point, I'd started caring about Dave.

Now I was stuck with a four-legged partner who was bound to put a crimp in my style. Yikes.

I smiled as he trotted out of the house, following his nose, and zeroed in on the cremated steak.

"Mojo," Tucker said suspiciously, "what's going on in that bruised head of yours?"

"Do you think you could grease the tracks and speed up my liquor license?" I asked. "I'd like to open Mojo's for business as soon as possible."

He blinked. Whatever he'd been expecting me to say, it wasn't that.

"No," he said. "I don't have that kind of influence, and if I did, I wouldn't use it."

That darned honor of his. I shrugged. Went on munching salad.

Daisy stepped outside and approached me shyly. "Are you my daddy's girlfriend?" she asked for the second time that night.

I almost choked on a cherry tomato. Looked to Tucker for help, but he was turning my steak over on the grill, with his back to us.

"No," I said.

"*Yes,*" Tucker said.

"Do you want to see my room?" Daisy asked, her eyes big as she studied me, probably wondering about the troweled-on concealer, which suddenly felt like a mask on my face.

"Sure," I said. "Why not?"

She took my hand when I stood up, and that did something peculiar to my heart. "Did you know my friend Gillian went to heaven?" she inquired as she guided me across the living room. Danny was lying on the couch, reading one of the early Harry Potter books.

My throat felt thick. I couldn't speak, so I nodded.

"I miss her," Daisy confided. "I miss my daddy, too. He's gone a lot."

I nodded again, and my eyes burned.

Daisy pulled me into a long hallway, pushed open a pair of double doors. "My mommy sleeps in here," she told me solemnly.

I couldn't look. Or talk.

"This is Danny's room," Daisy went on, like a little tour guide, a second or so later as we passed an open door. I glimpsed a lot of boy clutter inside—books, toy airplanes, a hand-held video game. "Daddy sleeps in here when he's home," she announced at the next doorway. "And my room is on the other side. That way, if any monsters come, Daddy's in the middle. No monster would *dare* try to get us when Daddy's around."

"Right," I choked out, ashamed, because through everything I was feeling ran a thin, sturdy thread of pure relief. Tucker hadn't been lying to me when he said he wasn't sharing Allison's bed. Maybe the setup really *was* platonic.

Daisy's room was the kind every little girl dreams of—or, at least *I* had when I was her age. Maybe a bit longer—like until last week. There was a white canopy bed, swamped in pink ruffles and piled with stuffed animals. The dressers and the nightstands matched the bed, the lamp bases were porcelain ballerinas and there were pictures pinned to a bulletin board on the wall.

I moved closer to examine them.

Tucker and Allison figured prominently in almost every shot. The Darrochs camping. The Darrochs at Disneyland. The Darrochs in front of a Christmas tree.

I wanted to cry, but that would have confused Daisy, maybe even frightened her, so I sucked it up.

"That's Gillian," Daisy said, standing on tiptoe to press a finger to the face in a school photograph. "I wish she'd come back, but Mom says she can't. Not ever."

I bit my lower lip. It was hard to look at Gillian's image, alive, smiling for the camera, unaware that she'd never get the chance to grow up. I looked away, my gaze bouncing off more photos of Tucker and Allison, finally catching on a shot of four figures standing in the Darrochs' swimming pool, on a sunny day.

Daisy, Danny and two girls in bikinis.

"That's Chelsea," Daisy said, pointing out the girl I'd met at Helen Erland's. "She's our babysitter. When she gets her new car, she's going to take us for a ride." Her finger slid to the other girl. "And that's Janice. She's Chelsea's best friend. And she's got *tattoos.*"

I became aware of Tucker's presence even before I turned to see him standing in the doorway of Daisy's room.

"Steak's ready," he said. "Daise, it's bedtime. If you hurry, you can beat your brother to the bathroom."

Daisy didn't balk. She tugged at my hand again,

though, and looked up into my face with an expression so innocent that it made me ache inside. "Which is it?" she asked. "Are you my daddy's girlfriend, or aren't you?"

"I guess I am," I said, embarrassed.

"Okay," Daisy replied in a that's-settled tone. Then she turned to Tucker. "Can I sleep in Mommy's bed tonight? I can brush my teeth in her bathroom."

"Sure," Tucker answered, sounding hoarse.

Daisy grabbed a pink nightgown out of one of her dresser drawers, took a stuffed unicorn from the fluffy menagerie on the bed and ducked past Tucker into the hall.

Danny was less amenable to the bedtime decree than his sister had been, and when Tucker stayed in the living room to argue with him, I went back to the patio to eat my steak.

Justin was sitting in one of the chairs at the glass-topped table, holding Dave on his lap.

I sat down in the chair I'd left earlier.

"Did you find Greer?" I asked, almost whispering.

"I think so," Justin answered, putting Dave down gently. "But it was hard, because she's not using her real name, and she doesn't look all that much like the picture you gave me. That's why it took so long."

I glanced over one shoulder, saw Tucker hurl a now-laughing Danny over one shoulder and start toward the back of the house. "Where is she?"

"In some farmhouse, I think. She stays mostly in the cellar."

I shuddered. "Is she being held prisoner?"

Justin sighed. "No. But I think she's scared. She acts nervous and won't come out of the cellar unless it's dark out."

"Where is this farmhouse?" I thought I knew, but there was always a chance I was wrong. It happened, now and then.

Okay, it happened a lot.

"I didn't check out the countryside—but there's a calendar upstairs, in the kitchen, with a picture of a lake on it."

Shiloh, of course. Greer's hometown. It sat on the shores of Flathead Lake.

"Is she alone?" I was still hoping Carmen was with Greer. That would mean she was alive, at least.

"As far as I could tell," Justin said. "She paces a lot and climbs up onto a box every once in a while, trying to see out the cellar window."

Greer had left her car behind, which was one of the reasons I'd been so convinced she'd been abducted. Now I figured she must have fled instead, rented a car or borrowed Carmen's and driven nonstop to reach western Montana as quickly as she had. But if that was true, why hadn't she called Jolie or me to let us know she was safe?

"Are you going there?" Justin asked. His gaze drifted past me, and I knew Tucker was back. He wouldn't see Justin, but he'd probably heard me talking to myself.

I nodded to answer Justin's question.

He leaned forward, covered my hand with his. "Don't," he said. "There's something really off about that place." Then, without saying anything more, he disappeared.

Tucker approached. "Who were you talking to just now?" he asked.

"A dead person," I said, very quietly.

"Gillian?"

I shook my head. "Justin Braydaven."

"The drive-by shooting victim." He pulled back the chair Justin had just vacated and sat down heavily.

"Right," I said.

I didn't like keeping secrets from Tucker, but I wasn't about to tell him Greer was holed up in a farmhouse outside Shiloh—probably the very place she'd run away from, as a teenager, after poisoning her stepfather's supper. I wanted to talk to her before the police did. I wanted to confront her with the information Beverly Pennington had given me, and demand an explanation. This time she wasn't going to get away with the I-don't-want-to-talk-about-it routine. If I was going to help her, she'd have to level with me.

"What did he say?"

There were moments when I wished I hadn't told Tucker I talked to dead people, and that was one of them. I was in a position where I had to lie, and I didn't like it. Not when it was Tucker I had to lie to.

"He wanted to tell me that his dog died," I said.

"Look at me, Moje."

I gulped, met Tucker's gaze. "Why did you insist on telling the kids I'm your girlfriend?" I asked. It was partly a diversion tactic, but I really wanted to hear the answer. "They're bound to repeat it to Allison, along with the news that I was here for supper and you gave me a present, and who knows how she'll react?"

Tucker sighed, tilted his head back, stared up at the star-strewn sky. When he looked at me again, his expression was weary. I remembered that he'd missed a night's sleep, too. "What would you suggest, Moje? Lying to them? Pretending there's nothing going on between you and me?"

"They're *seven,* Tucker. *I* don't even understand what's 'going on' between us. How could they?"

"Kids are a lot smarter than most people think. If you don't tell them the truth, they start speculating. Making things up." He paused, cleared his throat, watched as I tucked away another delicious bite of the steak. "You ought to stay overnight," he said. "You can sleep in the guest room."

"No way," I said.

"Mojo, listen to reason, will you? A crazy woman tried to run over you with a four-wheeler today."

"Tiffany's out of commission."

"And you probably have nineteen *other* mortal enemies waiting to take a whack at you."

"I've got the Glock."

"That is not reassuring. You don't know how to shoot."

I sat up a little straighter. "Actually, I had a lesson this morning."

"Where?"

I gave him the name of the target range. I didn't mention Max Summervale, though.

"One lesson," Tucker pointed out, "does not make you Annie Oakley."

I sat back in my chair. "I can't stay here, Tucker. Not in Allison's house."

"Then at least go and spend the night with Jolie."

"Her dog might eat my dog—or me. I once sat on top of a refrigerator for three hours, just to stay out of his slavering jaws."

Tucker sighed and shook his head. "All right," he said. "I'll call Chelsea and see if she can stay with the kids, and I'll sleep at your place."

"No," I said. Daisy and Danny were upset enough, with Gillian dead, Allison away from home and their grandfather having surgery in the morning. Daisy was afraid of monsters—unless her daddy was close by. A teenage babysitter wasn't going to keep the bogeymen at bay. "I'll be perfectly all right." I leaned down, patted Dave on top of the head. "You'll protect me, won't you, boy?"

CHAPTER FOURTEEN

TUCKER WALKED DAVE AND ME to the car once I'd finished my supper and helped him clean up the mess. He needn't have worried about me being alone in the apartment, although I didn't tell him that, because I wasn't *going* to the apartment, except to pick up the Glock, my phone charger, the bag of kibble and a couple of plastic bowls Dave could eat and drink from.

I was headed to Shiloh, Montana—with one stop before I hit the highway.

I drove straight to Beverly Pennington's condo and, even though it was late and the windows were all dark, I punched her doorbell at least a dozen times. When that didn't raise her, I pounded on the door itself, fit to shake that brass six loose from its shiny screws.

"She's not home," a voice said behind me.

I turned and found myself almost nose-to-nose with the dead security guard I'd let sit in my car during the last visit.

"Where'd she go?" I asked.

The ghost shrugged. "Left here in a hurry, with a couple of suitcases. That's all I know."

"Thanks," I said. I can't say I was surprised that Beverly had decamped. She'd probably given me the newspaper articles to spite Greer and then realized that possession of them implicated her in the blackmail scheme. And if she *knew* about the scheme, then she was part of it.

But maybe she'd simply been called away on some emergency, though that seemed unlikely. Estrangement or none, I didn't think she'd skip town with her son's funeral on the agenda.

I'd make some calls during the long drive to Montana, I decided. Stop at a couple of libraries or Internet cafés along the way, to stretch my legs—and find out whatever I could about Beverly Pennington.

I shifted my focus to the task immediately at hand.

Like most dogs, Dave loved a road trip. He made good company as we cruised north through the night. We got all the way to Kingman before we had to stop and spring for a bargain motel room, which was all my strained budget would allow.

The next morning we got up early, shared a drive-through breakfast and rolled on.

Montana is a long, loooong way from Arizona.

I had to backtrack a couple of times before I finally resorted to buying a map at a service station and figuring out a route.

Standing beside the car, I tried to summon Gillian, but she didn't appear.

I tried Justin. No luck there, either.

Fretful, I put a call through to Helen Erland at the convenience store in Cave Creek, fully expecting a rebuff, since she'd already fired me. Instead, she was cheerfully weepy; according to Vince's public defender, the county's case wouldn't hold water. Vince was coming home.

I had mixed feelings about that, to say the least.

I wasn't sure Vince was Gillian's killer. I *was* sure that he was a scumbag.

"Vince is going to help Chelsea pick out a new car," Helen said out of the blue. Maybe she was trying to convince me that he was a great guy, always ready to help a neighbor. More likely, she was just prattling, high on the news of his impending return to their double-wide castle, and didn't give a rat's ass what I thought. "She's been saving every penny she earns, and Vince wants to make sure she gets a good deal."

I said nothing.

"Well, thanks anyway," Helen said. I heard the write-off in her voice as she added a stiff goodbye. Chattiness aside, she had zero confidence in my abilities as a private detective, and I had only slightly more.

Maybe Tucker was right. Maybe I wasn't cut out to fight crime. And from the sound of things, the real money was in babysitting, anyhow.

It would be good, I thought, to have some time alone, with just Dave for company. No distractions.

Libraries proved to be few and far between on the road less traveled.

And there were no Internet cafés, either.

My cell phone began to ring around 10:00 a.m.— I wasn't in the mood to talk, since I knew who was calling. After that it went off at fifteen-minute intervals, as irritating as a smoke alarm in need of a new battery.

Since I still had a temple-pounder from the knock-down, drag-out with Tiffany the day before, and I was unsettled by the Helen Erland interlude, despite efforts to put her out of my mind, I began to feel downright grouchy. I finally fished the damn thing out from under Dave and scrolled through the message list.

Tucker, Tucker and Tucker again.

I thumbed the off button.

He'd know by now that I wasn't at the apartment in Cave Creek, but on my way to Shiloh. And he would be seriously pissed off. But there wouldn't be much he could do about it, besides rag on me via satellite, which I had just taken the obvious step to prevent.

I drove on.

And on.

Dave and I pulled into a rest stop someplace in Utah.

He peed.

I peed.

I tried to call Jolie, to ask her to check Beverly

Pennington out online, but I got her voice mail. No doubt she was on a crime scene someplace.

We drove on.

And on.

I fixed my thoughts on priority number one: finding Greer.

Dave and I ate lunch on the road, sharing pepperoni sticks I bought at another gas station.

By midafternoon I was missing Tucker and still a long way from Montana.

I switched on my cell phone and listened to roughly nineteen messages, all from him. It was like watching a whole season of some TV series you've already seen.

The last episode summed it all up. And there was even a cliff-hanger.

"Mojo," Tucker said, probably with his teeth clamped together, from the sound of his voice, "*call me.* If you don't, I swear to God I'll put an APB out on you and you'll end up cooling your heels in some shit-heel jail until I feel like bailing you out!"

"He can't do that," I told Dave. "This is America."

Dave looked unconvinced. His floppy ear perked a little; he was listening hard. Trying to puzzle out the human drama.

"Can he?" I asked.

I kid you not. At exactly that moment a siren sounded behind me.

"Shit," I said, glancing in the rearview mirror.

I had the Glock under my front seat. It was harmless, but the state patrolman cruising behind me with the light bar on top of his car flashing bad news probably wouldn't see it that way. I didn't have a permit, and that would be the least of my problems if the gun turned out to be illegal.

Trying to outrun the guy would not be smart, but I briefly considered it anyway. I hadn't had that much sleep, remember.

I pulled over, rolled down my window and sat up straight in the seat, smiling winsomely.

The stater whipped in behind me, got out of his car and ambled my way.

I had my this-is-America speech all ready, just in case Tucker had followed through on his threat to have me busted and held on some trumped-up charge.

"License and registration, please," the patrolman said. He was young, square jawed and good-looking. "Proof of insurance, too."

I got out the necessary cards and papers, which were in the console between the front seats. "Was I speeding?" I asked.

He didn't answer right away. Instead, he examined my driver's license, registration and insurance card, each in their turn, then studied my face.

"Call Tucker," he said.

I stared at him, openmouthed.

He grinned, tugged genially at the brim of his spiffy round stater hat. "If you don't," he said, "I'll have to ask you about the Glock you're probably carrying under the front seat. And I don't want to do that, because it will mean hours and hours of paperwork."

"This is America," I said.

"Last time I looked," the stater agreed affably. And then he just stood there, waiting.

"Can you do this?" I asked, already fumbling for my phone.

"Evidently so," he answered.

I speed-dialed Tucker.

"Hello," he said, and he sounded smug.

I blushed furiously. "Do all you guys know each other?" I demanded in a hissing whisper.

The stater grinned, handed back my license, registration and insurance card, tugged at his hat brim again and walked away.

Tucker chuckled. "It's a brotherhood," he said. "Where are you?"

"Somewhere in Utah," I replied, softening a little. Pissed off as I was, I was glad to hear his voice, too. "Were you *really* going to have me arrested?"

"I was hoping it wouldn't come to that."

"I'm not coming back to Arizona until I've talked to Greer," I said. "In person."

He sighed. "How do you know she's in Shiloh, Moje?" he asked.

"I just do."

"Carmen's been found."

I was still sitting alongside the road, and it was

a good thing. I was so startled that I might have piled right into the ditch if I'd been on the move. "Is she—?"

"No," Tucker said. "Carmen's fine. She's been hiding out with a shirttail relative in Phoenix, scared out of her mind."

"Did she say anything about Greer? About what happened—?"

In my mind's eye I saw Jack Pennington's corpse sprawled on the entryway floor.

"She's not talking," Tucker answered.

"What do you mean, she's not talking? She must have seen something—"

"I mean she's not talking. As in, she's practically catatonic."

I closed my eyes for a moment. "What now?"

"We wait," Tucker said.

I absorbed that, trembling a little, thinking of what Carmen must be going through, but desperately glad she was alive. Dave was so worried that he whimpered and perched his front feet on the console so he could lick my face. Either that, or he'd just developed a taste for concealer.

"Mojo?" Tucker said when I didn't speak.

"I'm here," I said weakly.

"Come home. Allison will be back tomorrow— her dad came through surgery just fine. If you still want to, we'll fly up to Montana together and turn the place upside down looking for your sister."

The stater whizzed by me, tooting his horn in

jaunty farewell. *We're a brotherhood,* the sound seemed to say. *Don't screw with us.*

"I am *not* turning around now, after coming all this way." Tears of frustration trickled down my cheeks, and I didn't bother to wipe them away. "You can have me arrested. You can do anything you want. But one way or another, Tucker Darroch, *I am going to find Greer.*"

"Easy," he said. "I'm on your side, remember?"

"Then why don't you act like it?" I scrubbed at one cheek with the back of my hand, and Dave took care of the other.

"Moje, this is how a person-on-your-side acts. God knows what you could be walking into up there, armed with nothing but moxie and a Glock you don't know how to use. *Let me help you.*"

"You can help me by not engaging in police harassment!"

"All right, all right. It was a little heavy-handed, siccing the state patrol on you, I'll admit that, but I was frantic, Moje. Come home. I promise, we'll fly up to Montana as soon as Allison gets back to take care of the kids."

"No."

Tucker thrust out a sigh. I knew, without seeing him, that he'd shoved a hand through his hair just then. I knew his jaw would be tight and his eyes narrowed. "Please." He ground out the word. "Cut over to Vegas and win a little money on the slots or something. I'll meet you there."

"Meet me in Montana if you want to." I sniffled. "I'll be in Shiloh."

"Moje."

"It's the best offer you're going to get, bucko. If you weren't such a good lover, I'd tell you to take a permanent hike right about now."

He chuckled again. The sound was raspy, reminding me of the way his face felt against mine— and other parts of my anatomy—when he'd been too busy chasing bad guys to shave for a day or two. "Okay," he said. "You win."

I blinked. "I do?"

"Yes. Go to Shiloh. And try to keep a low profile until I get there. One catch, though. If you don't check in with me every few hours, I'm going to get worried. And when I get worried, I do drastic things."

"Like?"

"Like having you busted, for real."

"You wouldn't dare."

"You know I would."

"I'll dump you if you do."

"No, you won't."

"What makes you think that?"

"You said it yourself. I'm too good a lover to throw over. If we were together right now, I'd go down on you and prove my point."

Heat surged through me. My nipples hardened, and I got damp. "I don't have time for phone sex," I said.

He laughed. "I'll be in Shiloh sometime tomorrow. Plan on a wild ride, cowgirl—no phone required."

I groaned.

Tucker laughed again. "Are you sure you don't have time for a little phone sex?" he teased in a low drawl.

At least, I *think* he was teasing. I didn't risk finding out. "I'll call you in four hours," I said. Then I hung up, drew a couple of deep breaths, squirmed on the car seat and got back on the highway.

He didn't call me again.

Good thing. If he had, I probably would have pulled over and stuck both feet against the dashboard while he talked me through two or three noisy climaxes.

Talk about your roadside attraction. *See the Amazing Orgasmic Woman, three miles ahead.*

It took Dave and me another fourteen hours to reach Shiloh, and by the time we pulled into town and checked in to the Lakeside Motel, we were too pooped to look for anybody. I did manage to ask the desk clerk if she'd seen a woman matching Greer's description—blond, slender, cast on her left arm— and she said no.

I figured she was probably lying—Shiloh is the sort of place where everybody knows everybody else—but there wasn't a damn thing I could do about it.

Dave had kibble for supper.

I had a chocolate bar scrounged from the glove compartment of my car.

Once I'd dined, I showered, tossed back the covers on the rent-a-bed and crashed.

It wasn't until the next morning, when I wanted to dress, that I realized I hadn't packed my usual trash-bag suitcase before leaving the apartment in Cave Creek. I was going to have to make do with the sundress and bra I'd been wearing for two days already, at least until I could scope out the local shopping opportunities. I chucked the panties, and not just because I knew Tucker was on his way.

One cannot fight crime in dirty underwear. It's too distracting.

So after Dave lifted his leg next to one of the picnic tables down by the lake and pooped for an encore, we got into the Volvo to cruise. No Wal-Mart and no Target, but there was a place called Nellie's Boutique. Nellie's, a small, narrow store-front that ran deep—all the way back to the alley behind it, as I soon learned—was caught in a time warp, circa 1955. The abandoned movie theater next door only added to the spooky nostalgia.

"Stay here," I told Dave as I got out of the car. As if he was going to crank up the engine and go joyriding or something. I dumped a bottle of water into one of the bowls I'd brought along, so he was good to go, for hydration purposes anyway. And he probably *would* go if I didn't get my butt back there pretty quickly and walk him again.

I'd parked across the street from Nellie's, leaving a window cracked so Dave could breathe, and as I was crossing, I had a totally weird experience—one I could not have predicted, even after making the acquaintance of several dead people and zooming out of my body that day at the shooting range.

For half a heartbeat, maybe less than that, I was back in that same darkened room, but this time there was an image on the screen instead of the spinning spiral. One small, pink ballet slipper, lying forlornly on the ground.

I knew it belonged to Gillian.

In the next moment I slammed back into my body.

I was standing in the middle of the street, with one hand over my mouth.

The honking of a car horn jarred me out of my stupor.

I turned, heart pounding, and waved apologetically to the driver of a muddy pickup truck. The guy behind the wheel, sporting a straw cowboy hat, smiled and raised an index finger in acknowledgment.

I hurried on, heading for Nellie's.

What had just happened here? Had my brain short-circuited, or was it residual fatigue, or the fact that I needed breakfast almost as much as I needed a fresh supply of underwear?

Maybe what I *really* needed was psychotropic medication.

I was understandably shaken, and there would be no making sense of the astral-projection thing until I'd had coffee and protein. I couldn't think straight without breakfast—or without panties.

A little bell jingled over the door as I entered Nellie's.

I made quick work of shopping, selecting two bras, three pairs of nylon panties and several cotton sundresses. A heavy woman with dyed red hair and makeup that looked thick enough to be peeled off her face in a single pull greeted me with a suspicious smile.

"Are you Nellie?" I asked as I forked over my ATM card to pay for the new wardrobe.

"Nellie's been dead for twenty years," she said. "I'm Sally Swenson." She bagged my purchases and handed back my ATM card, after studying my name on the front of it.

It was all I could do not to shinny into a pair of those new panties right there in front of the sales counter, I felt that vulnerable.

"You just passing through Shiloh, Mojo?" Sally inquired. Her tone when she said "Mojo," indicated that she considered it strange, but she didn't seem unfriendly—just curious.

I nodded, reaching for the bags. "Can you tell me where the Severn farm is?" I asked, trying to sound casual.

Sally's eyes widened. "It's out on Route 2, a mile or so past the cemetery," she said. "Nobody lives there now."

I was still light-headed, and I'd broken out in a cold sweat during my out-of-body experience. Normally I'm a pretty quick thinker, but I couldn't come up with a single viable excuse for wanting to visit an empty farmhouse.

"Oh," I said, hoping I looked smarter than I sounded—or felt.

Sally shuddered, as though a veil of cobwebs had just dropped from the ceiling and settled over her. "Somebody ought to burn that place to the ground," she said. "Nothing left but rats and bad memories. Kids go out there to drink beer and smoke dope. It's a public menace, that house, practically falling in on itself. Ask me, it would be a good thing if it did."

There were so many questions I wanted to ask, but I was a little off my game. I gripped the counter edge with one hand and leaned against it a little.

"Are you all right?" Sally asked.

"Fine," I lied. "What happened to Mr. and Mrs. Severn...and their daughter—what was her name?"

"Fred died. Alice moved away after that—married a forest ranger or something. Rick's been in and out of jail since that accident of his." Sally narrowed her eyes and peered at me. "What's your connection to the Severns, anyhow? You're not a reporter, are you? Or somebody from one of those tabloid TV shows?"

"I knew—Molly. Their older daughter."

"Well, if you have any idea where she is," Sally said, "you'd better tell the cops. She's wanted for attempted murder."

"I haven't seen her in a while," I replied.

Sally looked downright suspicious now. "She ruined a lot of people's lives, that Molly Stillwell. Fred senior's, certainly. She *poisoned* that poor man. Alice all but dried up and blew away, trying to take care of him. And as for Rick and Tessa—"

I grabbed hold of the name. "Tessa. What happened to her?"

"In and out of drug rehab. Married and divorced a couple of times. Last I heard, she was in a mental hospital in Missoula. Slashed her wrists with a broken bottle and almost bled to death. The police found her in an alley."

"Thanks," I said, feeling numb now, as well as dizzy.

I left, carrying the bags to the car.

Dave was glad to see me, but then, Dave was *always* glad to see me, which is definitely not the case with everybody.

I stood a moment next to the driver's door, breathing deeply.

Once I was inside the car, I snatched a pair of pink panties from the stash, jerked off the price tag and, after checking in all directions to make sure I wouldn't be observed, wriggled into them.

"There," I told Dave. "That's better."

Tucker was due to hit town anytime now, I reminded myself. The panties would be sliding back down around my ankles as soon as we were alone, and as badly as I'd wanted to put them on, I probably wouldn't protest. In the meantime, though, it was good not to feel naked.

Dave and I headed for the local pancake house, which had outside seating—picnic tables under a dented metal awning. Together we consumed the three-egg special with a short stack and crisp bacon on the side, although Dave's appetite was a little more delicate than mine, since he'd had kibble back at the motel.

We piled back into the Volvo and drove up and down every street in Shiloh. It didn't take long, since there weren't all that many, but I got a good sense of the place.

Next I found Route 2 and followed it for miles, but if the Severn farmhouse was there, I didn't see it. It could have been at the end of any number of dirt roads, with rusted rural mailboxes teetering at their weedy bases. Sally had mentioned a cemetery, but I couldn't find that, either.

I didn't think I'd go down in history as one of the great detectives.

Finally I turned around and headed back toward Shiloh, intending to ask directions—of anybody but Sally Swenson—to the Severn place.

There was a grassy, tree-shaded park in the center of town, fronting the lake, and it looked inviting. I decided to stop there and let my dog do his business while I thought about who I ought to approach, and what I'd say when I did.

I clipped Dave's leash to his collar and grabbed the half roll of toilet paper I'd snitched from a public restroom on the drive up from Arizona in case his business happened to be the goopy kind.

There was a modest stone fountain in the middle of the park, and an old man in overalls, a long-sleeved shirt and a billed cap sat on the edge, smiling as Dave lapped at the water. I was pretty sure the codger was alive, but the clothes made me wonder. They could have harkened from a variety of decades.

"Hello," I said.

"Howdy," he answered. "You from around here?"

"No," I replied. "Arizona."

"Long way from home."

I nodded. Dave was really sucking up the water; the sound nearly drowned out the old man's voice. "This is a nice park," I said.

"We like it."

Not a talker, then. I'd have to prod him a little.

"I guess you've probably lived around Shiloh for a long time."

He tilted his head back to study me more closely. "All my life," he said.

"You must have known the Severn family, then."

He nodded. "Talk about a bad-luck bunch," he mused.

"I've been trying to find their house," I said.

"Why would you want to do that? Nobody's there."

"I'm in real estate," I replied, inspired.

"You couldn't get a plugged nickel for the place, even if you put a dump-truck load of cash into renovating it first."

"I'm still curious." *And I think my sister is hiding in the cellar.*

The old man shrugged. Took a little notepad from his overall pocket, along with the stub of a pencil, which he touched to the tip of his tongue before drawing what appeared to be a crude map. "Mind you don't fall through a floor or something, snooping around out there," he said.

Blushing because he'd pegged me for a snooper, I studied the map. Three tiny crosses indicated the aforementioned cemetery, and he'd drawn a tiny stick house at the junction of two roads.

Dave stopped lapping at the fountain water and sniffed the grass around my feet.

"I'll be careful," I promised belatedly.

"I hope that's true," the man replied. "Because nothing else you said was. You some kind of cop or insurance investigator or something?"

I shook my head.

He gave a good-natured little snort of amusement. Then he spat, narrowly missing the dog, who didn't seem to mind. I let Dave off the leash, since there was nobody around besides the old man and me, but I was watching Farmer Brown from under my lashes the whole time.

About that time, Dave let out a yelp, and I looked up to see that he'd wandered some distance away. Now he was darting toward me, with two rottweilers on his trail, like the hounds of hell, closing fast.

Dave hit me like a bullet, scrambled right up my body. I clasped him in both arms, but the rottweilers kept coming. They were planning on having Dave for breakfast—and they'd chew right through me to get to him.

I looked around for an escape route and made two split-second determinations.

1) The car was too far away to offer refuge.

2) The old man was nowhere in sight, so I couldn't expect any help from him.

Dave clawed at me, frantic with fear, trying to climb on top of my head.

Holding him tightly, I stepped into the fountain, barely noticing the chill of the water as it bit into my legs. Gripping Dave in one arm, I used the other and both feet to climb the slippery statue in the center.

The rottweilers barked and snarled, their massive front paws on the concrete edge of the base of the fountain, their haunches poised to spring.

"Help!" I screamed. The statue was greased with mossy scum, Dave was wriggling in my all too tenuous grasp and I figured we had mere seconds before we slid down into the reach of those big teeth.

Out of the corner of one eye I saw a squad car screech to a halt at the edge of the park. A policeman leaped out, ran toward us. But someone else got there first. A man I didn't immediately recognize, being in a state of wholesale hysteria.

Tucker.

Reaching the base of the fountain, he grabbed the rottweilers by their collars and dragged them back. They struggled a little, but calmed when he spoke to them in a low, commanding voice.

The policeman huffed up, gun drawn. He spoke breathlessly into the radio mic on his left shoulder. "Eleanor," he growled, probably addressing the dispatcher at headquarters, "you tell Purvis those demon hounds of his got out again, and they've run some poor woman and a little dog clean up to the top of the statue in the park fountain! If he doesn't get over here, pronto, I might just shoot the both of these mutts!" A pause followed, while I clung to the statue and Dave clung to me, whimpering now. I stared down at Tucker, so glad he was there, I couldn't even speak. "Yes, Eleanor," the cop went on, "I *know* that I am the vice president of the Shiloh Animal Protection League. Call Purvis *now*. These dogs are a menace, and I mean to cite him good this time!"

Dave and I slid helplessly down the stone effigy.

Purvis's dogs growled ominously, but Tucker restrained them with ease.

Even with Tucker and the policeman there, I was afraid to climb out of the fountain. I was wet to the skin, which left my sundress see-through, since the fabric was so thin. It clung to me.

A person thinks crazy thoughts when they've nearly been devoured by rottweilers.

Here's what came to my mind.

Good thing I stopped by Nellie's for new underwear.

CHAPTER FIFTEEN

"MOJE," TUCKER SAID, when Purvis had rushed over
from his auto repair shop and collected his rottweilers, along with a loud lecture and a citation
from the policeman, "you can get out of the fountain now." He held out his arms to take Dave.

Sniffling, I buried my face in Dave's wet hide for
a moment, clinging to him. Looking back, I think
that was the moment he became my dog. We'd
bonded for good, in a moment of peril.

"Moje," Tucker repeated, his voice gentle and
quiet.

I surrendered Dave, then climbed out of the
water, dripping. I sneezed.

"I'm real sorry about this, ma'am," the policeman
said. His name, according to the tag on his uniform
shirt, was Joe Fletcher, and he was dark haired and
lanky, his features pleasantly rough-hewn. He
looked to be about Greer's age, and I wondered if
he'd lived in Shiloh long enough to know her.

I didn't get a chance to question him, but he gave
me his card, which I passed on to Tucker.

With a nod to Joe Fletcher, Tucker slipped the card into his shirt pocket, put an arm around me, carrying Dave in the other one, and squired us toward a rented SUV waiting on the far side of the park. The driver's door was standing open—that's how I knew it was his.

When Tucker arrived on a Mojo scene, he was always in a hurry.

"Thanks," I managed, shivering as a chilly breeze rolled up from the lake and made my wet clothes clammy.

"You need to dry off," Tucker said, ever practical.

"I have some clothes in the car," I said, referring to the Volvo.

"I'll get them," Tucker promised.

He settled Dave and me in the SUV, cranked on the heat and sprinted across to the Volvo to collect my shopping bags from Nellie's. I sat shivering in the front seat of his rental, grateful the seats were leather, not cloth, watching the windshield fog up.

Once Tucker was back with the bags—he'd paused to pick my purse up off the ground by the fountain on his way back—we headed for the Lake-side Motel.

There, inside my room, Tucker started a hot shower and peeled off my wet clothes. I was sneezing again, and my sinuses were already clogging up.

"I thought this would be different," I said.

"Me, too," Tucker answered, grinning slightly. "Get into the shower. Your teeth are chattering."

The water stung at first, but the steam was heavenly. Gradually the shivering stopped, but the old sinus passages didn't cooperate. About the last thing I needed was a bad cold—I had an investigation to conduct—but life, as John Lennon once said, is what happens while you're making other plans.

When I got out of the shower and left the bathroom, wrapped in a towel, Tucker had brought his stuff in from the SUV and dried Dave off, too. The dog was lying on the floor, cosseted in a couple of towels and the extra blanket from the closet shelf, with two mismatched eyes and his bent ear visible.

Tucker tossed me a sweatshirt from his suitcase, and I pulled it over my head. He'd turned back the covers on the bed, and I crawled in, miserable.

"I need to find Greer," I complained thickly. "I can't be lying around nursing a head cold."

Tucker leaned over me, pressing his hands into either side of my pillow, and kissed me on the forehead. I'd been up for a different kind of action entirely, but I knew, despite my protests, that it was going to have to wait. Along with a lot of other things—like tracking down my sister.

"You're sick," he said reasonably. "Get some rest."

"How could it have happened so fast?" I asked, whining a little. I figured I was entitled. "One plunge into a fountain, and I've got pneumonia?"

"It didn't happen fast," Tucker told me sagely. "And it's not pneumonia. It's probably been coming on for a while." He gave me another smack, this time on the end of my nose. "I'm going out for some stuff to make you feel better, and I'll be back before you miss me. In the meantime, try to rest."

I nodded. My throat began to ache, and my eyes were burning. My head felt twice its normal size, stuffed with something dry and scratchy, like old work socks. I closed my eyes, and when I opened them again, Tucker was back, slathering mentholated rub on my chest. Again, not the kind of chest rubbing I'd had in mind.

"Brought you some chicken soup," he said, once I was thoroughly mentholated. He propped some pillows behind me, and I sat up to sip the soup from a foam cup.

Emotion made my eyes sting again. If I wasn't careful, I was going to bond with Tucker, just as I had with Dave. Dangerous ground. Dave, being a dog, wasn't likely to reject me. Tucker, being a man, might do exactly that.

Sitting on the side of my bed, he rubbed my tears away with the pad of one thumb. There was no sound except for Dave snoring blissfully in the safety of his blanket and me slurping soup.

"Your timing is pretty good," I told Tucker, my voice heavy with congestion. "If you hadn't come along when you did, Dave and I would both be in bloody chunks by now."

"You're the one who saved Dave," Tucker told me. He paused, his mouth tilting up on one side in

one of those grins that always made me want to kiss
him. "I've never seen anybody climb the statue in
the center of a fountain before. Especially not with
a dog in one arm."

I smiled a little, though the memory made me
shiver again. "Pure adrenaline," I said, making a
stab at modesty.

"Finish your soup."

It was the kind with the short, stiff noodles
floating in it—my favorite—but I didn't have much
of an appetite. "When did you get to town?"

"Probably about five minutes before you headed
for the top of that statue," Tucker answered, rustling
in a paper bag on the nightstand, bringing out a
bottle of daytime cold medicine.

"Did you bring your laptop?" If I couldn't gum-
shoe, I could at least cruise the Internet. Maybe dig
up some stray bits of information that way.

Tucker tested my forehead for fever with the
back of one hand. "It's on the desk," he said.

"Can I borrow it?"

He sighed. "Sure," he said, and got up to retrieve
the laptop. Just before setting it on my thighs, he
pushed the button and it began to boot up.

"How are Daisy and Danny?" I asked while we
waited.

"Fine," Tucker said.

I knew he was hedging. "And Allison?"

"Scared," he admitted. "Vince Erland's out of jail."

"Helen told me," I said, watching as Tucker

turned the laptop around to type in his password. "You'll be glad to know she fired me."

"Now, why would I be glad about that?"

"Because you didn't want me interfering in the case."

He leaned forward, kissing my forehead. "Interfere all you want. God knows the *official* investigation isn't going anywhere."

"Any improvement in Carmen's condition?"

Tucker's jaw tightened. "Yes," he said. "According to her, she was working in the kitchen when she heard a loud argument in the front of the house, along with a scuffle. She went to see what was going on, and saw Greer shoot Jack Pennington. Greer was in a panic, and so was Carmen. Greer asked Carmen to drive her to a private airstrip, and she did. After that, she—Carmen, I mean—got scared and drove around in some kind of fugue state for hours. When she came to her senses, she was sitting in a cousin's driveway, with no memory of how she got there."

"You found the pilot," I deduced after absorbing all the Carmen info, watching Tucker through my eyelashes as I navigated to my Internet server's Web site and entered my password.

Tucker nodded. "He dropped Greer off outside Missoula. She had a rental car waiting, and took off right away."

"Are the Feds involved?"

"Not yet," Tucker admitted. "But it's imminent."

I nodded. Typed Beverly Pennington's name into Google, tempted, as always, to try out the "I'm Feeling Lucky" button. I didn't really expect to find anything.

Imagine my shock when I did.

"What?" Tucker asked, evidently catching my expression. When I didn't answer right away, he moved around me and peered at the laptop screen.

Beverly Pennington had something like three hundred references on the Web. Even assuming that most of them were about people who just happened to have the same name, it was intriguing.

I quickly discovered that her maiden name was Quaffly, and since there aren't a lot of Quafflys out there, it was an easy leap to her high school's online yearbook.

"What do you know?" I murmured, stunned. "Beverly graduated from Shiloh High School. She was prom queen, head cheerleader..."

Tucker frowned at the screen. "Quite a coincidence," he said.

"I don't believe in coincidences," I replied. Beverly was some ten years older than Greer, but they must have been acquainted. "Did I mention that I stopped by Mrs. Pennington the first's condo on my way here, and a dead security guard told me she'd packed her bags and split in a big hurry?"

"No," Tucker said, drawing out the word a little. "You didn't."

I typed in "Molly Stillwell" next, but all that

came up were the newspaper articles Beverly had given me. Molly had run away and left Shiloh far behind long before she could graduate from high school, but there were several undergrad pictures of her on the yearbook site and they confirmed what I already knew.

Greer and Molly were one and the same person.

I set the laptop aside and tried to get out of bed. Greer was hiding in the cellar of the Severn farmhouse—I knew that—and I had to get to her. I couldn't wait until I got over my cold, or for anything else.

"Whoa," Tucker said.

"I know where Greer is," I told him. "I tried to find the place today, but I couldn't, and then the whole Dave-and-the-rottweilers thing happened—"

"You're not going anywhere," Tucker informed me. "Tell me where she is, and *I'll* find her."

"Oh, sure. And you'll arrest her while you're at it! Or she'll see you and take off—"

"Moje, she's a *murder suspect.*"

"She's my sister!" I managed to wriggle past him, but when I got to my feet, I swayed. Whoa. *Way* woozy.

Tucker stood and steadied me. "Okay," he said. "Okay."

"Okay what?" I demanded.

"Okay, we'll go hunt down your sister. Together."

I felt for pockets I didn't have, since I was wearing Tucker's sweatshirt and nothing else. The map the old man in the park had drawn for me had probably been ruined when Dave and I plunged into the fountain, but it had been a pretty simple sketch, and I remembered it clearly.

"Let's go," I said.

"What about Dave?" Tucker asked reasonably. "He's had a rough day."

"He can come with us," I answered, figuring that would be less traumatic for the dog than staying alone in a motel room.

I put on dry underwear and another sundress and we headed for Tucker's rental. The sky, summer-perfect only a little while ago, was dark with rain clouds, and the wind was brisk.

It figured.

We found the house after about half an hour of searching—a small, gray, gloomy-looking place, curiously black-and-white, like the shack in *The Wizard of Oz* before Dorothy steps outside into glaring Technicolor and realizes she's not in Kansas anymore. The structure was engulfed in weeds, and there were tire tracks in what passed for a yard, but no sign of the car that had made them.

"We should have brought a machete," Tucker remarked as we made our way slowly through the grass jungle to a sagging front porch. "I keep expecting to run across a lost tribe of pygmies or hobbits or something."

The sky rumbled again.

Dave had wisely elected to stay in the car, but he

was peering through the windshield, his forefeet braced against the dashboard, probably willing us to come back.

I cupped my hands around my mouth. "Greer!" I called. "It's me, Mojo!"

The first spatters of rain began to fall, tapping at the tar-paper roof.

The deep grass rippled—maybe Tucker's pygmies/hobbits were stirring.

Thunder exploded overhead like a bomb, and I heard a faint yelp of dismay from Dave.

"I'm going in," I said, eyeing the house with some trepidation.

"Hold it," Tucker protested. "The floors are probably rotten. Let me go first." With that, he skirted the hideout, heading for the back door.

I scrambled after him, hoping my cold wouldn't escalate to black plague.

Hoping to find Greer.

A rusted-out wringer washer stood at a tilt in the yard, next to a leaning clothesline pole. I tried to square the Greer I knew, living the high life in Scottsdale, with the girl who had called this place home.

How she must have hated it.

Tucker was already inside the house when I caught up to him.

The kitchen was dark and smelled of mice and mildew, and the linoleum floor was peeling. The ceiling sagged, weighted with years of hard rains and deep snow—not to mention despair. Dust and

cobwebs hung like swags from corner to corner—
everything was filthy. The ancient gas stove, the
harvest-gold refrigerator, the chipped porcelain sink
with its pipes dangling like entrails, the cheap table
in the center of the room, all those things added to
the gloomy mood.

I stood on the threshold, hugging myself. I
wondered which place at that table had been Frederick Severn Sr.'s, and if Greer had really dosed his
supper with insecticide.

And if she had, why?

"The cellar," I said. "Justin told me she was
hiding in the cellar."

"Stay where you are," Tucker said, approaching
a door in the far corner, next to the fridge. "This
floor feels pretty spongy. God knows what kind of
shape the cellar steps are in."

I tested the floor with a toe and immediately
followed Tucker. He outweighed me by at least
forty pounds, so I figured if he didn't fall through,
I wouldn't either. Simple physics.

"We should have brought a flashlight," I said.

"Thank you, Nancy Drew," Tucker retorted,
clearly displeased to find me at his elbow. There
were only three steps leading down into the cellar,
as it turned out, and they were concrete.

At the bottom I peered over Tucker's shoulder,
waiting for my eyes to adjust to the dim light.

I saw a sleeping bag, a camping lantern, a bag
of Oreos and the newest issue of *Town & Country*.

But Greer was nowhere in sight.

"Maybe she's hiding in the woods or something," I said thickly. My sinuses were almost completely closed now, and the dank, dusty air in that cellar did nothing to help. "I should have come alone."

Tucker and I snooped a little, but we didn't find much. Obviously *someone* had been staying in the Severns' cellar. I knew it was Greer, but Tucker was probably thinking the sleeping bag and the lantern could belong to anybody.

Even without the copy of *Town & Country,* the Oreos would have been all the proof I needed. I checked the magazine for a subscription label, but there wasn't one.

"I'm calling Joe Fletcher," Tucker said.

"No," I argued, catching hold of his hand. "Not yet. *Please.* Just give me a chance to talk to Greer—"

"I'm not leaving you alone here, if that's what you're thinking. Suppose whoever has been camping here *isn't* Greer? What if it's some drifter?"

"How many drifters do you know who read *Town & Country?*" I countered.

Tucker gave me one of those looks that singe off your eyelashes.

I stuck out my chin. "We could wait."

"Right," Tucker said. "You're sick. It's raining the proverbial cats and dogs. And if your sister has been hanging out in this hole, ten to one she's not coming back."

"She's around," I insisted. "Somewhere."

"Or she's moved on."

Another clap of thunder shook the sky. Dust and dead bugs drifted down from the rafters overhead.

I thought about Dave, alone in the car and probably terrified.

Tucker took me by the hand and pulled me up the concrete steps, through the dismal kitchen and out into the rain. We ran for the car, but we got soaked anyway.

Dave was pathetically glad to see us, whimpering and trying to lick our faces—first mine, then Tucker's.

Neither of us spoke all during the drive back to the motel.

There, Tucker dosed me with a couple of aspirin and a capful of the cold medicine he'd bought earlier. He peeled my clothes off, put the sweatshirt on me again and put me to bed.

I was already drifting off when I heard him turn on the shower.

When I woke up, hours later, Tucker was stretched out beside me, naked and warm and sound asleep. Dave sprawled across my ankles, and the room was dim. The TV murmured, low, somewhere in the shadows, casting bluish light into the room.

"Tuck?" I nudged him.

He stirred, sat up and yawned. Grinned sleepily, his hair mussed. "Hey," he said.

"Hey," I said back.

Dave unpinned my ankles and walked the length

of my body to lave my face with his sloppy tongue a couple of times.

Tucker laughed and lifted the dog off me, set him gently on the floor. Got up to give him kibble and refill his water dish in the bathroom.

"Feeling better?" Tucker asked while Dave munched happily on the kibble.

"I must be," I said. "Because I'm starved."

Tucker ran splayed fingers through his hair. His clothes were drying on the back of a chair nearby, and he gave them a reluctant glance. I stayed where I was, enjoying the view. "Then I guess I'd better go scout up a pizza or something," he said.

"Or," I said, "we could call in the order and have crazy, sweaty, screaming sex while we wait for the delivery."

Tucker arched an eyebrow, as though considering the pros and cons of the idea, grinned and then dived back into bed.

An hour later we got around to ordering the pizza.

CHAPTER SIXTEEN

THE KNOCK AT our motel-room door seemed pretty forceful for a pizza-delivery person.

I scrambled out of bed and ducked into the bathroom, since I was bare-ass naked, and the Lakeside wasn't the kind of place where they provide robes. Tucker did the honors—after pulling on a pair of jeans and tugging a T-shirt over his head.

It was—and *wasn't*—a surprise to see Joe Fletcher, his hair dripping with rain, cross the threshold with a pizza box in his hands. Small-town cops do double duty in a lot of ways, but I wouldn't have thought delivering the pepperoni special with extra cheese would be in his job description.

I was beyond curious, and I briefly considered fashioning myself a towel toga so I could leave the bathroom without being charged with indecent exposure, but the selection on hand would have left a lot of skin showing. So all I could do was peek around the edge of the door with my ears perked.

"I've heard of some inventive ways of supplementing municipal budgets," Tucker remarked, getting out his wallet to reimburse Fletcher and, probably, to flash his badge. "But this is a new one. Join us?"

Joe Fletcher's mouth lifted at one corner in a laconic attempt at a grin. "I've eaten, thanks. Happened to be in the pizza joint having supper when the order came in. Since I wanted to talk to both of you anyway, I decided to run it over here."

"Have a seat," Tucker said after giving Fletcher his name.

I tried to get Tucker's attention, catching at him with my gaze and pulling. I wanted clothes so I could participate in the conversation without calling from behind the bathroom door.

He dug a sundress out of the bag from Nellie's and brought it to me while Joe Fletcher pulled back the only chair in the room and sat down at the desk.

Dave approached and licked his shoes.

I scrambled into the dress, sans underwear, and wished I'd had a chance to make the bed before Fletcher arrived. The covers looked as though they'd been caught in a wind tunnel, and it wouldn't have taken a trained law enforcement officer to figure out why.

Joe bent to ruffle Dave's ears. "Close call with those rottweilers today, buddy," he said with gruff affection. "Good thing Ms. Sheepshanks is a quick thinker."

I'd been pretty traumatized at the park myself, and didn't remember introducing myself to the lawman, but it wouldn't have been any great trick to find out my name. One call to the desk clerk at the Lakeside would have done it, or Sally Swenson could have gotten on the horn as soon as I left Nellie's and told him there was a stranger in town, asking a lot of questions about the Severn family.

Joe stood when I entered the room, a point in his favor. Tucker, meanwhile, had opened the pizza box and helped himself to a slice, severing several long strands of cheese in the process.

Dave, attracted by the excellent begging prospects, left Joe to trot over to Tucker.

"First thing I'd like to do," Joe said after shaking my hand, "is apologize for what happened at the park today. Purvis took the dogs out to his brother's place in the country—after I wrote him a ticket— so you won't run into them again."

"Thanks," I replied, sitting down on the edge of the sex-tousled bed, since there was nowhere else to light.

Joe sat down again, once I was seated, and cleared his throat. "I hear by the grapevine that you were asking about the Severn place," he said.

I nodded.

Tucker offered me a slice of pizza, and I took it. I wanted to make a professional impression on Joe Fletcher for some reason, but the condition of the bed tanked the whole plan. Besides, I was ravenous, so I went ahead and stuffed my face.

"I'm curious as to why you'd be interested," Joe told me.

Tucker, apparently in a cooperative, law-enforce-ment-brotherhood kind of mood, fetched the newspa-per clippings off the bureau and handed them to Joe.

Joe scanned them.

"Oh," he said.

"Tell him about Greer," Tucker said, elbowing me. "Or I will."

I had to swallow a mouthful of pizza first. While I was working on that, I gave Tucker a sidelong glare.

"Greer?" Joe asked, obviously puzzled.

I gulped, nearly choking. "My sister," I said.

"I've never heard the name."

"She would have been Molly Stillwell to you," I explained, belatedly returning Tucker's elbow jab with one of my own.

Joe's face changed. "Oh, Lord," he said.

I felt a little leap of hope, spawned by something in Joe's expression. "You knew her?"

"Sure did. We went to middle school together."

I nodded to indicate the clippings, still in Joe's hand, though he seemed to have forgotten he was holding them. "According to those articles, she was suspected of lacing her stepfather's supper with poison."

"If she did," Joe said, a faraway and thoughtful look in his eyes, "she had good reason."

My heartbeat quickened, and my breath caught. I was super-glad I hadn't taken another nosh of pizza, because I probably would have needed the Heimlich maneuver. "What do you mean?"

"My uncle Roy had this job before I did," he said, still reflective. "In those days, people didn't talk about 'other people's business' much, but I knew my uncle went out to the Severn place a couple of times, on domestic-violence calls. Molly was one of those kids who were always in trouble for one thing or another, shoplifting and the like." He glanced down at the articles, then set them aside on the desk. "You already know what happened to Rick. Tessa—the youngest one—she must have gotten the worst of it, though." Joe's face was bleak, and he ran a hand down the length of it. Shook his head. "That girl always looked like a deer caught in the headlights. She got so fidgety that Alice homeschooled her."

I bit my lower lip.

Tucker started his third slice of pizza and didn't contribute to the conversation.

"Do you think Mr. Severn might have been abusing Tessa?" I ventured. "Maybe Gr—Molly, too?"

"It's a possibility," Joe said.

A short, tense silence fell.

Tucker elbowed me again.

I told Joe about Greer's identity switch, Jack Pennington's death and her flight from Scottsdale.

"You know where she is?" Joe asked.

I hesitated.

Tucker picked up the ball and ran with it. "Indications are she's been staying in the basement of the Severn farmhouse," he said.

I rammed him with my shoulder.

A sad grin moved in Joe's brown eyes, but didn't touch his mouth. Watching me intently, he raised both eyebrows and drawled, "Clearly, you didn't want me to know that. Why?"

"Because you'll arrest her," I said. "And I wanted to talk to her first. This is a delicate situation."

"In what way?" Joe persisted quietly.

"Someone's blackmailing her," I answered after mulling over my options—which were nonexistent, it turned out—for a few moments. "And they've made some pretty heavy threats. Jack Pennington—the man Greer shot—was probably in on it. Maybe he was even the ringleader, but the original information must have come out of Shiloh."

"I'd bet on Rick Severn," Joe said, surprising me. "But he was killed in a jail fight almost three months ago. Believe me, if he found out where Molly was, and that she had money, he'd have wanted a piece of it, whether he was behind bars or not."

"Do you remember a girl named Beverly Quaffly?" I asked.

"She was Rick's high school girlfriend," Joe said. "Her dad broke it up, though. Sent Bev off to stay with relatives two days after graduation and, small towns being what they are, there was some talk that she might have been pregnant. The whole Quaffly family moved away not too long after they put Bev on the afternoon bus for Missoula. Far as

I know, she's never been back here, and neither have they."

Beverly had been Rick Severn's *girlfriend?* After seeing that house, and knowing the lifestyle to which Mrs. Pennington the first had become accustomed, post-Shiloh, it was hard to imagine her with a wrong-side-of-the-tracks bad boy like Rick.

On the other hand, bad boys are notoriously appealing, especially to girls barely out of high school.

Tucker's cell phone rang. He stopped eating pizza to answer.

I watched the color drain from his face as he listened.

"Something wrong?" Joe asked kindly when the call ended and Tucker just sat there, staring into space.

"Tucker?" I prompted.

He came to life. Got to his feet.

"Tucker?" I repeated, scared to death.

"Danny fell in the pool," he said, moving around the room like a sleepwalker on speed, gathering his stuff, his gaze never connecting with mine. Dave followed him fretfully from place to place. "Chelsea pulled him out, thank God, but he's in intensive care at Phoenix Children's Hospital, and he hasn't regained consciousness."

I put a hand to my mouth, tried to stand. My knees failed me, and I dropped back onto the edge of the bed.

Tucker finally located me with his eyes. "We have to go," he said.

I was crying silently. And I shook my head.

"Mojo," Tucker said, "I don't have time to argue with you."

"Go," I murmured.

"Come with me," he said gruffly.

Joe cleared his throat again and looked away, a man wishing he was elsewhere.

"I can't," I said.

"Why?"

The Darroch family would close ranks around Danny, and that was as it should be. But there was no place for me in that circle. I'd be an intruder, an outsider, someone who could only get in the way.

"Because I don't belong," I whispered.

Tucker didn't understand; I could see that in his face. His son had nearly drowned, and he had to get to him. And here I was, balking at going along.

"Go," I repeated.

He left.

Dave followed him to the door and whimpered when it closed in his face.

"I'm really sorry," Joe said, and I knew he wasn't just talking about Danny.

I sat with my eyes closed, listening to Tucker's SUV start up with a roar and screech out of the lot behind the Lakeside Motel.

"Is there anything I can do?" Joe asked quietly.

I nodded, and when I could speak, I said, "Yes. My car is still at the park. Could you take me over there, so I can pick it up?"

"Sure thing," Joe said.

Sure thing, I thought.

No such animal.

I KNEW JOE WOULD HEAD straight for the Severn place as soon as he dropped Dave and me off at the Volvo, but I didn't dare follow, not right away anyhow. Given the news of Danny's accident and Tucker's immediate departure for the nearest airport, my thought processes seemed to be short-circuiting all around. But I did have the presence of mind to know Joe would spot me if I tailed him too quickly, so I waited.

When half an hour had passed, I stopped cruising the streets of Shiloh and headed out of town.

Dave, who usually would have had his head between the seats, drooling on the console, was curled disconsolately on the backseat. Every once in a while he gave a sad little whine, low in his throat.

He was yearning for Tucker.

And so was I.

And there was nothing to be done about it— except wonder if I'd done the right thing, letting Tucker go back to Arizona alone.

My heart ached for him, for Allison, for Daisy.

And especially for Danny.

I stopped at the all-night market, bought a flashlight and batteries, and drove slowly along the winding country road Tucker and I had followed earlier that day. The rain had eased up, but there was mud, and I almost got stuck several times. I took a couple of wrong turns, but when I saw Joe's squad car lights flashing in the distance, I knew I'd found my way.

I parked, squinting through the windshield at the house. It was dark, but the cellar window was at the rear, and wouldn't be visible from the overgrown driveway.

I looked back, saw Dave crawl off the backseat and onto the floor and huddle there, crying softly.

"Everything's going to be all right," I told him, hoping it was true.

When I turned around again, to open the Volvo door and get out, I almost screamed.

Danny Darroch was standing just outside my car, clad in a swimming suit, dripping wet.

"*No,*" I whispered, staring, fumbling for the door latch.

Danny retreated a step, his eyes enormous. He spoke when I got out of the car, but I didn't hear his voice with my ears—it was an echo, inside my head.

I want my dad.

It was all I could do to remain upright. I wanted to drop to my knees on the muddy ground, double over and beat at the earth with my fists, but that wasn't an option.

"He's on his way home, Danny," I said.

It was raining again.

Danny wavered, like a reflection, and I realized

I could see *through* him, as though he'd been pro-
jected onto the night itself. I hadn't met that many
ghosts, up close and personal, but the ones I *had* encountered were all as solid as anybody else.

Did that mean—please, God—that Danny wasn't
dead?

I took a step toward him.

Don't touch me, he said in his silent voice.

My face was wet with tears. "Okay," I answered
softly. "You're dreaming, Danny. You're only
dreaming. Go back to—" I paused. "Go back to
your body."

Hope filled his small, freckled face. *I'm dreaming?*

I nodded.

He smiled, and then he was gone.

I fell back against the side of my car, one hand
pressed to my heart.

Rain pelted me, drenching my clothes and hair,
sogging up my shoes, washing away my tears. I'm
not sure how long I stood there, unable to move.

A sound from inside the house jolted me out
of my shock.

A shout?

A gunshot?

I couldn't be sure.

I opened the car door again, grabbed the Glock
case from under the seat and tried to remember how
Max had loaded a similar weapon at the shooting
range.

Joe Fletcher had been inside the Severn house

for too long, since I'd given him a half hour head start and then made the trip myself, using up another thirty minutes at least, because of the muddy roads and the wrong turns. Yet his squad car was still sitting there, with the lights whirling on top.

I opened the glove compartment, brought out the box of hollow-point bullets Bubba had sold me along with the Glock. Every few seconds I looked out the car window for Danny, but he was nowhere in sight.

I began to sweat, even though I was wet to the skin.

But I extracted the magazine from the Glock, loaded it with bullets and drew a deep breath. Holding the gun in my right hand, with the flashlight I'd purchased earlier pinned to my side with my elbow, I got out of the car and headed around the side of the farmhouse, toward the back.

A dim light glowed from the cellar window.

My heartbeat picked up speed.

I crept to the door, praying it wouldn't creak on its hinges.

It did.

I flipped on the flashlight, hoping to avoid the soft places in the kitchen floor. Below me, I heard voices—a woman's, a man's—but I couldn't identify them, or make out the words.

The entrance to the cellar stood open.

I tightened my grasp on the Glock, my finger already hooked in the trigger, and tried to see below.

You don't need a gun. This is Greer. Your sister.

That's what my brain said. My body kept the Glock in a death grip.

I moved onto the top step, bent to peer into the cellar.

Joe Fletcher was lying on the floor, groaning, his head bloody. I didn't know if he'd been shot or bludgeoned with something, but he was conscious. His gaze connected with mine, and he seemed to be willing me backward, out of the kitchen, out of the house, away.

Greer couldn't have done this violence—could she?

But she'd shot Jack Pennington. If Joe had scared her badly enough, she might have reacted instinctively.

Joe closed his eyes, shook his head slightly.

I tightened my hold on the Glock and stepped full into the cellar.

Beverly Pennington was sitting cross-legged on the sleeping bag Tucker and I had seen on our visit, idly thumbing through the copy of *Town & Country*.

Seeing me, she smiled.

"Here at last," she said.

I kept the Glock trained on her. Sidestepped toward Joe, crouched beside him.

"Where's Greer?" I asked.

"Probably dead by now," Beverly said. "I knew she'd come here. Back to the scene of the crime. And I was right. Imagine my surprise when *you* showed up, too."

Joe rolled slowly onto his back, blinking blood out of his eyes. I saw that he'd been relieved of his service revolver—and when I glanced up, Beverly had it trained on me.

"Where," I repeated, *"is my sister?"*

"I don't suppose it will do any harm to tell you," Beverly answered pleasantly, setting aside the magazine. "Since you'll be joining her soon. She's back there—in the little room behind the furnace."

I wasn't fool enough to look over my shoulder. "Why?" I said. "Why are you doing this?"

Beverly sighed prettily. "Everything got out of hand," she said, sounding regretful. "I didn't recognize her for a long time—Greer, I mean. But she looked like someone—and then it came to me. *Little Molly Stillwell.* The girl who'd poisoned her own stepfather, turned him into a vegetable. For a while it seemed like too much of a coincidence, both of us coming from Shiloh, and I was still drinking then. Still torn up over losing my husband to another woman. So I turned to Jack—my dear son—and told him what I suspected. He took it from there, and pretty soon we were funneling money into various offshore bank accounts." She paused, smiled fondly. "Alex was frantic, of course. It was delightful to see him falling apart that way."

Joe's hand found my right wrist, tightened around it. I knew he wanted the Glock, but I couldn't unlock my fingers. They seemed paralyzed.

"And then Alex got too close, didn't he?" I asked quietly. "So you and Jack decided to kill him, and frame Greer for the murder."

"Jack handled that," Beverly said. Her face, so placid before, suddenly hardened. "He must have gotten greedy, though. I know he had some idea that Greer had been siphoning off far more of Alex's money than she'd given us. He probably meant to kill her and eliminate the problem, but he wouldn't have expected her to fight back. Fool. I knew she would."

Joe squeezed my wrist again. Out of the corner of my eye I saw him looking at me, felt him silently pleading.

Beverly trained the service revolver on him, swung it to me and then blew out the cellar window. In that instant I managed to let go of the Glock. Joe grabbed it, sighted in on Beverly.

"Drop the gun," he said.

She laughed. Swung the revolver toward us again.

And Joe fired.

Beverly looked stunned. Her hands flew out from her sides, and the revolver went off again, taking out a chunk of the cellar wall. A crimson flower bloomed at the center of her chest.

And then she pitched over onto the floor, face-first.

Joe got to his feet, breathing hard.

I made a dash for the room behind the furnace. It was padlocked shut.

"Greer!" I yelled, looking around for something to use to pry the lock loose. "Greer! Can you hear me?"

Joe appeared, his head still bleeding, and thrust one shoulder hard against the ancient door.

It gave immediately.

The room was dark.

I remembered my flashlight, realized I must have dropped it.

Joe had one in his service belt, and he sent a cone of light spilling into the gloom.

Greer was lying in a corner, trussed in duct tape like a mummy, from her shoulders to her ankles. But her eyes were open, gleaming in the darkness, huge with fear.

"Greer," I said, landing on my knees beside her. "It's Mojo. Everything is okay."

She blinked. She was probably dehydrated, and her left arm was broken. The pain of being bound like that must have been excruciating.

I began to pick and pry at the tape.

Joe was on his radio. "I'm at the Severn place," he said. "I need an ambulance...."

I stroked Greer's matted hair.

"Mojo," she whispered, her voice a raw rasp.

"Take it easy," I murmured.

"Beverly..."

"Shhh," I said. "She's dead. She can't hurt you anymore."

Joe produced a jackknife and began cutting away Greer's bonds.

"Be careful," I told him. "She's got a broken arm."

He nodded.

A prickle danced up my spine, and I turned around. Beverly Pennington was standing in the doorway. I gasped, and Joe pulled the Glock out of his holster, where he must have automatically shoved it after shooting Beverly, and whirled.

I knew what he was seeing. Nothing.

I watched, appalled, as Beverly began to melt, like some gruesome statue in a burning wax museum. If there was a hell, she was in it.

She gave a terrible, piercing shriek, and then she was gone.

I looked at Joe and Greer, certain they must have heard the cry, but Joe was busy with Greer's bonds again, and she was staring up at me.

"Mojo," she explained, "sees dead people."

"She needs water," Joe said to me, probably thinking Greer was delirious. "I've got a bottle out in the squad car, along with a blanket. I'll go and get it." He swayed a little as he stood. He was covered in blood, and possibly seriously injured himself.

"You stay with Greer," I said. Frankly, I wasn't eager to go out into the rainy night alone, after all that had happened, but I wanted to check on Dave anyway, and I wasn't sure Joe wouldn't be leaving the scene in an ambulance himself, right alongside Greer.

But Joe refused.

"My dog…"

"I'll bring him in," Joe said.

Greer was free of the worst of the duct tape, but she lay still, cradling her left arm in its filthy cast.

"What happened here, Greer?" I asked after giving her a few moments.

She tried several times to speak, before she got a word out. "I was hiding—and she found me—"

"I don't mean that. I mean before. When you were Molly Stillwell."

"I didn't poison my stepfather," Greer said.

After all the secrets, all the lies, implied and stated, I believed her. "Who did? Rick?"

Greer shook her head. "Mom," she whispered.

"Why?"

"He was—he was molesting Tessa."

I gave Greer my hand, and she clung to me.

"And you?"

She looked away for a moment. "When I said I did something terrible…I meant I—I let him touch me. I was hoping he wouldn't bother Tessa."

My stomach roiled. "Did you tell your mother what was going on?"

"She—she didn't want to believe it." Greer ground out the words. "Not at first."

"It's okay," I said, blinking back tears of rage and pity. "We can talk about it later."

Greer nodded in relief and closed her eyes.

Joe came back with a blanket, a bottle of water and Dave at his heels.

I was so glad to see my dog that I started to cry again.

Joe spread the blanket over Greer, squatted to give her water from the bottle. "Careful, now," he said gently. "Little sips."

Dave scrambled into my arms, squirming, laving my face with his tongue.

"This was beeping when I opened your car door," he said, pulling my cell phone from the pocket of his bloody jacket. "I thought it might be important."

Tucker couldn't have gotten to Phoenix already, even if he'd caught the first plane out, but I wanted to hear his voice, even the recorded version.

I pressed the messages button.

"Moje?" Tucker said, his voice ragged. "I'm at the airport in Missoula. My plane's leaving in a couple of minutes, so I'll have to shut this thing off pretty soon. I just wanted to tell you—I understand. Why you couldn't come with me, I mean. Stay safe, okay? Look—I've gotta go. Here's hoping there'll be a message waiting when I land. Bye."

He was gone.

I felt as though everything vital had been jerked out of me.

Crying again, I keyed in his number. "Hey, Tuck," I said, my voice breaking. "We found Greer—Joe and I did. Call me as soon—as soon as you know anything about Danny's condition. I don't care what time it is. Just call."

I'd barely broken the connection when the phone rang in my hand.

I knew it couldn't be Tucker—he was in flight—but I said his name anyway.

It was Jolie. "Sorry I didn't get back to you," she said. "Sweetie chewed up my phone, and I had to get a new one."

"Greer is safe," I said, watching as Joe held her head and held the water bottle for her.

"You *found* her?"

I laughed, the sound soblike. "Don't sound so surprised. I *am* a detective, you know."

"You're a former billing clerk who owns a bar," Jolie reminded me. "How is she? Is she hurt? Did she say…?"

"She's in rough shape," I answered, "but I think she'll be okay."

In the distance I heard sirens, and I blessed the sound.

"You were expecting a call from Tucker?"

I started to cry again, hard.

"Moje?" Jolie prompted gently.

I told her about Danny's accident. I *didn't* tell her I'd seen the little boy, because I didn't know what it meant and because I didn't want Joe to overhear and think I was crazy.

"Oh, my God," Jolie said. "What hospital?"

"Phoenix Children's," I told her. "But Danny's in intensive care, Jolie. You won't be able to get in."

"I'm going over there anyway. Maybe I can find out something."

"I'd appreciate that," I said, sniffling.

"Look after Greer, and come home as soon as you can."

"I will," I promised.

We rang off.

The EMTs arrived first, and then the state police. They put Greer on an IV and took her out on a stretcher.

Somebody inspected the gash in Joe's head—it turned out Beverly had clubbed him from behind, with something heavy, as soon as he stepped into the cellar. He'd need a few stitches and an MRI, but he was walking around and acting pretty much normal.

I was questioned, but since Joe vouched for me, I was allowed to leave. Dave and I got into the Volvo and headed back to the Lakeside.

Dave immediately searched the place for Tucker, and that made me cry again. I supposed I should have gone to the hospital with Greer, but she'd asked me not to, and because I was emotionally exhausted, I'd agreed.

Jolie called when I was about to get into the shower.

"It's serious, Moje," she said. "Touch and go. They lost Danny once, but managed to bring him back."

My knees sagged.

Call-waiting clicked in.

"It's Tucker," I said. "I'll call you back."

"I'm coming up there," Jolie told me. And then she hung up.

I pushed another button. "Tucker?"

"The plane just landed," Tucker said. "Are you okay?"

"Never mind me," I said. "I'm fine, and so is Greer."

Tucker's voice dropped. "Moje, what if he dies?"

"We have to believe he won't," I answered. "Jolie's on her way here, so she can pinch-hit with Greer. I'll be home as soon as I can, Tuck. Hold on, okay?"

"I'd ask what went down, but I'm not sure I could stand knowing it right now."

"I'll tell you all about it when I get back. Just think about Danny."

"Allison says he flatlined once, Moje. Even if he survives, there could be brain damage."

In my mind's eye I saw Danny standing outside my car window.

I want my dad.

"Just go to him, Tucker. Make sure he knows you're there."

"Can I call you later?"

"You can call me anytime, Tuck. You know that."

Hold on, Danny. He's on his way. He'll be there soon.

"Moje, I—"

The call dropped.

The shower was still running.

I waited for Tucker to reconnect, but he didn't.

I stepped under the spray, and the warmth

affected me like a double shot of whiskey, swallowed in one gulp.

I dropped to my knees and then curled up like a fetus.

And I stayed like that until the shower water turned cold.

CHAPTER SEVENTEEN

DAVE AND I CHECKED OUT of the Lakeside Motel at eight the next morning and headed straight for Joe Fletcher's office. He was there, with a square bandage on the back of his head, looking good otherwise.

"Heading out?" he asked.

I nodded. Dave, on his leash, sniffed at the base of the water cooler, but behaved himself. "My sister's coming in on a ten-o'clock plane," I said. "She'll stay with Greer until she can leave the hospital."

Joe looked sad. "You understand that Greer could be charged with attempted murder?"

"She didn't poison Mr. Severn," I said. "Her mother did."

"Unless Alice confesses, or we can find some proof that she's the guilty one, Mol—Greer is in big trouble."

"I understand."

"The boy," Joe said. "Is he all right?"

I'd talked to Tucker around six that morning. "No change," I said.

"I guess the news could be worse."

I nodded, already edging toward the door.

"Take care," Joe said, bending to ruffle Dave's ears in farewell.

"You, too," I answered. "And, Joe?"

"Yeah."

"Thanks."

He saluted, and I left.

Two hours later, in front of the Missoula airport, Jolie tossed her suitcase into the back of the Volvo, with Dave, and jumped in on the passenger side.

We headed for the hospital. Jolie called ahead for an update.

Greer was in surgery—her arm had been re-broken during her ordeal in the cellar at the Severn farmhouse. Leaving Dave with Jolie outside the visitor's entrance, I took an elevator to the fifteenth floor, after getting the room number from the admittance clerk, intending to wait for Greer.

There were two policemen outside her door, but that wasn't what stopped me in my tracks.

It was the woman, dressed in a neat navy blue suit and wearing high heels, who was talking to them. She looked so much like Greer that I didn't need to ask who she was.

Seeing me, she fell silent, her expression curious.

"I'm Mojo Sheepshanks," I told her, and the policemen. "Molly's—friend."

"Alice York," Greer's mother said.

One of the policemen cleared his throat. "We're going to have to arrest you, Mrs. York."

I opened my mouth. Closed it again.

"I'd like to see my daughter first," Alice told the man. "Just let me wait here until she gets out of surgery and comes around. I'm not going anywhere."

The cops conferred, then agreed. Alice *wasn't* going anywhere. But they weren't, either.

I followed Alice into Greer's room.

"You confessed?" I asked quietly.

"Yes," Alice said.

"Why did you let Greer—Molly take the rap for you?"

Alice stood with her back to me, staring out a window. "I was a coward," she said. "When Molly ran away, I was glad she'd gotten out of that house. I only wish Tessa could have escaped, too. The gossip started almost immediately—everybody thought Molly had been the one to poison Fred, because of what he'd done to Tessa, and tried to do to her. I knew she'd land on her feet, so I let it ride."

"Wasn't it strange, staying there, in the same house where it all happened? Taking care of a man you'd tried to kill?"

"It was my form of penance," Alice said quietly. "He ruined so many lives. Tessa's, certainly. Rick's, too. God, how I hated him. When he finally died, I wanted to dance for joy. I was free. I prayed Molly was, too. But Tessa and Rick? There was no turning back for them."

I nodded, but said nothing. It wasn't my place to tell Alice that Greer—Molly, to her—wasn't out of the legal woods yet, even though she'd been cleared of Fred Severn's poisoning. She'd shot Jack Pennington and, while Carmen would probably testify that it had been self-defense, nothing about it would be easy.

For one thing, there was bound to be a lot of ugly publicity.

I wondered if Greer was strong enough to stand the stress, or if she'd crack up, as Tessa had. Things like that run in families. Believe me, I know. I have the half brother from hell. And I'm not speaking figuratively here, either.

Greer was a long time getting out of surgery, and when she did, she was unconscious. Alice stood over her, holding her hand, her eyes brimming with tears.

I left and went downstairs to relieve Jolie of Dave-duty.

"Go home," she said, handing over the leash. "I can take it from here."

"What about your job?" I asked.

Jolie grinned. "I decided I was overqualified. I'll be doing consulting work from here on out. Care to hire me? I'll give you the family rate."

"Please tell me you didn't get fired," I said. If she had been axed from the city payroll, it was my fault— I'd let the discovery of Alex Pennington's dead body slip to Tucker, after all. And while I was pretty sure he wouldn't have blown the whistle on Jolie, someone else might have overheard the conversation.

"Okay," Jolie answered cheerfully. "I didn't get fired."

"You're lying," I accused.

"Don't blame Tucker," Jolie said, "or yourself. It happened because I'm not very good at taking orders, that's all."

I still felt guilty. I have a black belt in that.

Jolie touched my arm. "Go on back to Arizona, Mojo. Tucker needs you, and you need to get Mojo's up and running. I'll catch up with you when I'm sure Greer is okay."

My throat tightened. I don't like goodbyes, even when they're temporary; all too often they turn out to be permanent instead.

I'd brought Jolie up to speed on the Greer situation on our way over from the airport. Now I added, "Her mother's up there, in the room. She confessed to poisoning Fred Severn herself, so Greer's okay on that score."

Jolie nodded, looked wistfully down at Dave, probably missing Sweetie, but she didn't say anything.

"Where are you going to stay, Jole?" I asked. "What will you do for a car?"

"I'll rent one, Moje," Jolie answered. I knew she wasn't quite herself—there was something very wrong—but she wasn't ready to tell me about it, or she would have. "And I can still afford a hotel, even if I am self-employed."

"I didn't get to tell Greer goodbye," I said.

"I'll give her your love, Moje. Just get going, okay?"

We hugged.

Dave and I got in the car and pointed ourselves south.

We were barely rolling when Tucker called. Instead of "hello," he made a hoarse, strangled sound.

Oh, no, I thought. *Please, no...*

But I said, "What? Tucker, what?"

"He's awake," Tucker told me. "Danny's going to make it, Moje. He's drifting in and out, but he's going to be okay."

I had to pull over to the side of the road, I was shaking so badly. "Thank God," I murmured.

"Amen," Tucker said.

"Dave and I are on our way," I told him.

"You can't get here quickly enough to suit me," he replied. "Call me again when you get within half an hour of Cave Creek. I'll be at the apartment waiting for you."

Emotion swelled in my throat. "I'll hurry," I promised.

"Don't speed," he said. "I'd hate to have to bust you."

I laughed, but tears of joy were blurring my vision.

We said goodbye, and I wiped my eyes with the back of one hand and got back on the highway.

I WAS WITHIN a hundred miles of home the next afternoon when Gillian suddenly appeared in the passenger seat. She folded her arms and gave me an accusatory look.

"It's good to see you," I said, and I meant it. I'd been worried about her.

She looked back at Dave, smiled at him with bleak affection and turned to me again, signing rapidly.

"Honey," I told her quietly, "I don't understand."

Her whole body moved with the sigh she gave. And then she put both hands out in front of her and made a shoving motion with them.

"Danny," she said laboriously, and pushed again, hard.

My blood went cold. "Are you saying somebody *pushed* him into the pool?"

She nodded.

"Who?"

She sat perfectly still.

"Gillian, were you there? Did you see someone push Danny into the pool?"

She shook her head.

"Then how do you know?" I asked, enunciating the words carefully.

She moved one hand, as though working a puppet. Making it talk.

"He told you?"

Again Gillian nodded.

"Does Danny's dad know, or his mom?"

No.

I remembered my encounter with Danny the night before, in the rainy darkness. I'd told him he was dreaming, and the chances were pretty good that he didn't remember the attack consciously. But a part of him did.

I pressed harder on the gas.

Gillian vanished, but not before I saw the pleading in her eyes.

Frantically I reviewed what Tucker had told me—that Danny had fallen into the pool, and Chelsea had rescued him. Who else had been at the Darroch house that day? Allison? Vince Erland? Who?

Allison would never hurt her own child.

Chelsea had been the one to *save* him, so she was out.

As for Vince, well, that was just frantic speculation on my part. If he'd been around, Chelsea would have called the cops.

A chill seized the marrow of my bones as a new realization struck me. The ghosts I'd met, with the exception of Beverly Pennington's, had been benevolent. But suppose there was another kind?

Half an hour out, as promised, I called Tucker.

He was at my place, as promised, making spaghetti sauce.

"Tuck," I said carefully, "did Danny say anything about—well—about what happened before he fell into the pool?"

"He doesn't remember," Tucker said.

"Could someone have—pushed him?"

"Moje, what are you getting at?"

"According to Gillian, Danny didn't fall into the water, Tuck. Somebody shoved him." I paused, gnawing at my lower lip. "Who was there when it happened?"

"Allison was inside, talking to her mother on the telephone. Chelsea and her friend Janice were on the patio."

"No one else?"

"No, not as far as I know." Tucker sounded worried again now.

The invisible-attacker theory was looking better and better. Or, more properly, worse and worse. "Where was Daisy?" I asked.

"In the house, with Allison," Tucker said. I didn't need astral travel to see him turning off the fire under the spaghetti sauce, shoving the pot off the heat.

"Go back to the hospital, Tuck," I told him. "I'll meet you there."

"Room 1205," he said. Then he ground out a hasty goodbye, and the call ended.

A little over an hour later I parked in the lot at Phoenix Children's Hospital, rolling a window down for Dave, and raced inside.

I practically collided with Allison as I got out of the elevator on the twelfth floor. She looked haggard, even gaunt, and there were deep shadows under her eyes. Seeing me, she opened her mouth to speak, probably to protest my being there, but then some second thought must have struck her. She pressed her lips together, shook her head once and got into the elevator I'd just stepped out of.

I held the doors open, delaying her departure. "Allison," I said, "where is Daisy? Who's with her?"

She blinked, as if confused by the question. After all she'd been through, I figured she was probably running on emotional fumes. "Chelsea is. Why?"

"Go to her," I said with an internal shiver. "And stick close."

Allison's eyes widened.

"Go," I repeated, and stepped back so the elevator doors could close.

After standing there for a few moments, trying to hold on to my composure, I hurried to 1205, and found Tucker there, pacing.

Danny lay sleeping in a bed, still and small and pale, hooked up to various monitors, an oxygen tube running into his left nostril. Except for the three of us, the room was empty.

I went straight into Tucker's arms, and he clung to me a little, burying his face in my hair. His cheek felt rough, since he hadn't shaved, and I smelled spaghetti sauce on his T-shirt.

A murmured word from Danny sent us both whirling toward the bed.

I bent over him, stroked his hair back from his forehead, worked up what I hoped was a reassuring smile. "Hey," I said.

"I saw you—" he croaked. "In my dream."

I kissed his cheek, too choked up to speak.

"It was raining," Danny went on.

I nodded. "It was raining," I confirmed.

Tucker's hand came to rest on my shoulder.

Danny closed his eyes, sleeping peacefully.

"What was he talking about, Moje?" Tucker asked, his voice very quiet, even for a hospital room.

I told him about seeing Danny the night before.

Tucker's eyes filled with tears as he listened. "It was pretty close, wasn't it?" he asked when I'd finished.

I bit my lower lip and nodded.

A movement in the corner of the room caught my eye, and I risked a glance.

It was Justin, and he looked scared and anxious.

I didn't even try to pretend, for Tucker's sake, that no one was in the room.

"She's got the little girl," Justin said.

My heart stopped, started up again. "Who, Justin? Where?"

"It's a campground or something. North of here, outside Carefree," he answered, adding a few details. I recognized the place, not so much from memory as by a visceral sense of already being there. "Mojo, you've got to hurry."

I nodded, caught hold of Tucker's hand and pulled, already moving toward the door.

"Stay here," I told Justin.

Justin nodded, looking uncertain.

Tucker didn't ask a single question until we'd gotten Dave from the Volvo and jumped into his SUV, with me chattering directions to the campground.

"Would you mind telling me what the hell's going on?" he demanded, zipping onto a north-bound freeway.

"Call the cops, Tucker," I urged. "We'll never get there in time."

He grabbed for the radio and did as I asked.

"Tell me what's going on!"

His cell phone rang before I could explain.

He answered, barking, "Darroch."

Allison's voice was a high-pitched buzz of energy. I couldn't hear what she said, but I didn't have to. I knew she'd gotten home and found Daisy gone.

The last thing I heard was Tucker shouting my name, and Dave barking frantically in the backseat.

I was out of my body again, speeding through a darkness much blacker than mere night.

CHAPTER EIGHTEEN

I LANDED WITH A THUMP.

Daisy was huddled in the corner of a starkly lit public restroom at the campground, plainly terrified. "I want to go home," I heard her say.

"We all want something, kiddo," said Chelsea Grimes.

I'd left my body behind, in Tucker's SUV, and I knew I was invisible. Focused consciousness, and not much more. I longed for my fists, my feet, a way to fight. A way to save Daisy.

"My daddy will come," Daisy said bravely. "He'll arrest you and throw you in jail—forever."

I tried to center myself around her, protect her somehow.

But I knew it was fruitless. I had no substance, no power.

"Maybe we shouldn't do this," Chelsea said, biting her fingernails. I wondered if Janice had pushed Danny into the swimming pool, planning to film his death with that damned video camera of hers. Chelsea must have panicked, and jumped in to pull him out.

"Like we could turn back now," scoffed Janice, a dark figure. "You heard the kid. She'll tell for sure, and if the cops get into your computer and find the Web site, we're finished."

Chelsea began to pace.

Outside the restroom a car door slammed.

"Somebody's here!" Janice snarled. "Hurry!"

I tried to scream, but I could feel myself fading, losing my grip.

I was pretty sure I was dead.

I landed in Tucker's SUV, and my own quivering body, with an impact that literally rattled my teeth and hurt in every joint and muscle, as if I'd fallen from the roof of a building and landed on pavement.

"Mojo!" Tucker yelled.

"Drive," I managed to say as everything around me began to come slowly back into focus. I was soaked with sweat and shaking with chills. "For God's sake, *drive!*"

"What just happened here?" he demanded. "Did you have a seizure or something?"

"I'll explain later," I said, wondering how long I'd been out of Mojo-central. We were speeding over the road into the campground.

Up ahead I saw a cluster of squad cars, light bars flashing.

But there was no sign of Chelsea or Janice.

No sign of Daisy.

"In there," I gasped, pointing toward the public

restroom, a small stone structure standing by itself in the desert landscape.

Tucker was out of the rig and running, practically before I lowered my hand.

I blinked, pushed open the passenger door and got out.

And then Daisy sprang out of a crowd of sheriff's deputies, and Tucker dropped to his knees on the ground, opening his arms to her. She launched herself into them.

Gillian appeared, a little distance away, watching the reunion.

I went to her, not to Tucker.

She looked up at me.

I held out a hand to the child, but she stepped back, shook her head.

She was already beginning to fade.

"Baby," I said brokenly, not caring who heard, "I'm so sorry this happened to you. I'm so sorry."

She was gone before I finished the sentence.

I stood numbly where I was, using all the strength I possessed just to keep from collapsing.

Allison arrived—I was vaguely aware of that. I saw her rush to join Daisy and Tucker. Take her daughter into her arms.

I looked around, saw Janice and Chelsea sitting sullenly in the back of one of the squad cars. I knew they weren't sorry for what they'd done—just sorry they'd been caught.

Pure, fiery hatred surged inside me. If I could

have gotten to them, I'd have clawed their eyes out with my bare hands. I'd have strangled them, and loved doing it.

Tucker approached, took me by the shoulders. "Moje," he said. And he pulled me close and held me tightly, and we sort of leaned into each other.

"I don't want to see dead people anymore," I wept, burying my face in his strong, Tucker-scented shoulder. "I don't want to see dead people *anymore!*"

"I know," he said gruffly. "I know."

I felt Allison watching us, met her gaze.

She took Daisy's hand and led her away.

I waited for Tucker to say he had to leave, too. But he didn't.

"Come on, Moje," he said, kissing my forehead. "Let's go back to your place and see if any new ghosts have popped in."

I blinked, confused. "What about Daisy?"

"She needs Allison right now, not me," he said.

I nodded.

We started, hand in hand, toward Tucker's SUV.

And then I remembered something I'd heard inside that restroom during my most recent out-of-body experience. I stopped, tightening my grip on Tucker's hand. "Chelsea's computer," I said. "There's a Web site—"

Tucker studied my face, then helped me into the SUV before going back to speak with one of the other policemen on the scene.

Dave stuck his head between the seats and whimpered.

"It'll be okay now," I told him. "It's over."

So much was over.

But other things were just starting.

I wanted a hot shower, and coffee—with a big slug of whiskey in it. I wanted to lie in my own bed, under a pile of blankets, wrapped in Tucker Darroch's arms, and sleep for a hundred years.

I wanted to pretend, if only for a little while, that the world was a sane and sunny place, and evil only a theory.

Tucker came back, and we went on to my place. Dave was glad to be home, and so was I.

Tucker and I took a shower together, standing a long time under the spray of hot water. Forgetting all about the coffee we'd planned to drink, we dried off, without a word to each other, and crawled into my bed.

We cuddled close, and when we made love we came together silently, with a slow, elegant grace.

And then we slept.

Tucker awakened me late that night. He was dressed, and I knew that meant he was leaving, going home to Allison and Daisy, or maybe to the hospital, to sit with Danny awhile.

He'd heated up the spaghetti sauce, though, and boiled up some noodles to go with it. We sat at the kitchen table, me in a bathrobe, Tucker in his movin'-on clothes, but neither of us could bring ourselves to eat.

He looked exhausted, haunted by the things he knew about the world and the way it works. He'd spoken to one of the investigators at the sheriff's office while I was still sleeping, and now he told me what I'd already suspected.

Janice and Chelsea had filmed Gillian's death— the proof had been found in Chelsea's computer. For a price, perverts could watch the clips.

"I don't want to live on this planet anymore," I told Tucker. "I want to find a place where things like this don't happen."

"We're stuck with this one," Tucker said, ever the pragmatist. "Might as well make the best of it."

I nodded, numb.

After we'd pretended to eat for a while longer, Tucker left, promising to be back as soon as he could.

I didn't expect to sleep that night, but I did, curled up with Dave in the middle of my bed, without waking up, without dreaming. In fact, when I opened my eyes I was in the same position I'd been in when I tumbled into slumberland—fetal.

I got up, yawning. Took a quick shower, dressed, put some coffee on to brew and took Dave down to the parking lot on his leash, a wadded paper towel clenched in one hand so I could dispose of the debris.

Once that was done, Dave and I hiked back upstairs and I washed my hands, then rummaged in drawers until I found the key to the bar downstairs.

It was time to drag the Mojo sign inside, open the box and admire it.

Dave went with me, trotting ahead into the saloon, sniffing the sawdust. I indulged in a few fond recollections of my friend Bert, raking spit lumps and cigarette butts out of that sawdust while we chatted.

Since I was feeling fragile, I figured I couldn't afford a lot of sentiment, so I dragged the big box inside and tore it open.

There it was, my name, in blue script. I plugged it in and got a major kick out of seeing it light up.

Inspired, I ducked behind the jukebox and plugged that in, too. After fishing around a little, I found Bert's stash of quarters in a cigar box behind the bar, and plunked them into the coin slot.

Brad Paisley was singing "Alcohol," and I was bellowing along, using the rake handle for a microphone, when I realized Dave and I weren't alone in the bar.

Max Summervale, my shooting instructor, was standing there, arms folded, head cocked to one side.

"Holy crap," I said. "You're dead, aren't you?"

Brad finished "Alcohol," and Randy Travis started to sing about "diggin' up bones." I thought it was oddly fitting, considering.

"I wondered when you'd notice," he replied.

"When?"

"When, what?"

"When did you *die?*"

Max considered the question. "Two years ago," he said.

"And now I suppose you want me to find your killer?" I asked, chagrined that I'd had two different encounters with the man and failed to notice that he was a ghost. It just shows you how much stress I was under.

Lest you think I was unsympathetic—I wasn't. Just burned out. I wanted to live a normal life, as soon as I figured out what that would look like.

On the jukebox Johnny Cash launched into "Folsom Prison Blues."

"Nope," Max told me. "I took the bastard out with me."

I stared at him, knowing I should have been relieved. And I wasn't.

"Then what do you want?"

Max grinned endearingly. "You need a partner," he said, spreading his hands wide. "Will a dead guy do?"

* * * * *

Turn the page for a
preview of A WANTED MAN
by Linda Lael Miller.

LARK MORGAN WATCHED slantwise from an upstairs window of Mrs. Porter's Rooming House as the stranger strode across the road from Jolene Bell's establishment to the barbershop, the dog walking close by his side.

The man wore a trail coat that could have used a good shaking out, and his hair, long enough to curl at the back of his collar, gleamed pale gold in the afternoon sunlight. His hat was battered, but of good quality, and the same could be said of his boots. While not necessarily a person of means, he was no ordinary saddle bum, either.

And that worried Lark more than anything else—except maybe the bulge low on his left hip, indicating that he was wearing a sidearm.

She frowned. Drew back from the window when the stranger suddenly turned, his gaze slicing to the very window she was peering out of, as surely as if he'd felt her watching him. Her heart rose into her throat and fluttered there.

A hand coming to rest on her arm made her start.

Ellie Lou Porter, her landlady, stepped back, her eyes wide. Mrs. Porter was a doelike creature, tiny and frail and painfully plain. Behind that unremarkable face, however, lurked a shrewd and very busy brain.

"I'm so sorry, Lark," Mrs. Porter said, watching through the window as the stranger finally turned away and stepped into the barbershop, taking the dog with him. "I didn't mean to frighten you."

Lark willed her heart to settle back into its ordinary place and beat properly. "You didn't," she lied. "I was just—distracted, and you caught me off guard."

Mrs. Porter smiled knowingly. There wasn't much that went on in or around Stone Creek, Lark had quickly learned, that escaped the woman's scrutiny. "His name is Rowdy Rhodes," she said, evidently speaking of the stranger who had just entered the barbershop. "As you may know, my cook, Mai Lee, is married to Jolene's houseboy, and she carries a tale readily enough." She paused, shuddering, though whether over Jolene or the houseboy, Lark had no way of knowing. "It's got to be an alias, of course," Mrs. Porter finished.

Lark was not reassured. If it hadn't been against her better judgment, she'd have gone right down to the barbershop, a place where women were no more welcome than in her former husband's gentleman's club in Denver, and demanded that the stranger explain himself *and* his presence in her hiding place.

"Do you think he's a gunslinger?" she asked, trying to sound merely interested. In her mind she was already packing her things, preparing to catch the first stagecoach out of Stone Creek, heading anywhere. Fast.

"Could be," Mrs. Porter said thoughtfully. "Or he might be a lawman."

"He's probably just passing through."

"I don't think so," Mrs. Porter replied, her face draped in the patterned shadow of the lace curtains covering the hallway window.

"What makes you say that?" Lark wanted to know.

Mrs. Porter smiled. "It's just a feeling I have," she said. "Whoever he is, he's got business around here. He moves like a man with a purpose he means to accomplish."

Lark was further discomforted. She barely knew her landlady, but she'd ascertained at their first meeting that Mrs. Porter was alarmingly perceptive. Although the other woman hadn't actually contradicted Lark's well-rehearsed story that she was a maiden schoolteacher, she'd taken pointed notice of her new boarder's velvet traveling suit, Parisian hat, costly trunk and matching reticules.

Stupid, Lark thought, remembering the day, a little over three months before, when she'd presented herself at Mrs. Porter's door and inquired after a room. *I should have worn calico, or bombazine.*

Now, in light of the stranger's arrival, she had more to worry about than her wardrobe, plainly more suited to the wife of a rich and powerful man than an underpaid schoolmarm. What if Autry had found her, at long last? What if he'd sent Rowdy Rhodes, or whoever he was, to drag her back to Denver or, worse yet, simply kill her?

Lark suppressed a shudder. Autry's reach was long, and so was his memory. He was a man of savage pride, and he wouldn't soon forget the humiliation she'd dealt him by the almost-unheard-of act of filing for a divorce. Denver society was probably still twittering over the scandal.

"Come downstairs, dear," Mrs. Porter said with unexpected gentleness. "I'll brew us a nice pot of tea, and we'll chat."

Lark wanted to refuse the invitation—wished she'd said right away that she needed to work out lesson plans for the coming week, or shop for toiletries at the mercantile, or run some other Saturday errand, but she hadn't. And she'd surely arouse Mrs. Porter's assiduous curiosity by jumping at the touch of her hand.

"Thank you," she said, smiling determinedly and under no illusion that Mrs. Porter wanted to "chat." Lark knew she was a puzzle to her landlady, one the woman meant to solve. "That would be very nice. If I could just freshen up a little…"

Mrs. Porter nodded her acquiescence, returned Lark's smile and descended the back stairway, into the kitchen.

Lark hurried into her room, shut the door and leaned against it.

After steadying herself and freshening up as best she could, Lark walked decorously to the top of the stairs, glided down them and swept into Mrs. Porter's spacious, homey kitchen. The huge black cookstove, with its shining chrome trim, radiated warmth, and the delicious scent of brewing tea filled the room.

"I've set out a plate of my lemon tarts," Mrs. Porter said, with a nod to the offering in the center of the round oak table.

Then the back door opened, and Mai Lee, Mrs. Porter's cook, dashed in, a shawl pulled tightly around her head and shoulders. She carried a grocery basket over one arm, with a plucked chicken inside, its head lolling over one side.

"Make supper, chop-chop," Mai Lee said.

"What did you learn about Mr. Rhodes?" Mrs. Porter said.

Mai Lee giggled. She might have been sixteen— or sixty. Lark couldn't tell by her appearance, and it was the same with her husband, who joined her each night, late, to share a narrow bed in the nook beneath the staircase, and was invariably gone by daylight. Both of them were ageless.

From the limited amount of information she'd been able to gather, Lark surmised that the couple was saving practically every cent they earned to buy a little plot of land and raise vegetables for sale to the growing community.

"He *handsome,*" Mai Lee confided when she'd

recovered from her girlish mirth. "Eyes blue, like sky. Hair golden. Smile—" here she laid a hand to her flat little chest "—makes knees bend."

"He smiled at you?" Lark asked, and could have chewed up her tongue and swallowed it for revealing any interest at all.

Mrs. Porter looked at her, clearly intrigued.

Mai Lee began hacking the chicken into pieces and nodded. "Through window of barbershop. I look. He wink at me." She giggled again. "Not tell husband."

The pit of Lark's stomach did a peculiar little flip. She'd seen Mr. Rhodes only from a distance; he might have been handsome, as Mai Lee claimed, or ugly as the floor of a henhouse. And what did she care, either way, if he winked at women?

It only went to prove he was a rounder and a rascal.

With luck, he'd move on, and she'd never have to make his acquaintance at all.

Lark picked up a book, a favorite she'd owned since childhood, and buried herself in the story. She'd read it countless times, but she never tired of the tale, in which a young woman, fallen upon hard and grievous times, offered herself up as a mail-order bride, married a taciturn farmer, slowly won his heart and bore his children.

The knock at the back door brought her sharply back to reality.

"Now, who could that be?" Mrs. Porter mused, moving to answer.

A blast of frigid air rushed into the room.

And there in the open doorway stood Rowdy Rhodes, in his long black coat, freshly shaven and barbered, holding his hat in one hand. Mai Lee had been right about his blue eyes and his smile.

Lark was glad she was sitting down.

"I heard you might have rooms to let," he said, and though he was addressing Mrs. Porter, his gaze strayed immediately to Lark. A slight frown creased the space between his brows. "Of course, you'd have to let my dog stay, too."

The yellow hound ambled past him as if it had lived in that house forever, sniffed the air, which was redolent with frying chicken, and marched himself over to the stove, where he lay down with a weary, grateful sigh.

Mrs. Porter, Lark thought with frantic relief, was a fastidious housekeeper, and she would never allow a dog. She would surely turn Mr. Rhodes away.

"It's two dollars a week," Mrs. Porter said instead, casting a glance back at Lark. "Normal price is $1.50, but with the dog…"

Rhodes smiled again, once he'd shifted his attention back to the landlady. "Sounds fair," he said. "Mr. Sam O'Ballivan will vouch for me, if there's any question of my character."

"Come in," Mrs. Porter fussed, fond as a mother welcoming home a prodigal son, heretofore despaired of. "Supper's just about ready."

No, Lark thought desperately.

The dog sighed again, very contentedly, and closed its eyes.

Mai Lee stepped over the animal to turn the chicken with a meat fork and then poke at the potatoes boiling in a kettle. She kept stealing glances at Rhodes.

"I'll show you your room and get a fire going in there," Mrs. Porter said, only then closing the door against the bite of a winter evening. "Land sakes, it's been cold lately. I do hope you haven't traveled far in this weather."

Lark stood up, meaning to express vigorous dissent, and sat down again when words failed her.

Mr. Rhodes, who had yet to extend the courtesy of offering his name, noted the standing and sitting, and responded with a slight and crooked grin.

The pit of Lark's stomach fluttered.

Mrs. Porter led the new boarder straight to the room at the back, with its fireplace and outside door and lovely writing desk. The dog got up and lumbered after them.

For a moment Lark was so stricken by jealousy that she forgot she might be in grave peril. Then her native practicality emerged. Even presuming Mr. Rhodes was not in Autry's employ, he was a stranger, and he carried a gun. He could murder them all in their beds.

Lark stood, intending to dash upstairs and lock herself in her room until she had a chance to speak privately with Mrs. Porter, but Rhodes appeared before she could make another move. She dropped back into her chair and was treated to a second look of amusement from the lodger.

Indignant color surged into Lark's face.

Mrs. Porter prattled like a smitten schoolgirl, offering Mr. Rhodes a tart and running on about how it was good to have a man in the house again, what with poor, dear Mr. Porter gone and all. Why, the world was going straight to Hades, if he'd pardon her language, and on a greased track, too.

Rhodes crossed to the table, took one of the tarts and bit into it, studying Lark with his summer-blue eyes as he chewed. He'd left his coat behind in his room, and the gun belt with it, but Lark was scarcely comforted.

He could be a paid assassin.

He could be an outlaw, or a bank robber.

And whatever his name was, Lark would have bet a year's salary it wasn't Rowdy Rhodes.